COMING OF ANGELS

BOOK 1

STRANGE HAPPENINGS

A JACK BRANDEN TRILOGY BY

M. J. BANKS

COMING OF ANGELS,
BOOK 1: STRANGE HAPPENINGS

by

M. J. Banks

Library of Congress Number: 2017901196
International Standard Book Number: 978-1-60126-525-8

Masthof Press
219 Mill Road | Morgantown, PA 19543-9516
www.Masthof.com

TABLE OF CONTENTS

DEDICATION

to Nicholas
and to all those
with autism.

CHAPTER 1

GOING HOME

December 1994

It was a bitter cold winter's night as I stood looking out of the window watching the wind blowing snow that had fallen that morning. The stars were quite visible as they glimmered against the dark backdrop of the sky, like well-faceted diamonds in a jeweler's showcase. I was exhausted from working on a piece for *INM* earlier that day and was looking forward to a great night's sleep, when all of a sudden, a bright light, which shone above the tree line, caught my attention. I could see it from the corner of my eye and was quite startled as I turned my head to get a better look. I walked to the door and opened it to get a clearer view of what was illuminating the dark, winter sky. I immediately became mesmerized by what I was witnessing. It was quite a sight to behold!

• • • •

Things are not always what they appear to be. The Middle East had quieted down and peace was imminent, or so we all thought. The Palestinians and Israelis were engaged in very serious peace talks that were monitored by the United Nations. The Middle East situation was out of control for several years, and the blood that was shed during this period was beyond what any of us had ever envisioned. The terrorist attacks had escalated after the war in Iraq started and suicide bombings were commonplace. What appeared to be a war of liberation for the Iraqi people became a military and financial nightmare for the United States and a violent nightmare for the Iraqis.

Terrorism had become the scourge of mankind and its occurrence increased with each passing day. Suicide bombings were the most typical, but no one would ever forget the event that made Americans wake up to this evil, 9/11. For decades, Europe and the Middle East had experienced many terrorist attacks, but Americans were always sheltered from the reality of it.

The bombing of the Twin Towers in New York on Sept. 11, 2001, completely changed all of that, living one's everyday normal life would never be the same. We realized on that day that we were just as vulnerable as every other country, and we were no longer the sheltered child. This one incident was a catalyst that began a chain of events which would lead up to the major event. One that no person on this planet could ever imagine and an event no one would ever forget. It would change the lives of all those who live on Earth, forever.

• • • •

My name is Jack Branden and I am a freelance writer. I have been following international events and writing articles for major magazines and newspapers all around the world. I have been a journalist since 1982 and have traveled to just about every country on this planet. Life was really good. I had a great career which afforded me the opportunity to travel and meet many people, some of whom were famous. I made great money and had the time of my life. I was recognized as a major player in the field of journalism and had won several awards for stories relating to international affairs such as the Middle East conflict and the violation of human rights. I was considered one of the major journalists reporting about terrorism in the Middle East and Ireland. Although I seemed to have it all, something was missing. I realized that life was about sharing and I hadn't done much of that. I came to the realization one night when I was alone in Paris that something had to change. There had to be more to life than living in hotels and jetting from place to place. I knew that it was a time for change and it had to be now.

I decided to return home to Philadelphia for the holidays. It was 1994 and I hadn't seen my family and friends in over three years. I made up my mind that I would be home for Christmas to spend time with my family. I came from a large family with four siblings and lots of aunts, uncles, and cousins. I was the middle child and the free spirit in the family. I have an older brother and sister and two younger sisters. I also have several nieces and nephews, some of whom I have never seen.

I really missed my family. My parents were wonderful people and it's funny how you don't realize that until you become a parent yourself. We were a typical, middle-class family living on the edge of the city. My dad worked for a tire manufacturer in Pottstown, and my mom was a housewife and mother. Life was great when I was growing up. We were so carefree as kids and always felt loved and protected. Our parents spent a lot of time with us and always took us to visit the cool places in Philadelphia during the summer, such as the Franklin Institute and, of course, the Phillies' games. At least one of our parents always came to our baseball, basketball, and football games. It's unfortunate that all kids were not raised in this type of environment. There again, I didn't know how lucky I was as a kid until I became an adult.

My brother, Rob, is the oldest in our family, and is married with three kids. He and his wife, Jessica, have been married since they graduated from high school in 1973. Neither Rob or Jessica went to college but they did, however, build a very successful business as bakers and have three bakeries in the Philadelphia area.

Claire is my oldest sister and the one who always made sure I brushed my teeth every morning and before I went to bed. She was the bossy one, so it's no surprise she ended up on Wall Street. She graduated from Wharton with a master's degree in business and moved to New York to forge a career in finance. She met her husband, Evan, in 1984 and got married a year later. Claire and Evan had their son Patrick, two years later.

My two younger sisters are Stephanie and Deirdre. They were very shy and quiet and always had a crush on my friends. Steph and Dee were only a year apart and were almost like twins. They worked as artists and eventually opened a gallery on Main Street in Manayunk. Steph married Jeff Martin, a contractor and they have two children: a daughter, Emily and a son, Nicholas. Dee was married for three years but is now divorced. She has no children but is very much the dotting aunt. Dee and Steph have become well-known for their artwork and have signed a huge contract with a home furnishing company to design the artwork for sheets, drapes, and ceramic ware.

• • • •

I arrived in Philadelphia on December 16th at 6 p.m. It was snowing lightly and I began to feel the excitement building in anticipation of returning home again. I was also excited about being home for a white Christmas. The cold weather and snow brought back warm, pleasant feelings of my childhood. Memories of snow days spent sledding down hills and ice skating made me smile. I remembered building snow huts with my friends and hanging out with my best friend, Randy Kalinski. Christmas was always the big holiday in our family. My mom decorated everywhere in the house and we always had big lights strung outside the windows and doors. I remember going with my dad and brother to buy a Christmas tree while my mom and sisters stayed at home and baked cookies. I loved it when we walked in the door with the tree and you could smell the cookies baking in the oven. Those were great times.

My family knew I was coming home for the holidays, but I didn't tell them exactly when I would be arriving in town. I really wanted to surprise them. I planned to stay at my parents' house while I was in Philly. I had plans to meet up with some old friends and visit family and hit some of the local bars while I was home. Little did I know that this visit home would lead to one of the most important decisions of my life and would change me forever.

The first stop I made when I arrived in Philadelphia was my brother Rob's house. His son, Michael, opened the door and howled when he saw me, "Dad, get down here! You'll never guess who just rolled in!"

• • • •

"Michael, I can't believe how you've changed! I guess you're a freshman at Penn State now, right?" I asked, as he crushed me with a bear hug. "Are you home for the holidays?"

In seconds, I was surrounded by Rob's family and Rob came into the room yelling, "Holy hell, when did you get in?"

"Just a few minutes ago. You are my first stop. Mom and Dad don't know I'm here." He was so happy to see me. I talked to his wife and kids and then Rob and I left his place and took off in his mini van to go to our parents' house.

Rob and I were always close even though he was four years older. We shared a room until he got married. I really looked up to him when I was growing up and it was always important to get recognition from Rob. After all, he was my big brother, my idol. We had not been in close contact for several years because our lives went in totally different directions. When I wasn't chasing down a hot exposé, I would have time to think about my family ties and realized how much I missed them.

"How was your flight?" Rob asked.

"It was a little bumpy and the flight took off late, but here I am, ready to see everybody and party through the New Year."

Rob laughed and said, "Sounds like a plan to me. Let's go out one night while you're home. We'll talk about old times."

"You're on, brother," I replied.

Rob and I arrived at our parents' house at about 8:15 p.m. I rang the bell and my dad opened the door to greet us. "Jack, Rob, I can't believe the two of you are here. I'm so surprised! Come on in and see your mother. Jack, I'm so glad you're home. It's been too long."

My dad gave me a huge hug and then called for my mother. Dad was having health problems; and he was starting to show his age. He was always very energetic and alive when we were growing up, but now he looked pale and tired standing before us. Dad's a tall man, 6 ft. 2 in. with a lean, almost lanky look. He still sported a full head of dark hair even at 64.

Mom, on the other hand, was only five feet tall and a little plump but always had a beauty radiating from her. She was in the kitchen baking

Christmas cookies and nut roll, and the house smelled of the most wonderful, sweet aroma. Christmas music was playing in the background and the sound and smell of Christmas triggered memories of my childhood. I felt like a ten year old again. Oh, the holidays. It is the most wonderful time of year.

Mom heard dad calling her, so she came into the living room to see who came to visit.

"Jack, Rob, I'm so glad to see you two together. It's been so long." Mom ran over to me and gave me a huge hug and kiss. She was so happy to see me. Tears appeared in her eyes. "Jackie, I missed you so much. Why don't you come home more often? Don't you miss us?" I looked into my mom's eyes and realized that time was going by quickly and all of us were getting older. I knew at that moment how important she was to me.

I really love my mom. She is the sweetest, dearest human being on this Earth. I remember how she would sit up with me all night when I was sick and she would sing to me. She would always get me ginger ale and ice cream to make me feel better. She was always there for all of us. She came to all the games we played including the ones where we warmed the bench. She always baked for the PTO and helped with the girl scouts and boy scouts when we were members. All of our friends loved mom. She was so nice to all of our friends. Even when we were fighting with someone, my mom would always try to resolve the issue. She's an amazing person and I appreciate her more each day.

Rob stayed for awhile and helped dad with a few things while I unpacked. I was very tired and looked forward to a good night's sleep in my old bedroom. My posters were still gracing the walls of my room and it made me chuckle when I saw them. I had posters of the Stones, Journey, Aerosmith, Queen, David Bowie, and Elton John along with posters of the Eagles' football team, the Flyers, the Phillies, and the Sixers. My room was literally wallpapered with posters and had not been touched since my youth. It was like walking into a time capsule.

I came downstairs and sat down with my parents and talked for several hours. They updated me on the sports scene in Philadelphia and what was going on in the old neighborhood. Many of the neighbors had passed away and the neighborhood was taking on a new look. It was becoming more diverse, with many different nationalities, however, it still maintained its old Philadelphia charm. The houses were sandblasted brick with black-shuttered windows. It still had the colonial flavor that Philadelphia is known for. We had a wonderful time talking and reminiscing, but I was so tired. I had to go to bed.

It was 6 a.m., Saturday morning and I was wide awake. Oh, the smell of fresh coffee brewing enticed me out of bed even though I felt so comfortable lying there. I dragged myself to the bathroom to wash my face and brush my teeth. That coffee was becoming more inviting, so I ran down the stairs to get a cup. Coffee is the fuel that keeps me going. It is my companion during those long, late nights when I'm writing an intense piece. Mom's coffee was the best, and so were her pancakes and waffles. She serves up a hearty breakfast, and I was long overdue for some good eating.

Mom and dad were sitting at the kitchen table when I came downstairs. I can't begin to tell you how great it was to see them after all this time. Mom smiled at me and got up to get me a cup of coffee and some pancakes. Oh, the melted butter and real maple syrup on pancakes were just what the doctor ordered. I sat down and we all started to talk about what was going on in our lives for the past three years. I told them I wanted to take some time off and be with our family. I felt it was time for me to settle down. My mom looked at me with a surprised look on her face.

"Jack, are you talking about getting married? I didn't know you were seriously seeing someone."

"I'm not seeing anyone and I wasn't referring to marriage. I meant that I wanted to see everyone and see all my nieces and nephews. I realize now that living on the edge is not all that it is cracked up to be. I didn't tell you about something that happened to me in Ireland a few months ago which caused me to re-evaluate my life." I paused for a moment and realized my mother's face took on an expression of real concern.

"I was caught in a crossfire when I was covering a story about the IRA, but a colleague of mine pulled me out of harm's way and saved my life. That single incident made me realize that I was not invincible and I understood at that moment, how important life was to me, which was something I had forgotten about while I was racing around the world."

My parents looked at me with shock on their faces. My dad said, "Jack, why didn't you tell us about this?"

"I didn't want you to worry about me."

Mom chimed in at that point and said she worries about me and all of her children every day of her life and that will never change. That's what mothers do, she said. We ended our conversation on a positive note and I said that I was going to visit Steph and Dee at their gallery to surprise them.

I drove down to Manayunk where Steph and Dee's gallery was located. The place had really changed since I was there several years ago. It had a lot of quaint shops and restaurants. It's a nice place to go and shop for unique things. Steph and Dee were working on some new artwork when I walked in.

"Hey girls, what's goin' on?" I said. Steph turned and looked at me as Dee finished with the painting.

"Jack, I can't believe you're here. When did you get in?" said Steph as she ran over to give me a hug.

Dee was just as excited to see me. "I'm so happy to see you. You look great! Have lunch with us and give us all the scoops on celebrities."

I helped them with a few things and then we went to a really cool restaurant down the street for lunch and laughed and talked for two hours. Steph and Dee had to return to the gallery, but we made plans to meet that night at Bailey's Bar.

I walked around the shops at Manayunk before I returned to my parents' house. The shops were decorated with Christmas cheer and it was like old times. There was a secondhand shop with all sorts of things that reminded me of my childhood. A Flexible Flyer sled was sitting in the corner just like the one I received for Christmas when I was nine. There were baseball cards and old Pez dispensers, and they actually had an old wood and glass display case with penny candy. Well, the penny candy now costs a dime, but it was a penny when I was a little kid. I got such a good feeling when I saw those things.

I spotted a vase on a table near the front window, which really looked a lot like a vase my mom had when I was young. It was green with vines and flowers on it which made a 3-D affect on the vase. I accidentally broke the one she had while playing with a ball in the house. She was upset, but forgave me soon afterward. I decided to buy the vase for her after feeling a moment of guilt for breaking the one she had when I was a kid.

I returned home around four o'clock and I gave the vase to my mom. She was so surprised when she opened the box. Tears welled up in her eyes and it was clear that she was very emotional.

"Jack, this is so beautiful. It looks like a vase I had years ago. Where did you get it ?"

"I saw it in a secondhand shop down the street from Steph and Dee's gallery. It made me think about the vase I broke while playing ball in the house. You know mom, I felt really bad about that and I still feel bad."

My mom laughed. "Jack, it was just a vase. You can always replace things like that. It wasn't my heart that you broke. That would have been more difficult to fix."

I smiled and kissed my mom on the cheek and went upstairs to shower. I was eager to get out and meet my sisters for dinner.

I arrived at Bailey's around 7 p.m. I hadn't been there for several years but the place didn't change. My brother Rob and his wife, Jessica, my sister Stephanie and husband Jeff, and Dee and her boyfriend Dave, were all there and it felt like a family reunion. I joined them at a huge table and we immediately started to laugh and talk about the really crazy things we did when we were kids.

All of us guys were talking sports when I noticed my sisters were at another table talking to two attractive women. One of the women was very pretty but very pregnant and the other was also very pretty and looked vaguely familiar to me. I started to stare at them and became very curious about the woman who looked familiar. She had such a radiant smile and beautiful, long, light reddish brown hair that was a few inches below her shoulders. She had a bright red sweater on and her eyes just glistened as she smiled and laughed with my sisters. I thought to myself that this was someone I would really like to meet.

I decided to walk over to the table my sisters were at and introduce myself to the two lovely ladies before the night was through. *Isn't it funny how brave you become when you have a few beers in you?* I was a little reluctant to just walk up to them but I had the perfect excuse to go over to their table. As I approached, the woman with the red sweater looked up and smiled at me and we locked eyes. I couldn't believe my reaction. I experienced a rush in the pit of my stomach. That was odd because I hadn't felt that since I was in college.

"Good evening ladies," I managed to say as I approached the table. "I'm Steph and Dee's brother Jack and I am very sorry to intrude, however, we are placing our order and I wanted to know what they wanted for dinner."

Stephanie turned around and said, "Oh, Jack, these are some friends of ours whom we met when Dee and I were in college. This is Leslie Ellis and her sister, Carrie Johansen. Leslie has remained a close friend of mine although I don't get to see much of her since she moved to New York." Steph turned to Leslie and said, "Jack lives in New York, too. Carrie and Leslie are meeting Carrie's husband and a friend of his for dinner."

I thought to myself, *this is not what I wanted to hear. Leslie waiting for her date.* I wanted to get to know this person and now I find out she was hooked up with someone.

"It is very nice to meet both of you. Leslie, have we met before? You look familiar to me. Perhaps I met you when I was at Penn?" I didn't know what else to say to her. I felt tongue-tied.

"Leslie did meet you several years ago at a fraternity party. She was there with me and Dee."

I don't remember meeting her then but it was probably because the night was a blur to me. My college years were a combination of hard work and hard play, and I drank more than my share of beer when I was at Penn.

I looked at Leslie and asked her where she lived in New York.

"I have a small apartment in Soho. It's a warehouse that was converted to apartments. Where do you live?"

"I have an apartment in the East Village, but I travel a lot and don't spend much time there," I replied.

"Carrie, when is your baby due?" I asked.

"Actually, I am overdue. My date was two days ago. I'm getting anxious to deliver this baby. I feel like the Good Year blimp!"

"You look great, in fact, you look very radiant and I'm sure you have been hearing that for the past several months. Don't they say that about pregnant women?" I said as I tried very hard to make conversation. "Would you ladies care to join us at our table until your guys arrive?" I said with sincerity.

"Thank you, but they should be here any minute. We really do appreciate the invitation," said Leslie as she smiled sweetly at me.

At that moment, I was completely mesmerized by her. I was determined to get to know her while I was in Philadelphia.

• • • •

Days had passed and Christmas had nearly arrived. I was busy shopping for gifts for family members when I bumped into Leslie at the mall.

"Hey, Jack, how are you?" she asked as she walked toward me.

"I'm a little exhausted from all of this holiday frenzy. I don't know how people do it. All this shopping from morning 'til night. It's not for me," I replied.

"Oh, you get use to it after awhile. The trick is to start early and get most of it over before December. Then you can kick back and socialize during the holidays."

I stood there looking at her and thinking how I would like to see her and wondering how to approach it. Lucky for me, she took the initiative.

"Jack, would you like to join me for a cup of coffee? I really need to sit down. I've been on my feet for hours and I need a break."

I couldn't believe my luck! "Yeah, sounds good," I replied.

There we were, sitting in Borders drinking coffee and having a great time. We were laughing about things we did when we were kids and when we were in college. We talked about our careers and the choices we had made. Leslie was a clothing designer with a sportswear company in New York. She had a small apartment in New York and came home to Philadelphia every other weekend. Leslie said she had read several of the articles I had written and admired my ability to go to dangerous places for the story. We both said it was odd that we lived near each other in New York and never crossed paths. Our apartments were actually only a few blocks away from each other.

Two hours had passed and I had to return to my parents' house for a holiday party. All of our extended family were expected to be there, and I hadn't seen most of them in years. I was having such a great time that I hated to leave, so I decided to invite Leslie to the party. She said she would be there and so we parted with the belief that we would see each other that evening.

I did feel comfortable talking to her. She had a certain quality that was difficult to define, and I found myself attracted to her. The chemistry between us was undeniable. She had beauty, brains, and a great sense of humor. She almost seemed too good to be true.

I was eager to see Leslie again. Here I was, surrounded by family and friends that I hadn't seen in a long time, and all I could think about was Leslie coming to the house. I found myself looking at the clock wondering when she would arrive. Finally, she showed up at 9 p.m. My sister, Steph, opened the door and was surprised to see her. I quickly went to the door and told Steph that Leslie and I ran into each other at the mall and I invited her to the party. My sister gave me a strange look and then grinned at me. I knew she could sense what was going on between us. I invited Leslie in and proceeded to introduce her to all of the family.

The house was all abuzz with laughter and conversation and the food was really great too. We were all having a great time, and I knew I didn't want this to end. I asked Leslie if I could see her again, after chugging down a few beers, and she said yes. She did mention that she had been involved with someone from New York, but the relationship had ended a month before and she knew it was time to move on. This visit home proved to be a turning point in my life and set destiny in motion.

Leslie and I saw each other a lot during this time and even went out together on New Year's Eve. We went to dinner and then clubbing with my brother and his wife. Leslie looked so beautiful that night. She wore a beautiful, sophisticated, black velvet dress with a low V in the back. Her hair was pulled up with curls falling and she looked very sexy without looking too provocative. She had the most beautiful, sparkling, hazel eyes and glowing skin. I found myself falling really hard and fast for her and I knew I was in trouble. I felt as though I had known her forever. I have always been a person who could control my feelings, but this was different. I had a strong feeling that we would be together from this point on.

CHAPTER 2

LOVE AND MARRIAGE

December 1995

Leslie and I continued to see each other when we returned to New York. We both traveled for business, but we called each other almost every day and spent as much time as possible together. We became close, and it became increasingly more difficult to leave her when I had to go abroad on an assignment. I had a reputation for cutting-edge investigative reporting and I was often in situations that were dangerous, especially stories in Lebanon in the 1980s and covering the conflict in Ireland in the 1990s.

Beirut was a hot bed of violence in the 1980s, and I was there between 1984 and 1987. I was in Beirut, Lebanon, in March 1984 when a car bomb killed 80 people and wounded more than 200, which was believed to be a CIA-backed attempt to kill the leader of the Hezbollah terrorist group. I was there when the CIA chief in Beirut, William Buckley, was kidnapped and killed by the Islamic terrorist group, Jihad. I was in Lebanon in 1985 when U.S. journalist, Terry Anderson, was abducted in Beirut and was later released. I was there in 1985 and 1986 when American students, Thomas Sutherland and Joseph Cicippio, were seized in Beirut by Islamic terrorists. They were both released in 1991. I was in Beirut when British journalist, John McCarthy and British church envoy, Terry Waite, were seized and later released in 1991.

The 1990s were just as violent. I covered the Irish conflict in Ireland and England from 1990 to 1994. I was there when the Irish Republican Army bombed the Baltic Exchange in London killing three and injuring 91 civilians.

I was there when conservative politician, Ian Gow, was killed in his home in England by an IRA bomb. I was chasing down a story about Islamic terrorism in London in February 1991 when the IRA fired a mortar at Downing Street, which was the residence of British Prime Minister John Major. Fortunately, there were no fatalities. I was in Belfast in 1992 when five Catholics were killed by Protestant terrorists, and I was in England when the London Financial District was devastated by an IRA bomb that killed one person and caused $1.5 billion in damage. I covered stories about the Chechen rebels and the car bombing at the World Trade Center in February 1993.

I reported on all of these terrorist acts and more, and received many journalist awards for breaking stories on terrorism. I have been on the run, chasing down stories for many years, but I felt that it was time to make some changes in my life. I had not had a personal life in so long and I was beginning to desire one after meeting Leslie. She brought new meaning into my life and I started to find myself taking time to smell the roses, as they say, and realizing that there are a lot of beautiful things in this world and that life isn't all death and destruction. I was actually becoming a bit more optimistic about life.

It was December 1995 when I asked Leslie to marry me. We were having dinner at a very expensive restaurant in Manhattan. I decided to wait until after dinner to ask her and to give her a ring. I had bought a princess cut solitaire at Tiffany's because I remembered her admiring one in their window. It was set in platinum and it was very beautiful. I wanted this evening to be romantic and memorable, because, after all, I found the love of my life and I wanted to make this relationship permanent. We started to walk down Fifth Avenue and we decided to take a carriage ride through Central Park. We had only been in the carriage a couple of minutes when I managed to make an excuse for her to reach in my coat pocket and then it happened.

She pulled out the Tiffany box and her eyes started to tear. She gave me a huge smile and said to me, "Is this for me?"

I looked at her and said, "Oh, the tooth fairy left that under my pillow with a note saying it was for you."

She laughed and then opened the box.

I said to her as she opened the box, "Leslie, I love you with all of my heart and I want to grow old with you." We had been seeing each other for a year and I knew she was the one for me. I never really envisioned myself married with kids, but my entire perspective changed on the subject. I found myself thinking about marriage, kids, a dog, and a nice house in the country. It surprised all of my colleagues when I told them I wanted to get married because I was always viewed as the eternal bachelor.

Leslie was shocked but was very happy. She told me that she was not sure how deep my feelings were for her. I am a person who holds back my feelings and people have often described me as aloof and very much in control of my emotions. I didn't know she was uncertain about my feelings for her, but surely she had no doubt now.

"Well, Leslie, will you marry me? I am crazy in love with you!" I said with great enthusiasm.

"Of course, I will marry you. I have never felt so alive and so complete as I do with you. I want to have a family with you. I want a house with a garden and cats and dogs and kids running around everywhere!"

"Well, I guess we should set a date and start planning a wedding," I said as I watched her gaze at her ring and then at me. I thought to myself how beautiful she looked in the dim lights of Central Park. I realized how fortunate I was to have met her and I firmly believed it was our destiny to be together. Life was good to begin with, but it just seemed to get better and better after I met her.

We discussed a wedding date and other plans, but couldn't agree on anything. I had been told that happens a lot with couples, and I was advised to let her have her own way with the plans. Weddings seem to be a bigger deal to women than it is to men. After much deliberation, Leslie decided that we should have a June wedding. I was fine with that, and she began to look for a wedding gown and a room for the reception. We both agreed that we should be married in Philadelphia at St. Peter's RC Church.

Tragedy struck Leslie's family in March. Her mother became very ill with pneumonia and died shortly after. Everyone was in shock. Her mother was always healthy, and no one could believe how ill Alice became that winter. Leslie was stricken with grief and could not continue with the wedding plans. She decided to take a leave of absence and move back to Philadelphia to spend time with her family. I came back to Philadelphia for the funeral and stayed two weeks, but duty called and I was off to the Middle East to cover a story. Leslie was very understanding about it, and before I left we made plans to get away in April.

Leslie and I decided to go to Paris for a week. Paris was so beautiful in the spring. We were having such a great time, and Leslie seemed to be handling the loss of her mother a lot better. We were sitting in a small café on the left bank when she got a serious look on her face.

"Let's get married while we are here," Leslie said with a very serious tone.

I was surprised because she had always wanted to have a grand wedding with lots of attendants and a grand reception and, of course, the long wedding Mass.

"I thought you wanted a big, fancy wedding?" I replied.

Leslie looked at me with such conviction and said, "I did but now it seems so unimportant after my mother's passing."

Truthfully, the thought of having a big wedding made me nervous. The idea of having a quickie wedding in Paris did appeal to me and had its merits.

"I'm game, if you are," I replied. "We can always have a big bash when we return."

She smiled at me, "You are the best. I really love you for so many reasons. I know that you will be a wonderful husband and I feel very fortunate to have found you."

"You know how I feel about you, so let's do it."

We managed to find a priest to marry us in a small chapel. It was a beautiful ceremony even though our family members were not present.

• • • •

When we returned to the States, we broke the news to our families. They were all disappointed, but were happy for us and wished us well. Our families got together and hosted a huge party with wedding gifts, lots of food, and even a wedding cake. Of course, the cake was made at Rob and Jessie's bakery and what a fine, delicious cake it was, with layers of chocolate and vanilla cake with thick, rich butter icing. It was an awesome party!

We stayed in Philadelphia for a week to spend time with our families and then returned to New York. We were ready to get back to work and start our new life together as husband and wife.

CHAPTER 3

RESEARCH

April 1996

Leslie and I found an apartment in New York, that was larger than what either of us had before. It was a nice apartment in Greenwich Village with exposed brick walls and a fireplace in the living room. It had a large kitchen and two bedrooms. It also had a small balcony where we were able to fit a table and chairs and lots of potted plants. I had to go to Europe on assignment for two weeks, but Leslie didn't mind because she was inundated with work and was involved with the design of new textiles for the fall line. Her sister, Carrie, who had a baby boy on Christmas Day 1994, was coming to visit Leslie while I was in Europe. They had planned to do some shopping and attend some Broadway plays while Carrie was in town.

I arrived back home on a Thursday evening only to find Leslie slumped over the toilet, vomiting profusely. I was very worried about her but she assured me it was just a stomach virus that was going around the office. The vomiting continued for a few days when I convinced her to see a doctor. She made an appointment for the next day and had a thorough examination. The doctor had her go for a blood test to see if anything showed up that was serious. Leslie received a phone call from the doctor two days later with some surprising news.

"Leslie, we got the test results back and it shows that your pregnancy test is positive," said Dr. Adams.

"You're joking, right doctor?" was Leslie's reply.

"No, I am not joking. Congratulations to you and your husband. I would like you to call Dr. Paul Jacobs' office tomorrow for an exam to determine how far you are with your pregnancy. He is a fine doctor and I'm sure you will like him. He's married with five children and his patients love him."

I saw the strange look on Leslie's face, and I asked her what the doctor said.

"He said I'm pregnant. Can you believe that?" she said with amazement. "I was so careful. I've been on the pill for a few years. I'm shocked."

"So am I, but I am also very happy. Aren't you?" I responded.

"Well, I guess when the initial shock wears off, I will be. I just didn't expect him to tell me that I am going to be a mother. It was a complete surprise."

All of a sudden, a rush of excitement came over me as I looked at her. I kept thinking that she was carrying my child. I felt very happy about it. I knew she would be a wonderful mother. She's caring, patient, sweet, and a million other things that a wonderful mother should be. A thousand things ran through my head, such as how our lives would change forever in ways we couldn't imagine. I went over to her and held her close to me. She was silent and still in shock from the phone call.

"Jack, are you ready for this?" she asked with concern in her voice.

"Les, is anyone ready for such an enormous change in their lives? We just got married a couple months ago and that alone is an adjustment, but that's what's so great about life. It's a continuous series of adjustments which is full of surprises, and somehow, humans manage to survive quite well through it all. Humans are the most adaptable species on the planet," I said in a reassuring tone. "I'm really excited about this. Trust me, everything will be fine. Didn't you say you wanted to have kids and a house out in the country with cats and dogs?"

"Yes, I did and I meant it when I said it, and I still want that. I'm so happy with you. I still can't believe I'm your wife. I know you are right about everything turning out fine. I was just surprised I got pregnant so quickly."

Leslie made an appointment to see Dr. Jacobs and I went with her to his office. The examination went well and he gave a prescription for vitamins and told her various things that were relevant to her condition.

We decided that it was time to look for a house, since our family would be expanding, but we didn't know where we should move. Should we buy a house in New York or Connecticut, or should we try to find a place near Philadelphia so we could be near our families?

We looked at several houses in three states and found exactly what we wanted. We found a stone farmhouse near Valley Forge, somewhat isolated in a wooded area. You had to drive up a narrow road to reach the property. It had several acres of land with it, and the features of the house were just what we were looking for. It had deep window sills, three fireplaces, original pine floors that were well preserved, and a huge kitchen with a walk-in fireplace. The house was built in 1778, and we loved it. It was close to our family and not too far from New York. We both decided that we could work from home and spend more time together. We had a child on the way, and it was time to do less traveling. I could cover stories stateside and Les could design from home.

We moved into the house in July. Leslie was three months pregnant and feeling much better. The nausea had subsided and she was looking more radiant every day. There was some work to be done to the house, but it could wait till after the baby was born. Leslie was really busy with decorating the house and working. She had very good reports from the doctor regarding her and the baby's health.

Things were falling into place. I started on some pieces for *International News Magazine.* They were told by an informant that things were heating up in Afghanistan and that a group of Islamic militants known as the Taliban were going to attempt to take control of the country. I also had an unusual offer presented to me by a friend, Kevin Leary, from Ireland. He called and asked if I would be interested in doing some work for a UFO documentary. The film would basically be about the debate over the existence of UFOs. I personally didn't believe in them and the existence of intelligent life on other planets, but I felt it would be a great opportunity for me, because I had never done work of this kind. It would also give me an opportunity to work from home.

• • • •

Kevin is a great guy whom I met a few years ago while covering stories on the Irish Republican Army. I told Kevin I would do it and I thought this assignment would be quick and easy. Little did I know that this subject was a heated debate that had been going on for many decades, ever since the 1950s with the Roswell incident. I thought it required a minimal amount of research, but I soon found out I was wrong. I was definitely not prepared for where this road was going to take me.

I had deadlines for both the *INM* articles and the UFO documentary, and soon discovered that I was not able to handle both projects. I did do one article for *INM* on the Taliban in Afghanistan, but declined any other work from them until I was finished with the UFO project. The Afghanistan assignment would have required me to spend a great deal of time there, and I wasn't prepared to do that at this time. I had a wife now and a child on the way and Afghanistan was much too dangerous. I needed to spend time at home with my wife, so the documentary project was perfect timing.

I started my research with the subject of crop circles and the theories behind them. Quite a few are manmade, in fact, at least fifty percent. There is a percentage that can't be explained. The molecular structure of the crops inside these circles are altered, and there is no explanation for this phenomena. There also seems to be a connection to Geometry with crop circles and a scientist actually discovered a new theorem after studying formations in England.

People have claimed to have made these circles starting in the 1960s, however, there were crop circles in other countries that appeared as far back as the late 1800s. I was never a believer in extraterrestrials or in the supernatural, but the more I researched, the more fascinated I became. Crop circles were interesting, however, the most interesting was yet to come. I must admit that the idea of extraterrestrials was really something I joked about, and always thought there was a logical explanation for all the things that happened which were attributed to them.

Roswell was a place that I really needed to visit, so it was my next stop on the UFO tour. I arrived there on a Monday morning and was given several names of persons who had relatives claiming to have seen UFOs and remnants of a crash. The crash that created such a controversy had allegedly taken place on July 4th, 1947, over a ranch in Roswell, NM. The rancher heard a tremendous bang that night during a terrible storm, so he investigated the next morning. What he found totally confused him. Strange debris was scattered across several acres of his ranch.

There were many pieces of metallic material that looked like it may have been remnants of a plane crash, however, the material had properties unlike that of any metal material known to man. The silver metallic material could be crushed inside your hand, but it completely flattened once released. The material could not be cut or burned. There were also plastic strips amongst the debris that contained markings which resembled hieroglyphics. He immediately contacted the sheriff's department and several officers came out to his ranch to see the debris firsthand. Not long after the discovery, military personnel from a nearby U.S. Air Force base appeared and closed off the property until all wreckage was confiscated.

One man claimed that when he was a child, he, his father, and two brothers were hiking when they came across a strange craft that had crashed in the desert near Roswell. The really bizarre thing about this story was that he claimed they saw human-type beings lying on the ground. They were all deceased except for one. He described them as small in stature, about the average size of a 12-year-old boy. They had large heads, no ears, a very small mouth, and unusually wide eyes. Their skin appeared to be grey in color and they wore tight-fitting garments that had a strange symbol on the front.

The being that was still alive was seriously injured and apparently communicated to them via mental telepathy. The people wanted to help this being but simply didn't know what to do. In a few minutes, Army personnel arrived and the man claimed that the military personnel forced them to leave. They were told not to reveal what they had seen, or else there would be serious consequences to them and their entire family.

I couldn't believe what I was hearing. This was too incredible for me to comprehend. I thought that it had to be an elaborate hoax that was passed on to the next generation. I decided to check records for that day in July 1947 to see what was recorded. I was very surprised to discover that a Colonel Blanchard had issued a press release stating that a UFO crashed on a ranch in Roswell. The release was later retracted and the story was changed to report that the foil-type material was debris from a crashed weather balloon. Roswell has been open for debate ever since.

Some of the other subjects I was researching included cattle mutilations, which were quite interesting, and the usual UFO sightings by average citizens. I had interviewed two ranchers in Texas who told me that they had several cows that were gutted and drained of blood. No one could figure out how it was executed. There was no evidence of blood surrounding the area where the cattle were found, and the removal of their internal organs were done with laser-like precision. It was a complete mystery to all who investigated the mutilations including a forensic team of veterinarians.

I also wanted to check the U.S. government's website to see if there was any documentation about sightings or other strange phenomena. What I found was information regarding a government agency, known as Project Blue Book, which investigated reports of unusual sightings and strange phenomena from 1952 through December 1969, when the project was officially terminated. Thousands of reports were collected and analyzed, but the agency concluded that there were no threats to national security.

I surely had my work cut out, and I had five months to prepare a comprehensive report for the documentary. I knew I had a lot more research to gather, but I didn't realize at the time that the most interesting research was yet to come.

CHAPTER 4

MISCARRIAGE

Summer 1996

I returned from my trip to Roswell only to find Leslie slaving away in the kitchen. It was a full moon and Leslie and I were having a nice intimate dinner in our newly-renovated enclosed side porch. Leslie really outdid herself with a fine Italian dinner of homemade bread, tossed salad, lasagna, meatballs, and an Italian pastry for dessert. We also enjoyed some wonderful Italian wine which I brought back from one of my assignments in Italy.

"Les, you really made a fine meal. A feast fit for a king. How did I get so lucky finding a wife with beauty, brains, and cooking skills," I said to her enthusiastically as I sipped my wine.

"I am so glad that you're home. I really miss you when you're away. I was thinking that maybe we should get a dog. What do you think?"

"I think that is a great idea. What kind of dog do you want?"

"I was thinking of a medium-size dog. Not too big, but not small. How about a Labrador. They are great dogs and they are suppose to be good with kids."

"Yeah, I like them. Let's get one. Maybe we could adopt one from the pound or some animal rescue group."

Les and I checked the newspaper over the weekend and decided to adopt a puppy from an animal rescue group. There were so many dogs that needed a home and we were advocates of adopting pets that have been abused or abandoned. We went to a place that turned out to be a farm where there were so many dogs. A female Lab was found roaming the streets and the group rescued her. She was expecting puppies and gave birth to eight.

Les fell in love with the smallest one in the litter. It was a female so we decided to take her. The man who sold us the puppy said he thought the puppies were mixed with golden retriever. She was so adorable and very affectionate. We were thinking of all kinds of names on the way home, and decided to call her Taffy because of her coloring.

Taffy quickly became a member of the family and we were very happy with her. She rarely had an accident in the house and she seemed to have very good instincts. She always knew when I was coming home. She would stand at the window about ten minutes before I came down the road no matter what time of the day it was. She just knew when Les or I were coming home. She was definitely Leslie's dog though. She followed her around and always laid at her feet when we were watching TV.

I was organizing my notes and information for the documentary when Leslie came into my office. Her sister, Carrie, and her were going shopping in Manayunk, and then they planned to have dinner with my sisters, Stephanie and Deirdre. It was three o'clock in the afternoon and she planned to return home by eight. That was fine with me because I needed to do some research on the internet and get started on the series of articles I was contracted to do. I started to research theories about UFOs when I stumbled across a lot of information about government conspiracies regarding the cover-up of alleged sightings and encounters. I did find it quite interesting even though I didn't believe in them. I did, however, believe in government cover-up. I saw plenty of that going on in Washington when I covered stories about terrorism and the CIA connection to some members of the terrorist organizations.

Leslie returned home at 8 p.m., right on schedule. She said she was going to sit in the living room and I decided to join her. I grabbed a beer out of the frigde and sat down on the sofa with her. I needed to unwind after sitting all afternoon at the computer. Leslie said she was feeling strange. She was very tired and she wanted to go to bed soon. I was concerned about that because she looked very pale, but I didn't want to say anything to her about it. I was ready to take a swig of my beer when she began to groan. She bent over slightly and said she was having severe pains in her stomach.

"Jack, I'm in a lot of pain. Please call the doctor."

As I got up to make the call, she cried out from the pain. "I'm taking you to the hospital now. Something is wrong and we are not waiting around to hear from the doctor."

I grabbed our coats and off we went in a hurry. She continued to moan from the pain and I admit that I drove way above the speed limit. I took her to the nearest hospital to our house. I was a nervous wreck, but remained calm. I didn't want her to know how worried I was.

"Jack, I think I'm losing the baby."

"Don't say that Leslie. Everything will be alright. You may just have indigestion and they will give you something to eliminate it."

"I know what indigestion feels like, and this is a lot worse," said Leslie.

"Stay calm, Leslie. The doctors will take care of this and you will be good as new," I said as I tried to reassure her.

A nurse took Leslie into a room in the emergency ward. I sat in the waiting room for two hours and it felt like an eternity. All sorts of things were going through my mind. Finally, the nurse came in the waiting room and said I could join my wife.

The doctor had just examined her and she was crying. I felt so helpless at that moment. Somehow I knew what had transpired and all I wanted to do was hold her in my arms and comfort her. The doctor motioned to me to go into the hall.

"Leslie, I will be right back," I said to her as I was leaving the room.

"Mr. Branden, I'm sorry I have to tell you this. Your wife has lost the baby. Has your wife been under a lot of stress recently?"

"No doctor, in fact she has been really happy and taking it easy."

"Well, sometimes there is a problem with the fetus and the body passes it. There are other times when women miscarry because their body simply rejects the fetus for no apparent reason. We will call her doctor and discuss it with her. She will get back to you and your wife with more information.

I'm sure she will want to examine Leslie tomorrow. We will admit your wife so we can observe her during the night. She is hemorrhaging badly and we want to make sure she doesn't lose too much blood or go into shock. You can stay with her when she gets into her room. Once again, I am very sorry for your loss."

"Thank you, doctor, for your help," I said in a very quiet voice.

I returned to Leslie. She was so distraught. *How do I comfort her when I am feeling so much sadness myself?* I knew I had to be strong for her.

"Leslie, the doctor said he was going to call your doctor tonight and he thinks Dr. Carlin will want to examine you tomorrow."

Leslie started to see Dr. Susan Carlin when we moved to Valley Forge. Her sister Carrie was a patient of her, and Carrie had highly recommended Dr. Carlin.

"Jack, I'm so sorry I lost the baby. I know how much you wanted to start a family and I feel so responsible for this."

I was shocked to hear her say that to me. "Leslie, it wasn't your fault. Please don't think that. These things happen. You are not responsible for your miscarriage. All I care about is that you are ok. You are the most important thing in my life. Everything will be alright."

Leslie sobbed as I hugged her. I knew this was devastating for her.

Dr. Carlin came to examine Leslie the next day. Les had lost a lot of blood and was very weak. Dr. Carlin examined Leslie and told her she had to rest. The doctor gave Leslie a sedative and motioned for me to follow her into another room.

• • • •

"Mr. Branden, your wife has lost a lot of blood, but she should be a lot better by this afternoon. I have her on a sedative and she will rest most of the day. She should be able to return home tomorrow. I really can't tell you for certain why the miscarriage occurred, however, about 20% of first-time pregnancies do end in miscarriage. The reasons are varied, but, at this time, I can't tell you why Leslie miscarried. She is in very good health and I didn't see anything unusual when she had her pre-natal check-ups. Was she experiencing any cramping, or was she under a lot of stress?"

"No, she was fine. In fact, she was really taking it easy. She cut back on her workload so that she could work from home for just a few hours a day. Everything has been going quite well for both of us," I replied.

"Mr. Branden, I will have my office set up an appointment for Leslie next week for a complete exam and I will see if anything looks unusual. Leslie should be sleeping now, so I will speak to her tomorrow about this when I check her to see if she is ready to be discharged."

I thanked the doctor and went to Leslie. She was sleeping quietly and I went home to shower and change my clothes. I had a lot of phone calls to make to let everyone in our families know what happened last night.

Leslie and I went to her doctor appointment the following week. Dr. Carlin gave Leslie a complete exam and afterwards, had a long talk with Leslie and I to let us know what the results were of the exam.

"Leslie, you are a very healthy woman in just about every way, however, it appears you have scar tissue on your fallopian tubes which can make conception very difficult. What I suggest is that you start trying to conceive in about a month or two, and we can see what happens. Many times it can take up to a year before women conceive when there is tissue present. I would like you to call me immediately if you have severe cramps or unusual pain. I will have Margaret set up an appointment for you in six months to check your progress. We will discuss what to do at that point if the scarring becomes worse and if you have not conceived by that time."

Leslie and I were both disappointed by what the doctor had to say. I felt bad but Les was really devastated by the news. She and I wanted to have children as soon as possible. Family was everything to us. We bought the house, got the dog, and we were ready for kids.

"Jack, how can this be? I didn't have a problem getting pregnant and I never had problems with my health."

"Leslie, do you think you should get a second opinion? I'm sure there are a lot of great doctors in Philadelphia who could give you a thorough exam and let you know what's going on."

"I think I may just do that for my own peace of mind," Leslie replied.

Leslie got a great recommendation from my sister and sister-in law regarding a Dr. Alex Johnson. They just raved about him. He delivered all of their kids and they were very happy with him. She went the following week for an examination, and Dr. Johnson confirmed what Dr. Carlin had said. I guess we will just have to try again and hope for the best.

CHAPTER 5

LESLIE AND MARCY

Autumn 1996

The autumn leaves were changing and I was busy working on my UFO research. Kevin came to the U.S. to discuss the details of the project and to arrange a meeting for all the principles involved. He was curious where everyone stood regarding material and deadlines. I had to return to New York for a few days to meet with him and to see some people at *International News Magazine*. They were still trying to assign me to Afghanistan to cover the Taliban, but I continued to refuse their offer. I thought that it would be beneficial to meet with them when I was in N.Y. and to let them know that I was still in the game but just not at this time.

I wanted Leslie to come to N.Y. with me because I thought the change in surroundings would lift her spirits, but she passed on it. She said she had to see the doctor and was concerned she had not gotten pregnant. Leslie had recently experienced severe cramping and heavy bleeding. She was going to have her younger sister, Marcy, accompany her to the doctor's office and have her stay a few days. Marcy was attending graduate school at Penn and was looking forward to spending time with Leslie.

I tried not to sound too concerned for her sake, but I was really worried about her. She had made the decision to hand in her resignation and take it easy. Although she had kept busy decorating and renovating the house, she still thought a lot about her miscarriage and was depressed over it.

I was planning to meet with a doctor who teaches at Columbia University while I was in N.Y. He was a psychiatrist with several patients who claimed they were abducted by aliens. I couldn't believe that I actually was going to interview someone like that because I thought alien abduction was a result of people hallucinating. I refused to believe such a thing was possible. Dr. Henry was highly intelligent, well-respected, and I think that was the reason I wanted to interview him. Surely a man with his credentials would not waste his time on nonsense. I later discovered that this meeting would prove to be most interesting.

I arrived in N.Y. at 8 a.m. on Monday and checked into the hotel. My schedule was busy. I had an appointment at *INM* for 11 a.m., and a late lunch meeting with Kevin and the other people involved with the project. We were meeting at Kevin's hotel and the meeting would probably last into the night. A member of the British Film Company (BFC) was also coming to see how things were progressing. Kevin was overseeing the documentary for them, and the British were very interested in subjects such as UFOs, psychic phenomena, and lots of other strange things which fall under the heading of paranormal.

My meeting with Dr. Benjamin Henry was scheduled for Tuesday at 10 am. I couldn't wait to hear what he had to say. I made a real effort to be serious when he discussed alien abductions and lost time experiences, which I had researched about a week before the meeting.

I still couldn't believe I took this assignment, but I did owe Kevin for saving my life. We were both covering the terrorism in Ireland and England and the evolution of the Irish Republican Army. I was in the middle of a cross-fire when Kevin pulled me into a doorway just as some bullets were fired in my direction. I would have been dead if it had not been for Kevin. We became very good friends from that moment on.

The meeting with Kevin and the others went well. Everyone's assignment was right on schedule, and the documentary would be ready to film in January. Kevin and I went down to the hotel lounge and had a few beers. Kevin said the BFC was really excited about this project and, if all goes well, there will be others.

"Jack, I have known you for a long time and I know what a great journalist you are. I would really like you in on other projects if this one goes well."

I was surprised at what he had just said. I hadn't seen Kevin for a few years and I didn't know he had such a high regard for my skills.

"Kevin, I'm flattered and you know how I like delving into a meaty story, but since I've gotten married, I have really slowed down. My priorities have changed, but I do appreciate your consideration."

Kevin looked at me with much surprise.

"This certainly doesn't sound like the Jack Branden I know. Jack, you don't have to lie down and die just because you got married. I'm sure you still have bills to pay. Besides, you could do all of your research stateside and get a lot of information online. You could do most of your work at home, and travel time would be at a minimum. It would be an ideal situation for you."

I thought about what he was saying, and it really did sound like a good opportunity for me.

"Let's see what happens with this project. I find certain aspects difficult to believe. It would be an ideal situation to work from home and that was my plan, but I was hoping to write a book about my experiences and do some freelance writing for newspapers and magazines."

I suppose I was not as optimistic about this project for the BFC as he was. Kevin looked me right in the eyes and said, "Jack, as you continue with your research, you will start to believe. No one was more skeptical than me and you know that, but I have seen things with my own eyes and I know there is more to this world than what we could ever fathom. As time goes on, you will understand what I mean, but for now, just trust me."

I was curious about his comment regarding things he has seen with his own eyes that made him a believer, so I asked him what he saw that changed his mind.

"Well, Jane and I were driving home from a Christmas party one night at about 2 a.m. when we noticed a bright object in the sky. I initially saw it in the rear-view mirror, so it was actually in back of our car. I pulled off the road and we both got out to get a better view. At first we saw only one bright object moving across the night sky, but then it was joined by two more bright objects. As they came closer to us, we could see that they were disc-shaped with colored lights completely around the perimeter. Each craft beamed down a spotlight as if they were conducting a search. This went on for a few minutes and then they came closer to us and hovered in one spot, almost as if to let us know they were aware that we were watching them. They abruptly took off a couple of minutes later and each craft went in a different direction."

"How did you and Jane feel during this sighting?" I asked. "Were you shocked, scared?"

Kevin paused for a moment to reflect on the question.

"Well, I think, it was a combination of both. We were shocked because we had never seen anything like this before and we never believed others who claimed to have seen UFOs. We were frightened because these objects came toward us and appeared to be aware of our presence. We didn't know what to do. We just stood there and watched. I think the greatest fear happened after we started to talk about what we just experienced. Jane was rather shaken afterwards so we got in the car right away and took off for home. Jane and I never discussed it with anyone. We didn't report it to the police because we didn't think they would believe us. After all, we just came from a Christmas party, and they probably would have thought we were drunk and seeing things," Kevin said in a very serious manner.

"Did you lose any time during this sighting?"

"I don't think so because when we got home, the clock in the kitchen was at 2:30 and the house where the party took place was about 15 minutes from our house."

It became clear to me at that moment that Kevin's obsession with UFOs and all the mystery surrounding them was motivated by a personal, profound experience.

We ended our conversation and I went to my hotel room and crashed on the bed. It was midnight and I wanted to call Leslie to make sure she was alright. I decided to call even though it was so late. I dialed our number and she picked up after the fourth ring.

"Leslie, I'm sorry if I woke you, but this was the first chance I got to call you tonight." Leslie sounded like she may have been sleeping.

"Hey Jack, it's ok. I just came upstairs. Marcy and I were catching up with each other as far as what has been going on in our lives." I detected something in her voice that disturbed me.

"Les, how was your doctor's visit?" Leslie took a deep breath and started to talk.

"She said that the scar tissue has increased and my chances of getting pregnant are practically impossible. I really don't want to discuss this over the phone. Let's talk about it when you get home tomorrow night."

I felt a knot in the pit of my stomach. "Les, you sound very tired, so I will let you get back to bed. I will be heading home as soon as I am finished meeting with Dr. Henry. I love you very much and I will see you soon."

"I love you too. Have a safe drive home. Goodnight Jack."

"Goodnight Leslie."

What a day it had been. The meeting with Kevin and the others involved with the project, the meeting with *INM*, Kevin telling me about he and Jane's UFO sighting, and now, the disturbing news from my wife. *I can't even imagine what Leslie must be feeling. I really have to get home to her. I almost feel like cancelling my appointment tomorrow, but I would only be postponing the inevitable.*

The next morning, I called Dr. Henry at his hotel and asked him if we could meet for breakfast. I didn't go into details but I explained that I needed to leave the city by noon. We met at the Plaza to have our discussion regarding alien abductions.

"Dr. Henry, you are a respected professor at Columbia University. How did you get involved with the subject of alien abduction?" I said with a tone of disbelief.

"Well Jack, I certainly hadn't planned to go in that direction, it just sort of happened."

"How did it all start?" I asked with great curiosity.

"It started several years ago with a family that I was counseling. They were all having anxiety attacks and recurring dreams of floating and being taken from their house in the middle of the night. I was very curious about it because all five members of the family were experiencing the same dreams, and they all had the same fear of the dark. I was totally baffled by the entire situation because conventional therapy was not working. I decided to try hypnosis to get to the root of the problem and the husband and wife agreed to it. One-by-one, the family members were put under hypnosis and they all repeated the same story. The husband, wife, and their kids, two boys and a girl, all claimed under hypnosis that a bright light appeared in the sky and it moved directly over their property. They went outside to see what it was and the next thing they knew, they were in a place that looked very sterile and very modern. Each one had the same account of being subjected to a physical exam and being told that everything would be alright and it would be over soon."

"Excuse me doctor, but do you really believe their story?" I asked with a skeptical tone.

"At first, I couldn't believe what I was hearing. I thought they had an elaborate hoax going on which involved the entire family, but then I realized it was a real event that took place. They were all under deep hypnosis, so they couldn't have been faking the experience. None of them remembered what had happened when they were out of the hypnotic state. The next session I had with them, I had a colleague observe, with the parents' consent, of course, and the same thing happened when they were put under. They repeated the same information in great detail"

Dr. Henry continued, "We both researched UFOs and alien abductions and discovered that there were a lot of reports on sightings and abductions, but it was a subject that was denied by the government."

I sat there in disbelief, however, I was strangely fascinated by what he was saying. The wheels were turning in my head and I sensed Dr. Henry picked up on that.

"Jack, I know this sounds far out there, but how would you like to observe a group meeting with abductees?"

I sat there and found myself speechless. On one hand, I was very interested in hearing what goes on at these meetings, but on the other hand,

I felt like I would be validating something as absurd as this. What should I do? I faced a dilemma.

• • • •

"Doctor, let me think about this. It is fascinating, but I really have to digest this first. Can I get back to you next week?"

"Sure, no problem. I understand how you feel. I've been there and it takes some time to accept this sort of thing. Here is my card. Please think about it and give me a call anytime. This particular group meets once a month and would welcome you at their meetings."

This was the most unusual trip to N.Y. I had ever made. In fact, it was the strangest trip I ever made, period. I called Leslie at noon and said I was leaving for home. I told her I should be home by 3 p.m. at the latest. She said she had something else to tell me when I arrived home. It wasn't anything bad, just different. I thought to myself that her comment was very mysterious and I was sure eager to return. I decided to stop and buy some roses on the way home to surprise her. She had gone through a lot recently and flowers would make her feel better.

I opened the front door and Taffy greeted me with a big sloppy kiss. "Hey girl, where's your mom?" I said to the dog as if she would answer me. I called Leslie's name and she came down the stairs. She was in the spare bedroom changing the sheets. Marcy was planning to leave for her apartment in the evening, and we were eating dinner together before she left. Leslie and I gave each other a hug and kiss, and we both said we missed each other.

"Here Les, I got these for you." I handed her the roses and she smiled and said that I was very sweet. Not exactly what a man wants to hear, but I knew what she meant. She told me that she was making dinner, and Marcy would be joining us. Leslie said she had so much to tell me at dinner, and asked me to run to the store to pick up some dessert.

The three of us had a pleasant conversation during dinner, but then Leslie said she wanted to tell me about something strange that happened to her and Marcy the night before. I was curious because of the way she said it. There was something in her tone of voice that was different.

"What happened last night?" I asked.

"Marcy and I were driving on a back road last night so we would get home quicker, when all of a sudden, we saw this really bright light in the sky. It looked like it was moving with the car. A minute later, the car stalled, and the next thing we know, it's over an hour later and we have no idea what happened in that time."

I must have looked at them as if I didn't believe them because Marcy chimed in.

"Jack, it was the strangest thing. One minute we are sitting in the car trying to start it and the next minute, or at least it felt like a minute, we were standing outside the car and neither one of us remembered getting out of the car. What do you make of that?"

How do you respond to a question like that? I know they don't drink, except for an occasional glass of wine. Nor do they take drugs, so I can rule that out. How do you explain not knowing what happened for an hour or more?

"Are you sure about the time? Maybe you were trying to start the car and didn't realize how much time had elapsed. You may have been frightened in the dark on a back road basically deserted."

Leslie got defensive and insisted that they did not try to start the car for over an hour.

"Jack, how do you explain the fact that we were standing outside the car? Neither one of us remembered even getting out of the car."

I sat there trying to make sense of this.

"What happened to the bright light?" I asked.

"I don't know. I just remember that it was gone when we were standing outside the car," replied Leslie.

Marcy chimed in at this point.

"Jack, I experienced the same thing Leslie did. I too was standing outside of the car. The whole thing is starting to scare me. I think I will stay here tonight and go back to my apartment tomorrow morning if that is ok with you. I don't want to drive home alone in the dark."

"Marcy, you can stay as long as you like. We love having you. Besides, we can always put you to work. Leslie said she wanted to start house cleaning. Do you do windows?" We all laughed and Marcy said goodnight to us.

Leslie and I stayed up a couple of hours. She reiterated what the doctor had told her about the scar tissue and that it would be nearly impossible to get pregnant. I tried to comfort her, and told her that we would work through this. There were options that we might consider and Leslie told me the doctor wanted to discuss them with us when we were ready. Shortly after that conversation we went to bed, but I had a difficult time falling asleep. I was thinking about Dr. Henry and what he had told me about his work. I was also thinking about Kevin's project and the opportunities that might arise from it, but mostly I was thinking about Leslie and how upset she was about what her doctor told her.

CHAPTER 6

THE GROUP MEETING

November 1996

It was November 1996 and I had a deadline to reach, plus I needed to contact Dr. Henry about the research on alien abductions. It was something I was trying to avoid, but I had to face up to it, because it was an important part of the documentary. Leslie appeared to be in better spirits lately. She had been working on the renovation of the house and it was really going well. She is so organized and she actually had a work schedule planned for the contractor to follow as to what had to be done first. She wanted to make sure that the work on the inside of the house was finished by Thanksgiving. This would be our first holiday season in our home and we wanted to make sure it was fit for entertaining.

I rummaged through my desk drawer and found Dr. Henry's card with his number. I gave him a call and discussed the possibility of sitting in on a group meeting with the alleged abductees. He said their next meeting was scheduled for the following Saturday at 1 p.m. at a church in the East Village. I jotted down the time and address and told him I would be there. I talked to Leslie about this meeting and asked her if she wanted to come to the city with me. She said that she had to pass on the offer. She had been taking a class on decorative painting, and her last class was that afternoon.

• • • •

I arrived at the meeting right on schedule. I had taken the train into the city and had planned to return home that evening. I was hoping to be home by 7 p.m. to have dinner with Leslie. I was very surprised to see 45 people at the St. John's Church for this meeting. Dr. Henry was there and he told me that there were many groups like this all over the country, and, in fact, there were international chapters.

The meeting started and Dr. Henry introduced me to the group and explained why I was present. He also asked each member to give their first name and their occupation. I didn't quite understand why he had asked them to say their occupation or profession, but I soon found out why. There were many professionals in the group, and I think he believed that it would add credibility to the claims if I knew they were professionals. Some of the people were related such as husband and wife, as well as families with their children. This particular group was formed ten years ago with six members. It has grown to 123, but due to the large number of members, they separated into other groups which meet on different days.

I sat there with recorder in hand and listened to the testimonials and was stunned to hear what they had gone through. I couldn't help but believe their stories because of their sincerity and I could feel their emotional torment. The fear that was present in some of these individuals was undeniable. *Something clearly happened to them, but what was it? Was it really alien abduction, or was it something that had happened to them on a more personal level?* I was on a mission to find out the truth. A common theme ran through the stories or experiences, and it was interesting. They all described the aliens in the same way—thin figures with no hair, large eyes, no ears, grey in color, and no verbal communication. Somehow these people received messages mentally.

I asked these people how the abduction began and one woman named Tracy said that she was driving home from a party late one night about three years ago, when all of a sudden her car stalled. She tried to start her car and then the next thing she remembered was that two hours had passed and she didn't know what had happened in that time. *I couldn't believe what I was hearing. It was a familiar story that I had heard before. It was the same experi-*

ence that Leslie and Marcy had several weeks ago when I was in N.Y. The shock must have been obvious to the others because Dr. Henry asked me if I was alright.

I looked at Dr. Henry and said I was fine and then I turned to Tracy and asked her what happened after that.

"I started to have strange dreams a few months after the incident occurred, so I went to a therapist because the dreams involved me running from strange people that I couldn't really see with the feeling of being captive and frightened. The therapist recommended hypnosis because she couldn't get to the root of the problem. While I was under hypnosis, I began to tell the therapist that I was taken on board a craft of some sort by some very strange looking people. They were about five feet tall or maybe even less than five feet, and they had large heads and huge eyes and were very thin. They did an examination and then they were probing my nose. The therapist had recorded the session, so when I came out of the hypnosis, she played the tape for me. I was horrified to hear myself describe in great detail the entire experience.

"I began to notice peculiar things after this session. I was having what I would call flashbacks of what I experienced. I also noticed that physical problems that I had most of my life had vanished. For example, I had terrible sinus problems which gave me severe headaches. I had apparently broken my nose when I was very young and there was a blockage which caused the sinus problems. I was scheduled to see my doctor to determine if the medication he prescribed was working and when I should schedule surgery to correct the problem. The doctor examined me and then studied the past records. He asked me who did my surgery and I told him I didn't have surgery. He said my nose had been repaired, and whoever did it had the skills of the angels. I asked him what he meant by that and he told me my nose was perfectly straight and my sinus passages were clear and I shouldn't have anymore sinus problems. The surgery was beautifully executed, in fact, the best he had ever seen."

I sat there in disbelief. I was thinking to myself that something like this could not be true. I moved forward in my chair and began to speak to Tracy.

"Tracy, you have no other explanation for this? Do you really believe these aliens abducted you and performed surgery on your nose?"

"I have no other explanation. I know I didn't go to a hospital and have surgery on my nose. There is no other explanation."

"Are you sure you didn't forget that you had surgery? Maybe you had outpatient surgery and just forgot?"

Tracy looked at me with a very defensive look on her face and said, "Don't you think I would have gotten bills from a doctor or a hospital for their services? Come on, Jack, when have you ever gone to a hospital for treatment and not received a bill for one thing or another."

I had to admit that she had a point. You can go to a hospital for a scrape that required just a band aid and you get several bills for just showing up at their door.

"Tracy, I apologize if I sound skeptical. I have never been exposed to this sort of thing and was not really aware of this phenomena," I said in an apologetic way.

I left that group session with a lot of food for thought. I just kept thinking about everything the members said about their experiences. People said they had implants in their legs and noses. Others had cattle that were mutilated, and people who had strange formations in their fields. I just couldn't get past the skepticism, but Tracy's experience really hit home. The lost-time incident that Marcy and Les had was so similar to what Tracy had described. It was really scary. Leslie didn't have any dreams or anything that would indicate that she may have been abducted. I didn't mention this to her. I didn't want to alarm her or her sister. I just couldn't believe that these experiences didn't have a logical explanation. *Could it be that people were reacting to a medication that would cause hallucinations?* I would have to do more investigating because I wasn't sold on aliens, yet alone alien abductions.

I got home about 7:30 p.m. and had dinner with my wife. We were having a glass of wine when she started to talk about a strange dream she had the night before. I didn't think anything of it until she started to give me details about the dream. Leslie said that she had a dream about her mother and that her mother told her she was going to get pregnant very soon.

"Jack, the dream seemed so real. She also said that Marcy would no longer have problems with her allergies."

My sister-in-law has had severe allergic reactions to many things. She almost died from a bee sting, and she also had a severe allergic reaction to medicine.

"I suppose the dream was a result of my disappointment that I had regarding the inability to get pregnant."

"You could be right about that, but we must not give up hope. Science has come up with some amazing things, so don't think that the situation is hopeless."

I attended a few more meetings with the abductees and the stories were absolutely unbelievable. These people were sincere in their beliefs, and they were credible individuals. But it continued to be difficult for me to comprehend the concept of aliens and especially abduction. *If this was true, why were they taking people? What was their motive?* Most of these people, who claim to have been abducted, were also tormented by their experiences. Many believe they had been abducted many times and some believe it started in childhood and continued through the years. They were frightened and felt they had no control over the situation. They believed they could be taken at any time again, against their will. *Will we ever find the answers to these questions?*

I wanted to interview people from other countries who also claimed to have been abducted, so I contacted Kevin to see if he knew of anyone in Great Britain who works with abductees. As usual, Kevin knew a few people and he gave me their names and phone numbers. I contacted a Dr. Judith Davies in London and she said she would be delighted to discuss this subject with me. Dr. Davies had been a psychiatrist for 25 years and has heard it all. I talked Leslie into going to London with me, and I said we could turn it into a mini vacation. We would go the beginning of December when London would be decorated for Christmas. Leslie said that it was a great idea, and she was looking forward to the trip.

CHAPTER 7

SWEET DREAMS

November 1996

Thanksgiving arrived and the inside of the house looked so beautiful. Leslie has a real flare for bringing a house to life and making it a home. It has such a warm and inviting feeling to it. We had invited several family members this year, and we were excited because this was our first Thanksgiving in our home. It would be a great time. Leslie bought a 25-pound turkey, and we went all out to ensure all of the traditional dishes were made. We planned on potato filling, several vegetables, biscuits, cranberry sauce, gravy, and of course, pumpkin pie. It would be a feast fit for a king!

Dinner went really well and everyone stuffed themselves with food. The men ended up in the family room to watch football, and the women were in the kitchen cleaning up and chatting. Leslie asked Marcy to come upstairs and see the renovations she made to one of the bedrooms. It was actually an excuse to get Marcy away from the others so she could talk to her alone.

"Marcy, have you thought about what happened to us that night the car battery went dead? I have been having strange dreams about mom and I want to know if you had any dreams that were strange."

"Les, it's funny you should ask. I did dream about mom a few times since that night. In my dream, she told me that I would no longer have allergy problems. The really strange thing is I haven't had any symptoms of allergy problems. I haven't coughed or sneezed or had any headaches or watery eyes since that night."

Leslie looked at her with amazement. “Marcy, mom also told me in my dream that you would no longer have allergy problems, and she also said I would get pregnant soon. You know what the doctors told me about the scar tissue. They said that I would probably never be able to conceive. I was wondering if there was some sort of connection with the dreams and our experience that night on that back road?”

“I was wondering the same thing. Have you told anyone about the dreams besides Jack?”

Leslie said no, and Marcy said she hasn’t told anyone either. They both agreed to keep it a secret for now.

That night, I helped Leslie put everything away when our guests went home. We went to bed at midnight and both of us were tired. Leslie was sitting in bed when she started to tell me about her conversation with her sister.

“Jack, I asked Marcy if she had any strange dreams after the night we were stranded on Brower Road and she said she dreamed about mom. She had the same dream as me regarding her allergies.”

“Leslie, aren’t you making more out of this then need be? Don’t you think it is normal to dream about your mother? After all, you were all very close.”

Leslie didn’t like my reply. She became very defensive and said, “We both had the same dream. That’s why it’s so strange. I can see you’re not interested in discussing this and that’s fine. Goodnight.”

Well, I just got a taste of the female version of the cold shoulder. I think I’m safe in saying that I made her a little mad. I would try and do some damage control, but we were both really tired, and it would have to wait till tomorrow.

I went downstairs the following morning and noticed that Leslie was not around the house. The dog was gone so I assumed she and the dog went for a walk. An hour later, Leslie came home with the dog. My assumption was correct, they went for a walk. I immediately felt the deep freeze. This was the first time we had a disagreement, and I hated the way she was handling it. She simply ignored me and that really bothered me. I thought I better fix this or she may not speak to me indefinitely.

"Les, is something wrong? Have I done something to offend you?"

She looked at me with ice in her eyes.

"I just get the feeling that you don't believe me when I talk about what happened to me and my sister. We lost an hour of time and we don't know what happened in that time. I'm a little concerned about that," she said with definite sarcasm in her voice.

"Les, I do believe you, but I thought that perhaps you worried about it too much. I guess I thought you could shrug it off."

"Jack, how would you feel if that happened to you?"

"Well, it was only an hour and it is possible that your timing was off. I wouldn't make a big deal out of it if it happened to me."

I could tell my comment was not appreciated, but I decided to drop it because it wasn't worth debating and ending up with a huge argument.

Leslie continued to experience strange dreams. She dreamed that her mother was rocking two cradles and singing a lullaby. She also had dreams about her and Marcy stranded on a road and floating away, and about bright lights that were blinding. She also had dreams of laying on a table in a dimly-lit room and having strange people poking her with instruments. I looked up dream interpretation on the internet, and one site interpreted the floating as the person feeling that they lack control over situations in their life and dreaming about your mother, who was deceased, was a good omen.

I spoke to Leslie about that and told her that if the dreams disturb her, then she should seek counseling. Leslie felt that she dreamed about her mother because she missed her and thought about her a lot now that the holidays were arriving. The dreams didn't disturb her, but she always forgot her dreams shortly after she awoke. Lately though she had been remembering them and that was unusual. I didn't find anything strange about her dreams. I had some really odd dreams on occasion myself, but I wasn't going to tell her that. I didn't want to upset her again and appear insensitive.

CHAPTER 8

LONDON TRIP

I received a call from Kevin, and he wanted to see Leslie and me when we were in London. He wanted an outline of the material I had so far so he could start on the project. He needed to organize all of the information from all of the team members so that he would have a cohesive flow to his documentary. I had been working very long hours on this project, which was kind of funny considering I originally expected this assignment to be a piece of cake. I had all the work finished for crop circles, UFO sightings, and cattle mutilation, but I was not finished with the alien abduction part. I had planned to finish that part by mid-December. I needed to conduct a few more interviews and do a little more digging and then I would be finished.

Leslie and I were getting the 8 a.m. flight from Philadelphia to London. We were both excited to fly to London, and Les planned on doing a lot of shopping while we were there. She was especially eager to see all the decorated shops and Christmas decorations on the streets and houses. We decided to stay for five days and do some sightseeing. She had never been to England and she wanted to see the British Museum, Buckingham Palace, Big Ben, Kew Gardens, and Westminster Abbey. She especially wanted to see the Poets' Corner inside the Abbey which is a burial place for such luminaries as Chaucer, Tennyson, Robert Browning, and Charles Dickens. They also have memorials for Wordsworth, Milton, Shelley, Keats, T. S. Eliot, Jane Austen, and the Brontë sisters. Sir Laurence Olivier is buried there too.

We arrived in London that evening, and we were tired. We settled into our hotel suite and started to unpack.

"When are you going to see Dr. Davies?" Leslie asked as she was turning the bed down.

"I have an appointment with her tomorrow afternoon, so we can sleep late and have brunch before I see her. Is that ok with you?"

Leslie looked at me and said that was fine with her.

"I thought you could do some shopping while I was with Dr. Davies and then I could meet you at her office building around 3 o'clock."

"Sounds like a plan to me. I can't wait to check out all of the shops. I am heavily armed with credit cards so this documentary had better make lots of money or else we will be bankrupt."

I looked at her with a grin and said, "If it doesn't, you will just have to peddle your wares on the street."

She looked at me shocked, and laughed, "My wares? I'm a married woman."

I looked at her and said, "I meant your designs."

We both had a good laugh.

Leslie and I went downtown to Dr. Davies' office. It was located several blocks from the shopping district. I told Les to meet me at 3 o'clock and then we would return to the hotel and drop off her bags and go to the British Museum. She said she would meet me then, and off she went with cards in hand.

I took the elevator to the eleventh floor of the Tower office building. Dr. Davies' office was in room 1123. The building was really elegant with huge windows and hardwood floors with oriental rugs. There were several chandeliers hanging in the lobby with antique pieces scattered throughout the place. Beautiful paintings graced the walls in the hallway. It was a very classy, old, English building.

I told the receptionist my name and that I had an appointment with Dr. Davies. She asked me to make myself comfortable while I waited for the doctor. I looked around the room and thought how expensive an appointment must be with the doctors in this building. The cost of the furnishings in this office alone had to be in the hundreds of thousands, and the rent was probably very high as well. The receptionist said the doctor was ready to see me, and she led me to her office.

"Mr. Branden, it is so very nice to meet you. I have read many of your books and articles and I confess, I am a fan of yours."

I was taken by surprise, and I chuckled. Dr. Davies was a professional looking woman with short, dark hair, and striking blue eyes. I would guess she was about 50 something. She was tall and had an authoritative air about her.

"Dr. Davies, it is a pleasure to meet you and I thank you for the compliment. You took me by surprise when you said that. By the way, please call me Jack."

"Very well, Jack, I understand that you are doing research on UFOs and alien abduction. Kevin Leary and I are old friends, in fact, we grew up in the same town in Ireland. He went to school with my younger brother, Matthew. We sort of bumped into each other about a year ago when he was in town, and we discussed what we have been doing through the years. Kevin asked me if you could interview me regarding the alien abduction part of the documentary, and I said yes."

"What is your experience with this phenomena, Doctor?"

"Well, Jack, about eight years ago I had some patients who manifested some strange behaviors and they didn't know why. For example, some patients had missing-time experiences at night, and as a result of that, they would make sure they were home before dark. We are talking about adult men and women who are professionals and who make lucrative salaries. Some of these people had strange marks on their arms and legs and couldn't explain where they got them. I was intrigued by their accounts and decided to do some research of my own. I placed an ad in the personals requesting that anyone with strange experiences should please contact me and I listed a phone number. I was flooded with calls within two days of the ad. I couldn't handle most of them, so I ran another ad to meet at a church hall to discuss their experiences. I was shocked when 122 persons arrived for the meeting. What started out as a fishing expedition turned into a support group for abductees."

I began to finally think that there must be something to this phenomena.

"Doctor, do you think that these people were sincere or do you think they just wanted attention, and therefore, fabricated their stories?"

"Oh no, they were real. I spoke to everyone individually and have sat in on many of their meetings, and I can tell you that people do not fabricate stories like these. They suffer real anxiety from their experiences, and I'm trained to know when people are delusional. Believe me when I tell you that this phenomena is real. Abductees do not, I repeat, do not want to be part of this. These abductions have wreaked havoc on their lives, not to mention their minds."

I started to think of my wife and what happened to her. I asked more questions.

"Doctor, what elements are typical in an abduction?"

She thought a moment and then replied, "Well, most abductees don't remember the experience on a conscious level. They have dreams of flying or bright lights and, more or less, they dream of small parts of the experience. They have fears of the dark that they didn't have before. Some people actually had physical problems corrected which would have required surgery. Some claim that they were taken several times in their lifetime which started when they were children. Many abductions happen within families."

"Have you used hypnosis on your patients or group members?"

"Yes, Jack, I have and that is what completely convinced me that all of it was true."

So many questions went through my mind when she said that hypnosis convinced her it was true.

"Doctor, why is this happening?"

"No one knows, but there are theories on it. First, I must tell you that most people think this is ridiculous and every government has denied it exists except Belgium."

"Belgium? What do you mean?"

"Belgium had a huge craft slowly pass over a couple of its major cities and the hovering craft was witnessed by thousands of people including the police and military. Belgium had some planes from their Air Force follow the craft and they observed that the maneuvers that it performed, the speed, and the angles that it made while in flight were not from any craft that was made on this earth. They identified it as a UFO and they are the only government who has issued an official statement which recognizes the existence of UFOs."

I was thinking in my head, *bravo for Belgium. At least there is one country in this world that is willing to tell the truth to their citizens.*

Leslie was doing a lot of window shopping in London when I was interviewing Dr. Davies. She later told me in great detail what had happened while she was walking down the streets and alleys of London. Les walked down one narrow alley when she came across a very small store front which had all sorts of stars and moons dangling in the window, and it also had a small sign which had PSYCHIC READINGS printed on it. The name of the shop was "The Harvest Moon." Les was always fascinated by that sort of thing, but had never gone for a reading. She decided to kill some time and go in and look around.

The shop had a real celestial, yet earthy, feel to it. There were lots of tie-dyed tee shirts and long skirts and lots of clothing made from flax. The smell of sweet vanilla and cinnamon was strong and strange, melodic music was playing very low in the background. The store also had homemade breads and baked goods and vintage-style jewelry and accessories. It was a quaint shop with a variety of different things. Les said she could have spent hours there just looking at some of the items.

A very friendly English lady about 45 years old greeted her as she entered the shop. She was a petite woman with long hair that was braided. She wore a gauze top and long skirt with several strands of crystal beads draped around her neck. The woman said her name was Brie and asked my wife her name. They struck up a conversation and Brie asked Les questions about where she lived and about her visit to London. Les asked Brie about the psychic readings. She wanted to know if she could have one. Brie was very excited and told her that she could have a free reading with any purchase.

Leslie laughed and said, "How about if I buy half of the contents of this store? I love just about everything you have."

"Well then, follow me," said Brie.

Brie led Leslie into a tiny room in the back of the shop which contained a small, round table, a tiny lamp, two chairs, and a deck of cards.

• • • •

"Have a seat and we will get started. I would like you to make a wish first, and then I would like you to shuffle the cards."

Leslie thought for a moment about her wish. Her first thought was a baby but she didn't know if she should wish for that since her doctor said she probably wouldn't be able to get pregnant. Leslie decided to wish for that anyway. Why not? After all, it is her reading.

"Ok Brie, I made my wish," said Leslie as she picked up the cards to shuffle.

"Leslie, I want you to shuffle as long as you want and then you must cut the deck into three piles."

Les complied and Brie picked up the cards and started to turn over 11 cards. She said she does the Keltic Cross method.

Brie started to tell Les what the cards meant.

"These cards are very interesting. The first card is the high priestess and that means that you are a very maternal and intuitive woman and you are greatly admired by men as having the ideal qualities for a woman. You recently had an unusual experience with a woman with brown hair who you are close to, and this experience will lead to many good things in your life. The Empress is in this spread and that is the fertility card. You will be giving birth by next year and there are two pages in this spread, so it may be twins. You had received some upsetting news in the past, but do not worry. Things will work out much to the surprise of a woman with very dark hair who has given you aid.

"You are married or involved with a man with dark hair. The two of you are very much in love and you recently acquired property. You and this man, will be receiving some exciting news shortly after the new year. I don't see you involved in a career. Are you currently working?"

Leslie sat there in disbelief. *How did she know all of those things?* She wanted to believe her about the pregnancy, but she knew what her doctor said and she didn't want to get her hopes up only to be disappointed.

"I'm not working right now. I resigned my position recently," Les replied.

"Well, you had a very important position which had an artistic side to it, perhaps designing. You gave it up for personal reasons. I don't see you returning to that position, in fact, I see you as a domestic diva in an older, large house with children, a dog, a cat or two, and of course, a husband which I think you already have."

Les laughed at the comment domestic diva. "I never wanted to be domestic, but I must confess that I am starting to feel really comfortable as a housewife."

"Leslie, I would like you to shuffle the cards again. Let's see what else is in store for you."

She shuffled the cards and was thinking that this was pretty amazing. *This woman didn't know her, yet she knew things about her. How was that possible?* Leslie shuffled and cut the cards. Brie started to lay out the 11 cards. The first card was the lovers card crossed by the two of cups.

"You and your husband are soul mates," Brie said as she continued to lay the cards out. "You lost someone very close to you this year. It is a woman, your mother. She is represented by the Queen of Swords. You dream about her and you will continue to dream about her. Think about those dreams because they are telling you something.

"Your husband is well-known. There is the five of wands which means he is working on something that will make him a controversial figure and he may meet opposition. He has a lot of courage and integrity and you will be very supportive of him. He will make a lot of money for some project he is working on, and it will lead to other things."

Leslie saw the death card and got a little upset. "What does that mean?" as she pointed to the death card.

"Oh, don't worry about that card. It doesn't mean physical death but rather change, transition, getting rid of the old and bringing in new opportunities. The world follows that card, which means the changes will be wonderful. Things will come full circle and all of your efforts will come to fruition. Your lives will change forever as one thing after another unfolds for the two of you. You've had a health issue but don't worry, it will be corrected in a way you could never imagine. You will be taking a secret journey and your consciousness will be raised to a higher level. Good things are coming your way."

Leslie sat there in amazement. "Thank you for the reading. I don't know what to say. You knew so many things about me."

Brie smiled at Leslie and said, "Leslie, you are going to have so many surprises coming your way, and your life is going to change so much that you will not believe it."

"Well Brie, I hope you are right about that. Now, let me exercise my credit card. I see so many things I want to buy."

They both laughed and went into the store.

Leslie and I met at Dr. Davies' office as planned. She was weighed down with lots of packages and she was very jubilant. I wondered if the shopping made her giddy. We headed for the hotel to drop off the goods and then walked a few blocks to a Chinese restaurant. It was at the restaurant that she told me about her reading.

I looked at her strangely and said, "A reading? Why would you get a reading? You don't believe in that stuff, do you?"

Leslie got a little defensive. "Yes I got a reading and you won't believe what she told me."

I smiled, thinking that it was just a folly, but I might as well listen to what she had to say.

"Well, what did she say to you that made such an impression?"

Leslie began to tell me the details of the reading and I have to admit, the reader knew a lot considering she was a stranger. It did bother me about what she said to Leslie about getting pregnant. I didn't want Les to be disappointed if it didn't happen, which is more than likely the case.

"Les, don't put a lot of faith in what she said. I would bet that most of what a reader says is untrue. They are vague about what they say, and I always thought they were just a con."

My wife looked at me with disappointment in her eyes.

"I know you are probably right, but I want to believe so much in all the good things she told me. You know how much I want children."

"I know and that is why I caution you. Leslie, what is meant to be, will be. If we are meant to have children, then we will. There are several options if you can't conceive. Right now, we are here to have a great time and enjoy London. Let's not worry about tomorrow."

"Yes, let's have a great time and take in all the sights we want to see while we are here," Leslie replied.

"Agreed," I said.

The next morning we went to breakfast and started on our way to some of the famous landmarks of London. We were on a mission to enjoy as much as possible before going home. We saw Buckingham Palace, the London Tower, Big Ben, changing of the guards, Westminster Abbey, and of course the Poets' Corner. Leslie is a big poetry fan so that was her favorite place in London. We skipped lunch to see more sights, so we were really hungry by 6 o'clock that evening. We decided to go to an English Pub near our hotel and enjoy dinner with a few beers. It felt like old times when we were first going out together. We were having the time of our life.

We had a couple of days left before we were to return home, so we spent as much time walking around London and taking in the sights as humanly possible. Picadilly Circus and people-watching was fun. We discovered streets that had a Dickens' Christmas theme and we went to the theater to see a play. It was one of the best times of our lives.

I had called Kevin and asked him to join us for dinner. He wanted my outline and I wanted to talk to him about the project. We made plans to meet at the hotel restaurant at 6 p.m. Leslie and I were at the restaurant right on time, but Kevin was a little late. It was about 6:15 when he arrived. He had brought his wife, Jane, along and I introduced them to my wife. We started to talk and then ordered from the menu.

Kevin and I began discussing the documentary. He told me that it was really coming together, and it should be right on schedule.

"Jack, how did you like Judy?"

I looked at him in a strange manner.

"Who is Judy?"

He laughed and said, "Dr. Davies. I've known her since childhood and she's Judy to me."

"Oh, she is a fascinating woman. I found the interview to be really interesting. She is quite convinced that alien abductions are real, but I'm still not convinced. Why wouldn't the government acknowledge UFOs if they were real and make it public?"

"It's all a cover-up. They're afraid of mass panic, I suppose. I also think that if people knew about aliens, that would make all of the politicians look like they were on the same level as the rest of us, and you know how egotistical they are."

We both started to laugh at that comment. Kevin started talking again in a more serious tone.

"Seriously, Jack, you know how the government covers up things so the public doesn't know what is really going on. There would be a rebellion if people knew the truth about all their secret dealings. They would never let something like this get out. Jack, you are one of the greatest investigative reporters of our time. You should really delve into this and find out why the government is not revealing the truth about this subject. You went to Roswell and interviewed people. You know what they told you about the way the government intimidated them and their family members."

I thanked Kevin for the compliment, but told him that I'm not convinced that UFOs are real so how could I investigate something that I didn't think existed. He said that he thinks someday I will be convinced, and God help the government if I decided to find out the truth. All of us had a good laugh over that because I am like a bulldog when I want to explore something. I won't let go until I obtain the information I want.

CHAPTER 9

THE DOCUMENTARY

Early 1997

Leslie and I returned to the States exhausted, but we both agreed it was one of the best trips we had ever taken. Before we knew it, the holidays came and went with much celebration. Our families gathered together, and it was a wonderful first Christmas for us as a married couple. We celebrated the new year with a lot of champagne. We enjoyed a pleasant New Year's Eve party at a hotel in downtown Philadelphia, and stayed the night. It was a wonderful holiday season for both of us.

January 1997 arrived and Kevin was ready to screen the documentary. I had sent him all of my material before Christmas and he worked non-stop to compile it. The documentary was scheduled for a private screening for all those involved with the project and the people from the BFC. Leslie and I were flying to London to view it, and then return home the next day. We didn't want to stay longer because of weather conditions. My wife was also feeling a little tired lately, and she just wasn't in the mood for traveling.

We went to the screening of the film and viewing it in its entirety made me think differently about the subject of UFOs and extraterrestrials. I felt like I was objective and logical, but somehow seeing everything together made me think that these things may very well be possible. The evidence was right there in front of me. The crop circles, the cattle mutilations, people giving first-hand accounts of what they had seen in the sky and on the ground were proof. Credible people talking about abductions and having medical exams and corrected physical problems without the aid of a doctor or hospital personnel surely made me think that there must be some truth to this. Why would all of these people lie? Individuals from around the world who were professionals, military personnel, and people who were very normal with no history of mental illness told of their experiences. What would they gain by fabricating these stories? When I really thought about it, it made me realize that it required a lot of courage to come forward and tell the world what happened to them. After all, they were setting themselves up for ridicule and most likely, the majority would think they were crazy.

The film appeared a week later on the BFC, and received great reviews and a high viewer rating. Everyone involved with the project was amazed with its popularity. It turned out to be a phenomena and the film received a lot of press. The press took a poll after the documentary aired to find out how many people believed in UFOs and the existence of intelligent life on other planets, and they discovered that 65% of those polled were believers. What a surprise! We never expected the percentage to be that high, and we certainly didn't expect such a positive response to the documentary. We received calls to appear on talk shows to discuss the film. The BFC decided to distribute it worldwide as a result of its popularity. It seemed to have the makings of a classic.

• • • •

Leslie continued to feel tired, and she started to feel nauseated as well. She was convinced that she had the flu so she made an appointment to see the doctor. She went to see Dr. J. D. Ventura, who had treated members of her family for years. He gave Leslie a thorough exam and suggested that she take a pregnancy test. Leslie was stunned when he said that, however, she stopped at a pharmacy on the way home and picked up a test. Leslie's stomach was in knots as she was ready to read the results. The test read positive for pregnancy. She couldn't believe the results and decided to keep them to herself until she saw her gynecologist. She made an appointment to see Dr. Carlin the next day.

She told Dr. Carlin about the positive test and how she had been feeling lately.

"Well, Leslie, let's take a look." Dr. Carlin paused and said, "This is interesting."

Les didn't know why she said that, but she surely was curious.

"Leslie, it looks like you are pregnant. Congratulations to you and your husband. I'm almost finished with the exam and I would like you to come over to my office so we can talk about this."

Leslie was concerned about what the doctor would say about her condition.

"Leslie, you are definitely pregnant and the scar tissue that was on your fallopian tubes has completely healed. I can't explain it because it is something that just doesn't happen, but it did happen to you. I am baffled by this but I am very happy for you and your husband. In any case, I will monitor your pregnancy very carefully and I want you to take it easy and do not exert yourself. I don't want you to be under any stress, so please relax and think pleasant thoughts. Do you have any questions?"

Leslie was still in shock. "I'm pregnant. I can't believe it, but it's true. Doctor, I don't know what to say. I didn't expect this, but I am thrilled. I can't wait to tell my husband. Thank you so much for the great news."

Leslie returned home and announced the good news from her doctor.

"Jack, that card reader told me I was going to get pregnant soon. She said although I had upsetting news in the past, things will work out much to the surprise of a woman with very dark hair who had given me aid. That must have been Dr. Carlin that she was referring to because Dr. Carlin was completely surprised that I'm pregnant and she told me that the scar tissue has completely healed, which is really surprising. Brie said we would have twins. Wouldn't that be wild having twins! I'm so excited about this."

I hugged Leslie and told her that I was very happy too. I also told her not to get ahead of herself because one baby would be wonderful. We both said that we should go out to dinner and celebrate, and then we could break the good news to our families.

Everything was going well. Leslie felt really good and her pregnancy was progressing smoothly. Dr. Carlin gave her a due date of September 27th.

Leslie was scheduled for an ultrasound the next week to make sure everything was fine. I went with her and much to our surprise, the doctor told us that Leslie was carrying twins.

Leslie started to laugh. "I told you so. She's right again."

I thought to myself, *here we go again.* The doctor asked her what she meant, and Les said it was a private joke.

"Everything looks good and I want you to come for a check-up every four weeks and as your pregnancy progresses, I will have you come in more often," Dr. Carlin said. She was very emphatic about Leslie taking care of herself and gave her specific instructions.

"Well Jack, now do you believe what Brie told me?" Leslie said as we were driving home.

"I can't deny the fact that she predicted you would get pregnant with twins. What else did she tell you?" I asked with sincere curiosity.

"Well, she knew I had problems but said I shouldn't worry because things will turn out well. She also mentioned a strange experience with my sister which would lead to many good things. I wonder if she meant that time my sister and I had that experience on Brower Road? She described you and said we were soul mates."

I laughed and said jokingly, "Soul mates? Poor you for ending up with someone like me for a soul mate."

Les, as quick as always, said, "Yeah, that's what I was thinking." We both laughed about it.

Leslie continued, "Jack, she knew about my mother dying and she knew I was dreaming about her. She told me the dreams that I have will have meaning and now that I think of it, my mother was rocking two cradles in my dreams. That had to mean twins."

• • • •

I was amazed at what she was telling me. I didn't want to hear about her reading before, but now I was interested. "Did she say anything about me other than being your soul mate?"

Les thought a minute then said, "Yes she did. She said something about you being well-known and making a lot of money on a project that you were working on. She also said you would meet with opposition, and you would become controversial."

We had finally reached home. I stopped the car and turned to my wife and said, "I would be controversial? I wonder what she meant by that? Well, she was right about one thing." Les asked me what that was. "I get a percentage of the film's profit when it is distributed to theaters worldwide. The way the popularity of the documentary is going, we should end up with a rather nice chunk of money."

Leslie looked at me and smiled. "Do you mean I won't have to go back to work?"

I looked at her and said, "That's right Mrs. Branden. You get to stay home and watch soaps and eat bon bons."

"Ha, ha," she said as I started to laugh. "I don't think I will have much time for soaps with twins demanding all of my time, but I will always have time for bon bons."

"That's my girl," I said.

Leslie's morning sickness continued during her pregnancy, and she was tired most of the time. It was amazing how fast the five months had passed. Les was doing well overall, and she had gained about 15 pounds so far. She really looked very pregnant, but beautiful none the less. It is true that pregnant women have a certain radiance about them. My wife really glowed.

I was working on some articles for a few magazines, and was earning a nice salary from my work. It certainly wasn't what I had done previously, but it paid the bills. I was also collecting a lot of money from the UFO documentary. It had become a huge success much to everyone's surprise. I decided that I would wait until after the twins were born before I would accept a more demanding assignment. I wanted to make sure I was around if Leslie needed me. I remembered what happened with her first pregnancy, and I was cautious about this one even though she was doing well.

Leslie made a new dish for dinner. She definitely was becoming a domestic goddess. She really took to cooking and seemed to relish in her new life. We talked about babies and how our lives have changed and where we were going from here. We both agreed that life seemed to be really good and we hoped it would continue that way. We had no idea how demanding twins would be, but somehow you always get through it. We would later find out first-hand how true that was.

CHAPTER 10

THE TWINS

September 1997

I received a call from Al Banken at *International News Magazine* congratulating me on the BFC documentary. He wanted to know if I could do an assignment for *INM*. I asked him what he was looking for and he said he needed someone who could cover the Taliban in Afghanistan. He felt I was the best person for the job and wanted me to take the assignment. There were times when I really missed the fast pace of serious journalism and flying around the world to chase down a story but now was not the time. I told Al that I had to decline but that I really appreciated the offer. He told me to call him if I reconsidered the offer. He would like to work with me and even if he gave the assignment to someone else, he has some other high-level assignments that would be coming up later in the year. I told him I would keep that in mind.

Time was drawing near for the twins to be born. We had no idea what the sex was and we didn't care. We just wanted healthy babies, and we prayed very hard for that. Both of us were raised Catholic and went to Catholic school for 12 years. We were well-versed in prayer and the saints. My wife was more religious than me and had great faith in novenas. She often prayed to St. Jude for help and guidance and insists that her prayers were answered by him when she became pregnant. I wish I had that sort of faith, but the truth is, I don't. I can't explain the fact that she became pregnant after being told by doctors that conceiving would be unlikely, but I'm sure there are thousands of couples in the world who were told the same thing and whose wives eventually became pregnant and gave birth. Anyway, I was really happy and excited that we were going to be parents in several months.

It was mid-September and the days were getting cooler. Leslie's belly was really big and it looked as though she would give birth any day. She was uncomfortable and was hoping she would go before her due date. Leslie had an appointment to see her doctor that evening. I wanted to go with her, but I received a call from my mom asking me to come over to their house and help my dad with a broken water pipe. Leslie insisted that I go, saying she would be fine. Her sister, Carrie, was going to the doctor with her. Leslie and Carrie left our house in separate cars at six o'clock. I went to my parents' house to help my dad and hung around till 9:30 p.m. I called home at 8:00 but no one answered. I figured Leslie and Carrie grabbed something to eat before she came home.

I had gotten home at 10:00 and Leslie was just getting home as well. I asked her how her appointment was and she said that everything was fine, but the doctor said she doubted that the twins would be born before the end of the month.

• • • •

"Leslie, did you and Carrie go to dinner after your appointment?" I asked.

"Yes, as a matter of fact, we did. We had dinner at Finelli's. I was really hungry for Italian food and Carrie was too."

"What time did you get there?" I asked.

"We got there around 7:30 and we were out of there by 8:30. The lasagna was excellent."

"Les, did you go anywhere else?" I asked.

"No, we both went right home. Why do you ask?" Leslie responded.

"Finelli's is only ten minutes away from here. Did you have car trouble?"

Leslie looked at me strangely. "Jack, I didn't have car trouble. Why are you questioning me? I came right home."

"Leslie, it is past 10:00! You should have been home before 9:00."

Leslie got a really strange look on her face. It almost looked like the color drained from her countenance.

"Jack, it can't be. I came directly home." She looked as if she remembered something and looked at me. "There was something odd that did happen on the way home from Finelli's. I saw a really bright star in the sky and I remembered looking at it when I was at a stop sign on Farm Ridge Road. I blinked my eyes and it was gone. I sat there thinking how strange that was that a star disappeared in the blink of an eye. Then I continued to drive home and I forgot about it."

"Honey, I'm really concerned about you. This is the second time you've forgotten what happened to you for about an hour. Maybe you should see someone about this. You might be having a seizure or you may be passing out. I think we should discuss this with a doctor."

Leslie was a little annoyed with me and she became defensive. "I think you are overreacting. I'm fine. The doctor would have detected a problem by now. I'm sure I lost track of time and we left the restaurant later then I thought."

• • • •

Leslie continued to have strange dreams about her mother and other things. She had a dream where her mother was rocking two cradles with pink ribbons and she was singing an Irish lullaby. My wife thought that meant we would have twin girls. She also had a dream about floating away and not being able to stop and another dream about being in a strange dark place where she saw shadows of people but could not see their faces. She was disturbed by these dreams at times, but chalked them up to being pregnant. She also had problems sleeping because of all the kicking the babies were doing. She was feeling very uncomfortable and gained 40 pounds during her pregnancy. Les was quite irritable for the last month. Both of us were extremely anxious for the birth of the twins. The nursery was set up with two cribs and we were ready.

September 27th came and went and still no babies. Leslie was really irritable now. Her feet started to swell and she was always tired. She looked like she was ready to explode. We decided one night to eat Chinese food, so Les called in the order and I went to pick it up. It was September 29th and while I was driving home from the restaurant, I thought about how I wished she would be going to the hospital soon. She was now two days past her due date and she was miserable. I returned home 30 minutes later to find my wife in the bathroom moaning.

"What's the matter?" I asked when I ran into the bathroom.

"My water broke. We have to get to the hospital fast. I think I'm in labor. I called the doctor ten minutes ago and she said she would meet us there. I'm starting to have a lot of pain."

I grabbed her bag that she packed for the hospital two weeks ago and out the door we went in quite a hurry. Leslie was taken to a room and Dr. Carlin examined her. "Leslie, you are completely dilated and it's time. The nurse will prep you and take you across the hall to the delivery room. I will see you there."

In the delivery room, I was so nervous, in fact, more so in that room then I was in areas that were bullet-ridden by terrorists. I prayed that everything would be alright as I stood there. Dr. Carlin proceeded to instruct Leslie to breathe and go with the contractions naturally. Leslie was trying very hard not to scream, but it was obvious that she was in a great deal of pain. I felt so helpless standing there holding her hand. I wish I could have experienced some of her pain so it would be easier for her.

The doctor said Les was doing fine and she should hold on. One of the babies was coming and the doctor announced that it was a beautiful baby girl. The doctor called the time of 9:26 p.m. for the first baby. One of the nurses took the baby and started to clean her off. Dr. Carlin announced that the second one was coming. The births were amazingly quick, much to my surprise. I never saw a baby born before and it was quite an experience. I was in total awe of the entire process. Before I knew it, the other baby also made its debut.

"Well folks, looks like you have another girl. Congratulations!" Dr. Carlin said as she showed Leslie our second daughter. The time for her birth was 9:38 p.m. The nurse took the second baby and cleaned and weighed her. Both babies were a nice size for twins. The first baby weighed six pounds, twelve ounces. And the second baby weighed six pounds, eight ounces.

• • • •

I heard Dr. Carlin and one of the nurses talking about the babies. Dr. Carlin said something to the nurses like that was unusual for both babies to have that. I wondered what she was talking about. She didn't say it with an urgent tone of voice but rather a curious tone. I immediately walked over to the doctor and asked her what was wrong. By this time the babies were cleaned off and wrapped in blankets, ready to go to the nursery.

Dr. Carlin turned to me, "Mr. Branden, nothing is wrong with your babies. The pediatrician will be giving them both a thorough examination and she will be able to discuss their health, but from what I can see, they look fine to me. Their breathing is steady, their color is good, and they both had a good healthy scream when they entered this world."

"Doctor, I heard you say to the nurse that it was unusual for both babies to have that. What were you referring to when you made that comment?" I asked with concern.

The doctor looked at me strangely and said, "Oh, both of your daughters were born with a caul. That is highly unusual for one child to be born with a caul, yet alone two."

I didn't know what she was talking about.

"What is a caul?" I asked.

The doctor proceeded to explain that a caul is an extra layer of skin over a baby's face. It's peeled off at birth. It occurs in about one in 10,000 births. It is unusual, but not harmful. It just happens and no one knows why but there are no after-affects such as scarring or skin problems, in fact, many parents report that their child's skin is exceptionally beautiful even as they go through their teenage years. I also noticed that both of your babies have a little mark behind their right knee. It is very small and I'm sure it is nothing, but your pediatrician will let you know.

Leslie was in her room and had rested for a couple of hours. I was sitting aside of her making calls to our families and telling them the good news. One of the nurses who was in the delivery room came to see how my wife was doing.

"Mrs. Branden, how are you feeling?" the nurse asked.

"I feel fine. I feel a little tired and sore, but otherwise, I feel good," Leslie replied.

"Well, I must tell you both that your babies are the talk of the nursery. We are all amazed that both of your babies were born with a caul."

I confess I didn't know why she said that. "What is so special about an extra layer of skin over a baby's face?" I questioned.

"A caul is an extra layer of skin and is a rare occurrence. It is believed that a child who is born with a caul, also known as a venician veil, has psychic powers. It is also believed that if you press the caul in a Bible, the psychic abilities will be greatly intensified. I have saved the veils for you and you are free to do what you want with them, but I strongly recommend that you press these cauls in a Bible."

I couldn't believe what I was hearing. Come on, psychic abilities, please. I chimed in saying that we appreciated that she saved them, but we really won't be needing them.

My wife got a little upset. "Jack, perhaps we had better take the cauls. What harm would it do?"

Leslie thanked the nurse for the advice and for keeping the cauls.

"Leslie, you don't believe in that, do you?" I asked with surprise in my voice.

Leslie was quick with a response, "Jack, you laughed when I told you about my reading and look at all of the things that happened that Brie predicted. I have to stand my ground on this one. Something is telling me deep inside that I should keep those veils and press them in a Bible. We need a family Bible of our own and this is a good excuse to get one."

How could I argue with her. After all, she just gave birth to two healthy daughters and gave me the most wonderful gift of all. I thought that I better humor her and let her have them. What harm could it do to keep them. I looked at my wife and said in a resigned way, "Ok, you win. You can keep the cauls."

The twins were brought into my wife's room. We each held one. Oh, how beautiful they were. I couldn't take my eyes off them. It just amazes me that two people together can make such wonderful, little beings. Nature is so unbelievable. We sat there holding them when we realized we hadn't officially named them. We tossed some names around, but finally decided to name the babies after our mothers. My mother's name was Anne, and my mother-in-law's name was Alice. We decided to give both the middle name of Elizabeth just like their mother's middle name. Alianna Elizabeth Branden and Annaleah Elizabeth Branden sounded really good to us. Allie and Annie would be more like it for their informal names, and it has a good ring to it. Allie was the firstborn. She was the biggest one and would probably be the more aggressive of the two. She certainly had the loudest cry.

• • • •

We took the girls home the next day. My mother volunteered to stay a week to help out with the twins. I went to the Catholic shop to purchase a family Bible so Leslie could press the cauls in it. We were so excited to get home. The dog missed us and really jumped and squealed when she saw us. Taffy was staying with my parents while Les was in the hospital. My dad had brought Taffy home when he dropped my mother off. He stayed for awhile to see Allie and Annie and then headed home. My mother was such a great help. She spoiled us with her home cooking and even got up during the night to help take care of the babies. I often wondered what I would do without her. She has always been there for us kids and now as adults, she is still here for us. I often reflect on how I'm surrounded by such great people in my life.

Two weeks had passed and our family members started to visit us. They were all excited about the twins. We were bombarded with gifts for the girls, but our favorite gift came from my sister, Stephanie. She had ordered handmade sweater sets and baby blankets from Italy. She also had little gold rings for the girls especially made with their initials engraved on the front of the rings. Steph had told us that she had a friend who worked at the hospital and she had told my sister about the twins born with cauls.

"Jack, this is so exciting. Your daughters should be very gifted. They are so sweet. You and Les are very blessed."

Steph was always the one in the family who was concerned about everyone, and was always the first one to offer help when needed. She was always so thoughtful and a truly beautiful person.

Leslie's sister, Marcy, stopped by to see her sister and the twins. She had bought two white christening gowns trimmed in satin and lace for the girls. Leslie was so excited to see Marcy and she loved the gowns.

"Marcy, thank you so much for the christening gowns. They are absolutely gorgeous," Leslie said with much excitement.

"You are so welcome. I am so happy for you and Jack. I know you both wanted children and here they are. Two beautiful, healthy babies. You two are really lucky, but you both deserve a wonderful family."

"You are so right about being lucky. I know I have been fortunate and I am so grateful for the life I have and the family I have like you and Carrie and Jack's family. Life is so good."

• • • •

Marcy and Leslie were looking at the twins when Leslie leaned over and whispered to Marcy.

"Marcy, have you had any strange things happen to you since the car stalled out when you were here last winter?"

"No, I haven't and, in fact, I no longer have dreams about mom. I must confess that I avoid driving on country roads at night because of what you and I went through. It did freak me out losing time like that, but I got over it. I'm sure it was a one-time strange event and won't happen again. Have you had any lost-time since it happened to you and me?"

"Actually, I did. Carrie and I went to my doctor appointment and then went to Finelli's for dinner and I lost about an hour on the way home from the resturant. Jack made me aware of it by questioning me about the time I got home. Finelli's is ten minutes away but it took me over an hour to get home."

"That's scary. What do you think is happening to you that you are losing about an hour at a time here and there?"

"I don't know but I hope it stops. Jack said I should get checked out by a doctor because I may be having seizures."

"Well, we both didn't have a seizure the first time you lost time. I'm glad it hasn't happened to me again, but it frightens me that it happened again to you."

"I think I may have to stay in at night and schedule my appointments in the morning. I don't like this happening to me, but I'm almost afraid to find out what is happening during this time."

Marcy and Leslie spoke for awhile about other matters and then Marcy headed home. Leslie attended to the twins, and then she and I went to bed early. We were both exhausted from all of the excitement.

CHAPTER 11

BACK TO WORK

March 1998

The twins were thriving and so was Leslie. Motherhood really agreed with her and I never saw her so happy. It was difficult to believe that six months had already passed. It seemed as though the twins were born only a couple of months ago instead of a half year. Allie and Annie were growing and their pediatrician, Dr. Jacobson, reported that they were doing well and developing at the normal rate. Life was good, but I was a little bored with the work I was doing. The fluff pieces I was working on just didn't do it for me. It was time to get started on a more challenging piece.

I had received a call from Kevin Leary who was coming to the States on business. He congratulated us on the birth of our twins and asked me to meet him in Philadelphia. He wanted to see our family and discuss some matters with me. It was great to hear from him and I immediately invited him to stay at our house while he was in Philadelphia. He declined the invitation because his wife, Jane, was coming, and she wanted to do sightseeing downtown. Apparently his wife is fascinated with the American Revolution. He did, however, agree to come to dinner at our home. Kevin had told me he was involved with another project and wanted to see if I would like to work on it with him. I asked for details about the project, but he said he would give me the skinny on it when he sees me in a week.

I was sure curious about this project, and the mystery that surrounded it. The timing was perfect, and I was ready for something new and exciting. The twins were settled into a routine, and I was needed less and less around the house. I mentioned the phone call to Leslie and she almost seemed relieved at the possibility of me getting involved with a project that would keep me out of her hair.

"Jack, this sounds intriguing and I think the timing is perfect. I know you have been antsy lately. You are not accustomed to staying in a house 24 hours a day. I know you are bored and need something to really motivate you. I think this is it. I can't wait to find out what it is," Leslie said after I gave her the news.

"You are so understanding. I am starting to get bored, but not with my home life. You and the babies and Taffy keep me on my toes but as far as work goes, I feel stagnant and I need something to get me excited again. Kevin has always been involved with exciting projects and I'm sure this will be a challenge," I said as I gave Leslie a kiss.

Kevin called as soon as he arrived in town. He and his wife were staying at the Four Seasons Hotel. I met Kevin and Jane for lunch and we decided to get together the following night at our home for dinner. Jane sounded excited to see Allie and Annie and, of course, Leslie. Jane and my wife really hit it off in London when we were there for the premier of the UFO documentary.

• • • •

"So, Kevin, what is this new project? You really have me curious," I said.

Kevin started to whisper, "Jack, keep your voice down. I don't want anyone to hear what we are saying. I don't want to discuss it now, but I will tell you all about it at dinner tomorrow night. You have to give me directions to your place."

I wondered what could be so secretive about this project that he wouldn't even talk about it in a public place.

"Well, if you give me a piece of paper and a pen I will draw you a map and write down the directions. So how have the two of you been since I last saw you?" I asked. I didn't know what else to say for fear he would not answer me in a normal tone of voice.

"Things have been going great. The BFC documentary raked in lots of money, as you know, and we are all celebs in the UK. Ireland especially loved the film, and people actually stop me on the street and ask for my autograph. Can you believe that! The film has the makings of a cult classic," Kevin said with much enthusiasm. "I can't wait for the next one. It should be even better."

Now he really had me curious, but I resisted the temptation to press him for details.

"So what have you and Leslie been up to?" Kevin asked.

"Well, the twins keep us busy, and we have been home a lot. I've been working on some fluff pieces for magazines, but I'm going crazy with boredom. I need something to get me back where the action is. Don't get me wrong, I like being home with Les and the babies, but you know how it is. I need to have something to investigate and do the writing I had always done before I was married. I feel like I've been on vacation long enough, and now it is time to return to where the action is."

"Well, I think I can help you with that, and I will let you know what I mean tomorrow," Kevin responded.

His vagueness was driving me crazy. I cannot stand secrets, and I guess that is why I have always been good at investigative reporting. We finished lunch and I told them I would see them tomorrow night at 6:00 p.m. They left for South Street, and I returned home.

Jane and Kevin arrived right on schedule the next evening. Leslie had made surf and turf, a large salad, pasta, and fruit pies for dessert. She is a fantastic cook. Leslie showed the twins to Kevin and Jane and introduced them to our dog, Taffy, who keeps guard over the nursery. We then sat down for dinner. Kevin and his wife just raved about Leslie's cooking and we all indulged far too much. I opened a bottle of vintage wine and Kevin started to tell me that a close friend of his brother was in the British Intelligence and had told them about the international cover-up of extraterrestrials.

"Jack, I think you and I would make a great investigative team, and our findings could make an extraordinary film. I think this is serious business and we must get to the bottom of it. The documentary we did only asked questions. It didn't provide answers. People want to know the truth," Kevin said with intense sincerity.

I looked at Kevin strangely and said, "Kevin, do you really believe in all of this stuff? I'm still not convinced that UFOs and extraterrestrials exist."

"Well, apparently British Intelligence believes in it because according to sources, cover-ups in Britain and the U.S. are going on and they are suppressing information from Russia. Russian military and scientists claim that they have possession of a craft and have been doing tests on this craft for some time including reverse engineering. You know what was going on in Roswell! You investigated it yourself for the documentary. Jack, don't you want to know the truth?"

As I sat in my chair pondering Kevin's question, I remembered the people I interviewed regarding alien abductions, and how sincere they were in their accounts of alleged abductions. I still wasn't convinced, though, and didn't want to spend a lot of time and energy on this. What is truth anyway? Life was really great for me and I didn't want to do another fluff piece.

"Kevin, I appreciate your offer, but I don't want to continue with this subject. I want to move on to something with more meat. I was thinking about going back to covering terrorism or covering the political scene. I do appreciate the offer though."

Kevin looked disappointed. "Jack, there is more to this than what you see. This is big. This is international. This is probably the biggest secret the governments are keeping of all time. People have the right to know what is happening. Look Jack, I think you are the person for this job. I want you to think about this in the next few months and give me an answer. I would like you to talk to Robert Jennings, a former member of the British Intelligence. I think you will see things in a different light. Here is his phone number. He is waiting for your call."

Kevin and Jane left our place at midnight. They were returning to England the next day. I thought about giving Jennings a call, but decided against it for now. I had other things to do. I contacted Al Banken at *International News Magazine* and told him I was interested in covering politics or something international. He was excited and asked me to come to N.Y. in a couple of days. I agreed and told Leslie I was going to N.Y. to discuss working for *INM*.

"Jack, will you be traveling a lot oversees?" She seemed really concerned.

I wanted to calm her so I said, "I told Al I didn't want to travel a lot and I told him I don't want to be away from my family for more then a couple days a month. Al said it wouldn't be a problem." Les looked relieved.

• • • •

Months had passed and the job with the magazine was going well. I had covered the bombings of the U.S. embassies in Kenya and Tanzania which occurred almost simultaneously. The FBI held Osama Bin Laden responsible for the bombings and accused Bin Laden of declaring Jihad, which is a holy war, against the U.S. They found out that Bin Laden founded Al-Qaida that year to promote Islamic fundamentalism. There was a lot of buzz going on in the journalistic community that terrorism in the Middle East was on the rise and it was not just centered around the Jews and Palestinians. Other factions were emerging and a holy war was waged against the western world. These Islamic fundamentalist groups were recruiting young boys and training them in camps, many of which were in Afghanistan. The name Bin Laden was tossed around in the intelligence circles as the one who posed the greatest threat. The recruits were taught that suicide was an honorable way to die for the cause. We didn't know at the time just how destructive this man would be and how his desire to destroy the infidels would affect all of our lives.

Covering terrorism was exciting work. I had traveled to the Middle East for two weeks, which made Leslie very nervous. She was concerned for my safety, but I assured her that everything would be alright. She had the twins to look after and they were approaching their first birthday and were starting to walk. I promised Leslie that I wouldn't leave the country again till next year. I would continue to work from home and travel only to N.Y.

or California on occasion. I only traveled a little but it was enough to satisfy me. I needed to have some involvement oversees with my job. I was starting to feel like I was part of the excitement and was kept up to date on everything that was going on in the world. I was receiving more calls and given more assignments. I felt like I was back again.

CHAPTER 12

ANNIE

1998

It was Sept. 29, 1998, Allie and Annie's first birthday. I was amazed at how the time flew by and how much they had grown. They were two very healthy girls and they never had colds or illnesses of any sort. They didn't even have reactions to their immunizations. They never had fevers from teething or so much as a cough or sneeze. Dr. Jacobson was impressed with the fact that the twins were never sick; in fact, he thought it was quite unusual. Allie was the more aggressive of the two. She was the first to walk and she started to say a few words, but Annie was more quiet and withdrawn. She was content to sit in the play pen and play with her toys. She had started to walk shortly after Allie but she didn't interact as much as her sister. We were so happy with our little family. It seemed as though we had an almost perfect life.

The twins did have strange behavior at times though. Leslie had noticed that on a few occasions they were looking at the sunshine that was shining through the window in their room for a long period of time. They almost looked like they were in a trance. They would smile and make sounds as if they could see someone. They even stretched their little arms out as if to touch someone. My wife was very concerned about that behavior but I told her that children see things with their imagination and it was normal. She was not so sure.

• • • •

I received a call from Kevin Leary asking me if I had reconsidered his offer. I declined once again but told him to keep in touch if he starts to work on another project. I told him I had been working on terrorism in the Middle East and he should consider doing something on that subject. Kevin had been out of the loop regarding world affairs since his UFO documentary. I was hoping he would abandon that pursuit for something more tangible. Kevin was always a great investigative reporter and filmmaker, and I felt he was wasting his talent on this UFO thing.

Months had passed and we were in the dead of winter. Everyone seemed to have the flu around us. I got sick and was put on antibiotics because of a fever and a really bad cough. I was so congested that I feared Leslie and the girls would get the same thing. Much to my surprise, they didn't get sick. The twins got through the winter without even a sniffle. Leslie didn't get the flu either. I was so glad because it would have been difficult for me to take care of Annie and Allie if their mother was confined to bed like I was. It was strange, though, that they didn't even catch a little cold. I was glad they were so healthy, but it still seemed odd to me. Leslie was always getting colds before we were married, but she hadn't had a cold since the twins were born.

Easter arrived and the weather was great. Spring was finally here after a long, snowy winter. Leslie dressed the girls in cute sailor dresses. They were such good babies, always agreeable and never any trouble. Allie started to talk a lot and form sentences, but Annie still didn't talk. Annie continued to withdraw while Allie developed an outgoing personality. She was very interactive, but Annie barely made eye contact. We started to be concerned with Annie's behavior. She was different from Allie, but we felt she should be talking by now. Dr. Jacobson said that she was not at the stage of development that her sister was, and he too seemed concerned because she should be talking and interacting. He wanted us to take Annie to the Children's Hospital for tests.

It was late summer when we took Annie to the hospital for tests. A doctor named Ruth Parsons tested Annie and she said she thought Annie may have a form of autism. She said that we will know better after Annie turns age two. She asked us to return in six months for more tests. Leslie and I didn't know much about autism. Our idea of an autistic child was someone who had tantrums and injured themselves. We knew Annie wasn't like that, so we decided to look it up on the internet before we took her to her next appointment at the hospital.

The holidays came and the twins were now two years old, and celebrated their third Christmas. They loved the decorated Christmas trees with bright lights, and especially liked Santa. The twins left a dish of cookies and a glass of milk for old St. Nick, as they patiently waited for Santa to leave toys under the tree.

After the holidays were over, we noticed that Annie became increasingly more withdrawn and developed a fixation for lining up objects in a row. She also began to make a loud noise. The best way to describe it was to say she constantly said ah. She also developed a sensitivity to certain sounds. She would put her hands over her ears and cry if she heard a really loud noise. She started to flap her hands a lot and walk on her tippy toes. She was constantly moving around. She also began to rock back and forth. This disturbed Les and I, and we were eager for her appointment with the specialist in January.

Allie seemed to be in tune to Annie and she would play with her and pull her out of her shell. Allie was amazing for a two year old. She was always helping her sister, and would show Annie how to eat with a spoon and how to drink from a cup. These simple actions seemed to be difficult for Annie.

We took Annie for her appointment at Children's Hospital of Philadelphia. Dr. Parsons tested Annie for over an hour, and concluded that Annie was indeed autistic. We were devastated when she told us, but we suspected it for some time. The doctor explained to us that autism was a developmental disorder that affects physical, social, and language skills. Children with autism are often adverse to displays of affection and physical contact. They don't like change and build a comfort zone around themselves that they don't venture out of, and when they are out of their comfort zone, they may display behavior such as tantrums. The doctor gave us more information and suggested that we join a support group for parents with autistic children. She also told us that although the cause was still unknown and there was no cure, there were therapies that were proven to be very successful and many autistic children could be taught to lead a fairly normal life. She told us that autism was on the rise and there was a lot of research going on regarding this neurological disorder.

Leslie and I felt helpless. We were never around anyone with autism and we didn't know how we would handle raising an autistic child.

"Jack, I feel like it's my fault. Maybe I did something wrong when I was pregnant," Leslie said with an emotional voice.

I turned to her and held her hand, "Les, it's not your fault. Allie is perfectly fine so you didn't do anything when you were pregnant. You ate well, took vitamins, and didn't smoke, drink, or do drugs. How could it be your fault? It's just one of those things that happens in life and we just have to deal with it. It will be difficult at times, I'm sure, but we can handle it."

We were driving back home from Children's Hospital when we saw something very bright moving against the dark sky. We were on Brower Road at the time and all of a sudden the car went dead. I kept trying to start the car but had no success. The bright object in the sky appeared to get closer and the next thing I knew, the car started up and the object was gone. I turned to Leslie and said how strange that was. She commented that it was similar to what had happened to her and her sister a few years ago. In fact, it was almost at the same place. We proceeded to travel home and thought nothing of what had happened. The car was running well and I thought it stalled because of the bitter cold temperature.

When we arrived home, our dog was crying as we approached the door. She ran out the door as soon as we opened it. She really had to urinate. She seemed like she had been holding it for a long time. I thought that was strange since we were only gone a couple of hours. I got Taffy back into the house when I heard Leslie yell my name.

"Jack, look at the time." She sounded frantic.

I looked at my watch and it said 8:15. I thought something was wrong with it. I looked at the grandfather clock and the time was the same.

I looked at Leslie and she said, “Jack, we just lost two and a half hours.”

I didn’t know what to say. “There must be an explanation,” I said.

“Well I would love to hear what it is. This is the third time this has happened to me and now it has happened to all of us. Something is going on here. I’m glad this happened to you because now you know I wasn’t imagining it.”

Once again, I didn’t know what to say. *How could we lose two and a half hours?* This will work on my mind until I find out what happened to that time.

CHAPTER 13

DR. DAVIES AND LOST TIME

January 2000

It was January and we had just experienced lost time. Now I knew what Leslie was talking about when it happened to her. I wish I had taken her more seriously. Kevin had just called to ask if I was still freelancing and I said yes, but I may reconsider his offer. I told him about what happened to us last week and how it was driving me crazy not being able to remember what happened for two and a half hours. Kevin sounded excited and suggested that I talk to Judy Davies. She was the psychiatrist that I talked to in London who worked with alien abductees.

"Kevin, why would I talk to her? We haven't been abducted."

"How do you know? You can't remember anything that happened to you and your wife and daughters for two and a half hours. Don't you think that is bizarre?"

I said I thought it was but I didn't know what to do to refresh my memory. Kevin suggested hypnosis and said Judy could hypnotize me and Leslie and get to the bottom of this mystery. I told him I would think about it.

Leslie and I decided to try the hypnosis route. We knew something was missing and we were anxious to find out why both of us could not account for two and a half hours. Kevin and Dr. Davies were coming to the States and she would be putting us under, as they say, at our house. We had dinner when they arrived and shortly after Leslie put the girls to bed and Dr. Davies started the hypnosis session with Leslie. She had me go into another room so I would not be influenced by what Les would say. Dr. Davies started to put her under hypnosis and Les went under very easily. Dr. Davies had a tape recorder and started to ask questions.

"Leslie, what happened on Tuesday night last week after you and Jack left Children's Hospital?"

"We were driving down Brower Road and we were talking about Annie when the car stalled."

"Did you notice anything after the car stalled?"

"We saw a bright object in the sky and Jack commented on it. It started to come toward our car and it hovered over it."

"What did this object look like?"

"It was a huge, round object with a low humming sound and bright lights rotating around it. It was amazing."

"Leslie, what happened next?"

"We took the girls out of their car seats, stood outside the car, and then we were inside a strange place. There were strange-looking people there. They were very thin and very pale. They didn't look like us. They had gray-colored clothing that fit close to their bodies like tight spandex. They were shorter than me. The one person said, 'Hello Leslie, it is good to see you.'"

"That person knew you? Who was he or she?"

"I had been with them before. Twice. They did something to me the first time and they said I would be able to have children now."

"Leslie, what happened to you the second time?"

"I was pregnant and they said they were checking me to make sure everything was alright with my babies."

"Did they say why they were checking you? What was their purpose?"

"The taller person, he said his name was Rolf, said that I had a specific purpose and that my daughters would be very special and they would be important to others."

Dr. Davies seemed really intrigued by this. She paused for a moment and then proceeded.

"Did they say why your twins would be so important?"

"He said that I would know in time but I should not worry because everything will be alright."

"Did they say they would see you again?"

"No," replied Leslie.

"Where were the twins and Jack during this time?" Dr. Davies asked.

"Two people took the girls and Jack to another room."

"How did you feel when you were in that place? Did you feel like you were there against your will?"

"I did feel that I had to do what they said, but I wasn't afraid of them."

"Did they examine you this time?"

"Yes, they inserted something in me and I saw something that looked like a big syringe filled with what looked like blood. I think they withdrew blood from me."

"What happened next?"

"They said they would take us back. They said everything was good."

"Leslie, when I count to five, you will awaken. One, two, three, four, five. Leslie, how do you feel?"

"I feel fine. What happened?" Leslie asked.

"I will tell you later after I work with Jack."

Dr. Davies walked into the study where I was waiting for her.

"Jack, are you ready?" asked Dr. Davies.

I replied that I was and asked about Leslie. Dr. Davies said she was fine and she would let us hear the tapes after she was finished with me. She then proceeded to put me under and question me.

"Jack, what happened last Tuesday when you and Leslie were coming home from Children's Hospital?"

"We were driving down Brower Road and the car stalled."

"What happened next?"

"I saw a very bright light in the sky and it looked like it was coming toward us."

"Did you know what this object was?"

"Not at the time."

"What happened next?"

"We were staring at this thing and then we got the twins out of the car seats."

"Why did you do that?" asked Dr. Davies.

"I don't know. It was strange. A thought entered my head that I should take them out of the car seats."

"What happened after that?"

"We were looking at this round, large craft hover over the car and then we were in it."

"How did that happen?"

"I don't know. I saw a beam of light and then we were in it. It was in an instant."

"What did it look like inside this craft?"

"It was very sterile looking. Kinda like stainless steel and lots of white."

"Were there people inside this craft?"

"Yes, they were thin, little people in grey clothes. They were weird looking. They had a slit for a mouth and no ears."

"Did they talk to you?"

"Yes, but it was more like mental telepathy. They didn't verbalize."

"What did they say?"

"They said they needed to check us. They were monitoring us for changes."

"Changes? What did they mean?" Dr. Davies asked in a curious manner.

"I don't know," Jack replied.

"Where were the twins and your wife?"

"They were in another room."

"Did they examine your body?"

"Yes, and it felt like they took blood from me."

"Did they do that to Leslie and the twins?"

"I don't know. They were in a different room."

"What happened next?" asked Dr. Davies.

"They brought Leslie and the girls in the room and said we were going back."

"What happened then?"

"We were back in the car and proceeded to drive home."

"Jack, when I count to five, you will awaken. One, two, three, four, five."

Dr. Davies asked me how I felt and I said I felt fine. She and I went into the kitchen and Leslie and Kevin were sitting at the kitchen table drinking coffee. Dr. Davies proceeded to play the tape for us. I couldn't believe what we were hearing. What a shock it was to hear about being abducted. I ridiculed people who made that claim and now I was one of them. Leslie was visibly shaken as she listened to the tape. *What was the purpose of the abduction? What did they mean when they said the twins were special and that they would be very important. The entire experience seemed surreal. What do we do now?*

Dr. Davies and Kevin said goodnight and headed back to Philadelphia. Leslie and I talked about what happened and both of us were in disbelief. We wondered about who those beings were and what they meant about the twins. Leslie expressed that she was frightened and hoped it wouldn't happen again. The investigator in me started to be very curious about this experience, and I decided right then that I would dig into this and find out as much as I could about this phenomena. Perhaps Kevin was right. This subject needed to be investigated so the truth could be learned about what is going on. *Who knows about this? Is the government aware of alien abduction and if so, are they covering it up?* I had to pursue this for my own peace of mind and Leslie's.

CHAPTER 14

THE LADY IN THE LIGHT

April 2000

Three months had passed since Dr. Davies hypnotized Leslie and I, and I was still no closer to an answer. I had read a lot about UFOs and alien abductions, but I still didn't know why they were here. There were theories about cross breeding, about aliens needing fresh DNA in order for them to survive but none of these really made sense to me. Some people believed that aliens were going to take over our planet because their own planet was drained of all its natural resources and they needed a place to inhabit. They were clearly superior to us in technology and intelligence so it would be easy for them to destroy us and take possession of the Earth if that was their plan. I just didn't buy that theory either. I started to wonder how much the government knew and how much information was in their possession that they were not releasing. Did they know why this was happening?

Kevin called again to ask how we were. I told him we were fine, but Leslie was having strange dreams again. She had a dream that her mother was standing in a bright light and was telling her that she and her family were protected and that she should not worry about the changes that were going to happen. Leslie also had other dreams about her mother, but couldn't remember them except for one dream that she had where her mother thanked her for naming one of the twins after her. Kevin asked if I had done any research on aliens, and I told him I had looked up possible reasons for aliens being here. I told him what I had learned and also that I didn't believe it to be true. He told me to keep working on it because he wanted me involved with his newest project. He knew I would really get into it since I had a personal experience with the subject.

Leslie and I occasionally discussed her experiences, but she really didn't want to talk about it. She said thinking about it frightened her and she would rather get it out of her mind. It's funny how I became the one who was probing for answers, and she was now the one who was side-stepping the issue. She was curious, though, about the identical mark that the twins had behind their knee. The doctor said he thought it might be a birth mark but wasn't sure. The marks didn't have anything abnormal about them as far as being harmful to the girls. He said we shouldn't be too concerned about them, but I have to admit that they are strange looking. They almost look like a small brand of some sort.

The twins were approaching age three and Allie was talking volumes. Annie still wasn't talking, and Dr. Parsons suggested we get therapy for Annie. She referred us to an agency that evaluated children with autism and matched the children with therapists. We were assigned four therapists who worked with Annie weekdays from 8 a.m. to 4 p.m. Annie was also placed on a special diet which eliminated all wheat and dairy products. Many autistic children have food allergies which affects their behavior. Annie was immediately placed on behavior modification programs that used a reward system. It also consisted of highly-structured, skill-oriented activities, and intense one-on-one training with the therapists. Play therapy was also used to help with emotional development which improves social skills and learning. Leslie and I were given training so that we could work with Annie on weekends. We were very fortunate that Annie was diagnosed so early. She showed much improvement in a few months. She started to maintain eye contact and responded when you called her by name.

The twins were now three years old and had developed distinct personalities. They continued to stare at the sunlight, but now Allie started to talk to the light and Annie was calm and fixed on the light. She didn't manifest the symptoms of autism. One day Leslie walked into the girls' bedroom and saw our dog sitting aside of Annie staring at the light too. Allie was holding a conversation with the light and Annie was smiling and shaking her head yes. Les went over to them, but Allie and Annie were totally oblivious to her. She called their names but they didn't budge. She even called Taffy and the dog ignored her. This went on for a few minutes and then Allie said goodbye. Leslie stood there looking at the twins not knowing what to say or do. She decided to ask Allie some questions to see if she could find out what was going on.

"Allie, tell mommy who you were talking to."

"Sofa," Allied replied.

"Sofa? Who is sofa?" Leslie asked.

Allie smiled and said, "She is a lady who comes with the sun. She talks to me and Annie."

Leslie was really curious. "Allie, what does she say to you and Annie?"

"Mommy, she said we are special and she sings to us. She tells us stories."

Leslie was really curious now. "Allie, what kind of stories does she tell you?"

Allie thought for a moment and said, "She tells us about heaven."

Leslie and I had a conversation about this.

"Jack, what do you make of this? Should we be concerned, or do you still think it is an active imagination?"

"Well, I don't think it is anything more than an imagination at work. Don't forget, they have a writer for a father. They come by an imagination honestly."

"Jack, you should have seen Annie. She was focused on the light and didn't manifest any autistic behavior. She smiled and paid attention to whatever it was they saw. How would Allie know about heaven? Did you talk to her about that?"

I thought for a moment and said I didn't tell them about heaven, but I told Les that they probably heard that word mentioned on television. Leslie decided that she would keep an eye on the girls when they were in their room to see if these incidents with the sunlight continued.

CHAPTER 15

ERIC, CLAUDE, AND ANTOINE

Time passed quickly as I was doing a lot of traveling for my research. It took me to Washington, D.C.; Roswell, New Mexico; and New York. I decided to contact an old friend of mine, Eric Newman, who worked for the Defense Department. Eric and I grew up in the same neighborhood, played football and baseball on the same team, and were together in most of our classes at school. We also had classes together at Penn, played racket ball and basically hung out together when we were in college. We were always great friends and have kept in touch through the years. I introduced him to Carolyn Massey, the girl he ended up marrying after we graduated from the University of Pennsylvania.

Eric worked for the government right after college graduation. His father had worked for the CIA for many years and had just retired last year. I called Eric at home to see if we could meet when I was in Washington. I planned to be there in October and had something I wanted to discuss with him. He said that would be great and we set a tentative date for a Thursday.

I drove down to D.C. and gave Eric a call. We met for lunch in downtown D.C. We hadn't seen each other since the twins were born, but he indicated that things were going really well for him and that he may be moving to a job at the CIA. He and his wife have one son age five and he was telling me about all of the things he was doing. Eric congratulated me on the UFO documentary, and I felt it was the perfect time to tell him about our lost time experiences.

"Eric, I know you are going to think I'm crazy when I tell you this, but keep an open mind. Leslie and I had a strange experience a few months ago which involved lost time. We were coming home one evening from a doctor appointment for one of the twins when the car went dead. We saw a bright light in the sky and commented on it. The next thing we remembered was that the bright light was gone. When we arrived home, two and a half hours had elapsed that we could not account for."

Eric looked at me strangely. "Jack, that is some story. I know you well, so I know you're not making it up."

"Eric, this gets better. A psychiatrist that I know personally put Leslie and I under hypnosis and we both told the same story of being abducted by aliens. Both of us said we were subjected to physical exams and they said the twins were very special and very important. They took blood from us and said changes would happen, but not to worry about it."

• • • •

Eric was silent for a moment then asked me why I was telling him about this experience. I told him that I thought he might know something since he works in the Pentagon and has a high-security clearance.

"Jack, I really don't know much about this sort of thing, but if I did, I wouldn't be able to tell you anything. I can tell you, however, that there have been rumors going around Washington on occasion and I have heard that there have been actual sightings by the military and I have heard about alien abductions but it is all hearsay and not official."

I knew something was going on and now I was sure the government knew a lot about it. Eric got a pensive look on his face, leaned toward me, and began to speak in a very low tone, almost like a whisper.

"Jack, if I were you, I would keep these things to yourself. I feel I need to warn you as a close, longtime friend. I don't think the government looks favorably on those who make claims about UFOs and abductions. You know how they completely deny things like that, and they have discredited those who have made claims of UFO sightings. Pilots have lost their jobs because they filed reports regarding UFO sightings while they were in flight. Military personnel were discharged when they made reports of UFO sightings, and they were told never to tell others about the sightings if they valued their lives. The government can be very intimidating when it comes to certain situations."

"Eric, I appreciate the advice but I can't deny what happened to me personally," I said.

"I understand, but, just be careful who you discuss your experience with because you are a high-profile individual who has a lot of credibility. I personally don't understand why the government is so adamant about UFOs, but they are. On one hand, they deny their existence, but on the other hand, they make life miserable for people who report seeing them. If they don't exist, then why do they care what people report? I'm just saying that you should be careful."

I replied that I would take his advice seriously.

I returned home that night and told Leslie about my conversation with Eric. His vagueness, whether intentional or not, reinforced my belief that something was going on and the government was fully aware of it. I was more determined than ever to find out what the government knew about this phenomena. I thought perhaps I could contact someone with the Belgian government since they went public with their conclusions regarding UFO sightings in their country. I decided to contact Kevin Leary to see if he had any names for me.

Kevin was glad to hear from me, and was excited that I had a change of heart regarding the UFO phenomena. He gave me the names of two people in the Belgian government, Antoine Rousseau and Claude Bonnet, whom he felt would cooperate with me. I called these men and they both agreed to see me when I went to Brussels. I was impressed with their honesty and couldn't wait to meet with them. We set a tentative date for October 28th and I booked a flight and hotel room as soon as I got off the phone. Leslie wasn't thrilled about me going abroad, but she said she would get over it as long as I brought back some Belgian chocolates. I told her I could do that. I told her I would only be gone a few days, and she was more understanding after that. I think the chocolates helped too.

• • • •

I arrived in Belgium the evening of October 27th, settled into my room, and ordered something to eat. The next morning I called Antoine and Claude and we set up a meeting for that afternoon at my hotel. I was so eager to meet these two that I almost felt like a kid at Christmas. I met them in the lobby of the hotel and we properly introduced ourselves. We then went into the restaurant and had something to eat and drink. Antoine and Claude spoke very good English, which was really great considering that I hadn't spoken French in years and my French was rusty. I explained to both that I was working on a project with Kevin and I wanted to know more about the UFOs that were sighted in their country.

"Kevin Leary suggested that I call you gentlemen so I could find out what position your government has taken on UFOs. What can you tell me?"

"There have been several sightings in our country and thousands of people have seen them. Our Air Force tracked several of these craft and we have basically taken the position that these craft are not of this world. There is no air craft on Earth that can maneuver the way those crafts could and the Belgian government has acknowledged their existence. They have issued a statement that they are investigating this phenomena and will release a report to the citizens of Belgium," replied Claude.

"Have there been any reports of abductions?" I asked.

"Yes. We have received several reports and that is also being investigated," replied Antoine.

"You gentlemen know that I am from America and our country completely denies the existence of UFOs and anything at all to do with the phenomena. I have to tell you that I have a personal interest in this. My wife, two daughters, and I had a lost-time experience one evening in December and we were later put under hypnosis to determine what had happened. We were subjected to physical exams by these aliens. I gotta tell you that I never believed in UFOs at all until this happened. I have to find out what they want just for my own satisfaction. I don't want to make a big issue about this, but I just want to know why they are here and why they abduct people."

"Antoine and I both have a background in military intelligence. We currently work for the Ministry of Defense, but our government believes that people have a right to know the truth about this subject and they have been completely honest with their findings. We have investigated several theories, but we still don't know the real reason why they are here."

"What are the theories out there regarding this phenomena?" I asked.

"One theory is that aliens are scientists who are researching our planet. Another one is that they are cross-breeding with humans to produce a new race because their species is weakening and is on the verge of extinction. Another theory is that their own planet is no longer inhabitable and they would like to take possession of our planet," replied Antoine in a very serious voice.

"These theories have not been proven and no one really knows what their intentions are. They are so much more advanced than us," Claude interjected.

Jack was digesting what Claude and Antoine just shared with him.

"I believe that they are far superior to us in terms of science and knowledge. I may be naïve, but I don't think that they are here to destroy us and take possession of our planet. Let's face it, they certainly have the means to be able to do it and I think they would have done it by now if that was their intention."

"I agree with you. They would have done something by now. I believe there is something much greater at work here and someday we will know what it is," replied Antoine.

I continued my conversation with Claude and Antoine and we ended our talk with a promise to keep in touch and to let each other know if we acquire any other information regarding aliens or UFOs. I had a good feeling about them and felt they were honest and as interested in this matter as I was.

• • • •

I left Belgium the next morning and I was glad to be heading home. Leslie greeted me at the door and the girls were right behind her. I received warm hugs and kisses from everyone, even Taffy. I also noticed someone else at the door—a tiny, orange tiger-striped kitten that could fit in the palm of a hand.

"Leslie, who's this little guy?" I asked.

"That is the newest member of our family and his name is Freddie cat."

"Where did you get him?" I asked.

"Well, the other day Taffy was at the window, barking and carrying on, so I looked to see what got her attention and there he was, sitting on the front lawn as big as can be. So, I had to go out and take a look at this cute little ball of fur. When I picked him up, he really started to purr. Well, you know what a sucker I am for kittens and puppies. I immediately took him to the vet and had him checked out. The vet thought he was about eight weeks old and gave him shots and a clean bill of health. The girls just love him. Annie plays with him a lot, which surprised me. We definitely have to keep him since she responds to him so well."

"I agree," I replied.

I was sure glad to be home, and told Leslie all about my conversation with Claude and Antoine and what position the Belgian government took about UFOs. She was relieved to know that someone official believed in this phenomena. Unfortunately, I was still no closer to why this was happening, but at least Les and I weren't alone in this. It felt good to know that a government came forward and was honest with its citizens about recognizing the fact that something was happening.

CHAPTER 16

VISIONARIES

November 2000

It was November 2000, and the presidential election had just taken place with a lot of controversy surrounding the election. The voting process appeared to be compromised and people were in an uproar about citizens in some states denied the right to vote. So much was going on here in this country and abroad. The Middle East was heating up again with rumors of terrorist attacks in the U.S. Apparently, there was a lot of chatter going on in the intelligence arena about it.

I was contacted by Al Banken who wanted me to do some investigation to see if I could find out what was going on in the intelligence community regarding the terrorist threats. I declined the request because I wanted to stay focused on the UFO phenomena. I needed to find out what was going on for my own peace of mind. I also didn't want to go abroad at this time because I had plenty of research to do here, however, I did inform Al of the information I had received from a fellow journalist regarding the chatter that the intelligence community was getting regarding a terrorist attack. I recommended that he contact this journalist, Reggie Johnson, and ask him to do a story on it. Al thanked me for the info and said he would contact Reggie the next day.

Leslie had to go to the dentist to have a filling replaced, so I was home watching the girls. It was 2:00 p.m. and they were in their room taking a nap. I heard the dog bark upstairs so I went up to see what was going on. The twins were in their room and Taffy was sitting there with them. Allie and Annie were staring at the window, and the room was just filled with sunlight. There was also a mild scent of lavender that filled the air. They were smiling and talking to the light. The dog was quiet, but also staring at the window along with the cat, who was laying on Annie's bed. They were all focused on the bedroom window.

Allie and Annie were both saying "yes" and shaking their heads. Annie was very still and not making any strange sounds. She seemed so different in this state. Allie said she would tell her mommy and daddy about the visit and Annie said something about a bear. That was really unusual because Annie doesn't talk, but she spoke clearly in this trance or whatever you would call this state. Leslie had told me about this when she saw the girls talking to a light at the window, but now I was witnessing it myself. I have to say that this was the strangest thing I had ever seen. It rates right up there with our lost-time experience.

I stood there watching, resisting the urge to go to touch the girls. I wanted to observe what was happening. The episode lasted for about 15 minutes from the time I came into their room, but I didn't know how long it went on prior to my entrance. The girls became aware of me when the light faded from the room. I asked them what was going on and Allie said Sofa came to see them. I asked her what she said, and Allie told me that the lady asked them about their teddy bears and what the names were and she asked about Freddie.

"Daddy, Sofa is so pretty, just like mommy," Allie said with enthusiasm.

"Allie, what else did she say?" I asked.

"Daddy, she said something bad was going to happen and there would be a loud noise and something would fall down."

I wondered what she meant by that, and then I realized that I was talking to a three year old with a vivid imagination. I can't explain what happened and how even the cat and dog stared at the window, but there couldn't possibly be someone in the room talking to them because I didn't see anyone.

Leslie finally came home around 5:00 p.m. She went grocery shopping after her appointment. I helped her with the grocery bags and I told her about what happened to the girls that afternoon.

"Les, I think we may have to get a professional opinion on what is happening to the girls. I am baffled by their behavior. I know I thought it was just their imaginations, but after seeing for myself what went on in their room, I have concluded it is far more serious then active imaginations."

Leslie looked at me and said, "Wasn't I concerned the first time it happened? Why is it that when I told you about this, you shrugged it off as nothing and now that you have seen it, it's a problem. I don't know if you realize this, but you always down-play what I say about things until you experience them for yourself. You did the same thing when I had that lost-time experience, but it was a different story when it happened to you. When are you going to start treating me as an equal and stop treating me like some empty-headed person who doesn't have a brain?"

I was taken back by what she had said, and told her I always felt she was a very intelligent person and always considered her as an equal.

"Leslie, I apologize. You know how my mind works. I'm a skeptic and I have to see it to believe it, but I promise I will never doubt your judgment again. Strange things are really happening to us and I have a feeling they are all connected. We really have to get to the bottom of this and find out what it all means. Maybe I should contact Judy Davies and ask her what she thinks about all of this. Perhaps she has encountered something like this before. She's a psychiatrist and I value her opinion. She's very professional but she has an open mind. What do you think about contacting Judy?"

Leslie thought for a moment and said she thought it was a good idea. Even though she agreed with me, I could still sense some tension in the air.

After our conversation ended, we noticed the girls were unusually quiet, so we called for them but got no response. The dog didn't even come to us when we called. We quickly went in each room to see where they were, and found them upstairs in my office. Annie was playing with my computer and Allie was watching her. I yelled at Annie, but she ignored me. I ran over to her, thinking she was ruining my computer, when I stopped dead in my tracks at what I saw she was doing.

• • • •

Annie was typing words on the screen and I was astounded at what I saw. She had actually typed sentences. I was completely stunned at what she wrote. She typed the following: Sophielia is the angel who comes to our room. She tells us things that will happen and she said we are very special because we can see her, but no one else can. She said she will visit us a lot and tell us things that will happen and we must tell mommy and daddy so that others will know. Bad things will happen and good people must protect themselves. She asked us about Taffy and Freddie and she said she knew about what happened to us in December. Sophielia said she will come again soon.

Allie was standing beside Annie and watching her type on the keyboard. I asked Allie if Sofa was really Sophielia and she said yes. I told her what Annie had written and asked her if it was true and she said yes. Leslie and I just looked at each other. We were speechless. Our autistic child, who didn't speak, wrote like someone with an education. She wrote better than some adults that I know. Annie was never taught to spell words much less write sentences. *How can this be? Is she a prodigy?* This day was full of surprises. *Now what do we do?* Leslie and I talked about what we just witnessed. We were too shocked to make any decisions, and we both agreed that we have extraordinary children and we would decide later what to do about that.

We discussed our daughters for a few days before we decided to call Dr. Davies for some advice. We explained to Judy what had happened and she said she would like to see the girls and do some tests to see if there were any neurological abnormalities. She asked us to bring them to London for the tests and everything would be discrete. We trusted Judy, so we made arrangements to take the girls to London the following week.

It was the first week of December and London was decorated for Christmas. We decided to stay for a week so that we could go over the test results with Dr. Davies and take the twins sightseeing. Leslie was nervous about the tests and prayed that everything would be alright. I was worried too but tried not to show it.

We met Dr. Davies at a London hospital. She appeared glad to see us and greeted us with a smile and a hug. She had seen the twins in April and she commented on how much they had grown and how cute they were.

"I have made the arrangements for the twins, and a nurse will be taking them to the third floor for the PET Scan. You can wait outside the room for them," Dr. Davies explained.

We were eager to find out what was wrong, and it seemed like an eternity while we waited for them. The twins were returned to us, and Dr. Davies said it would take till the next day to receive the results. Dr. Sean Buckley, a top neurologist, and she would look at the tests, and then she would call us at the hotel and let us know when we could meet with her to discuss the results.

Leslie and I decided to take the girls downtown to see the toy stores and look at all of the Christmas lights and decorations. Santa was at Harrods and so we took them to see him. Annie was afraid, but Allie went right over to him and sat on his lap. Santa asked her name and asked Allie what she wanted for Christmas, and she said she wanted a baby brother. Santa laughed and asked her if she would like a doll or a sled and she said no, just a baby brother. He looked over at Les and me and said he would see what he could do about that and winked at us. We found that quite amusing. Allie had never previously mentioned a brother to us. I questioned Allie about asking for a baby brother and wanted to know why she said that. She told me that Sofa said that she and Annie would have a baby brother some day. I didn't ask anymore questions and dropped the subject cold.

The girls really enjoyed the bright lights and the music, and especially liked the animated displays in the large department store windows. They were quite enchanted by it all. We continued to walk down the streets in the shopping district when Leslie saw that quaint little shop, the Harvest Moon. Leslie said she wanted to go in the shop to say hello to Brie. We went in to find the place sparkling with all sorts of glittery ornaments and lights. There was a beautiful Christmas tree decorated in a celestial theme. There were tiny angels dressed in glittery costumes and shiny stars all over the tree. There were also tiny twinkle lights in gold, white, and silver. Allie and Annie were truly mesmerized by the tree and the entire place. I heard Allie say to Annie that the one angel looked like Sofa. She still couldn't pronounce Sophielia. Annie picked up an angel that was in a basket and looked at me with her big brown eyes as if to say, may I have this. I picked her up and said to her that I would get it for her. She smiled and gave me a big hug. She has a real sweetness about her.

• • • •

Brie greeted us in a warm, friendly matter. She welcomed us in her shop and wished us a Merry Christmas.

"Brie, do you remember the reading you gave me four years ago?" Leslie asked.

Brie replied that she remembered some of it and acknowledged that she predicted Leslie would have twins.

"Your daughters are so beautiful. You must feel very blessed."

Leslie introduced me and the girls to Brie and said how beautifully magical the shop was decorated. Leslie started to pick out all kinds of things to buy. It was a good thing I brought my credit card with me. We had such a nice time at her shop and the girls seemed absolutely fascinated with it. Brie asked Leslie how long we would be in London and Les told her we would be here for a few more days. Leslie didn't tell her why we made the trip to England. Brie told Leslie to stop by for a reading if she had time, and Leslie said she just may do that. We said goodbye after Leslie spent a couple hundred pounds and wished Brie a Merry Christmas.

That evening we went to dinner in a fine restaurant. We had a wonderful meal and then we retired to bed. The next morning, Dr. Davies called and said she didn't get the results yet, but that she would have all of the information in another day. Leslie asked me if I could watch the girls while she did a little shopping and I said I would. I took them to the children's museum and we had a great time.

• • • •

Leslie had a lot to tell me when she returned to the hotel. It was dinnertime by then, so we decided to order in instead of eating in a crowded restaurant. After dinner, the girls played with toys we had bought that day and Leslie told me she went back to the Harvest Moon for a reading and she began to tell me about it.

"Jack, you won't believe what Brie told me. She said we were concerned with the twins' mental health but we shouldn't worry because they were fine. She said they have gifts that others don't have and they are very unique little girls. She reminded me that she had told me that when I had the first reading. Brie said they have a guardian watching over them and they will always be safe. She also said that we would have another child, a boy."

That made me think about what Allie said to Santa Claus at Harrods. She said she wanted a baby brother.

"Imagine my surprise when Brie told me that. She said we would have a son by this time next year," said Leslie.

I was taken back by what my wife was telling me. *We hadn't given much thought to another child because of the problems we had with Les miscarrying and her difficulty getting pregnant and Annie's autism. A son sure would be nice, though.*

"Les, I know how accurate she was the first time she gave you a reading, but let me caution you again. What will be, will be. If we are meant to have a son, we will. I hope she is right about the twins, though, but I guess we won't know till we hear from Judy with the test results."

At that moment, the phone rang and it was Dr. Davies. "Jack, I would like to see you and Leslie tomorrow morning at 10 a.m. The test results came back and everything looks normal, however, there is something I would like to discuss with you. Don't worry, it isn't anything serious."

I confirmed that we would be there and said goodbye. I told Leslie what Judy said and she felt relieved but puzzled as to why she wanted to see us. The next day we were at Dr. Davies' office.

"Come in and have a seat," she said to us. "Jack, Leslie, I believe you have extraordinary daughters. There is nothing wrong with them neurologically or psychologically. We did plenty of tests and the conclusion is that they are very intelligent and gifted. I have read about people who had similar experiences, such as seeing apparitions of the Virgin Mary. They are considered visionaries and the Catholic Church acknowledges that this phenomena has occurred in such places as Fatima, Portugal; Lourdes, France; and Mexico. Your daughters are far too young to invent these things and the experiences they had sounds like they were in a state of what is known as ecstasy. You may want to read about the apparitions that have allegedly taken place. There have been many and they all are of either the Virgin Mary, Saints, or Angels. It seems that almost all of them are prophetic in nature."

• • • •

Dr. Davies threw us for a loop. *Is it possible that our daughters were messengers? They were so young so how could this be possible?* Leslie and I just looked at each other. We didn't know what to say.

"Judy, what should we do?" I said.

"Jack, I suggest that you and Leslie keep close watch on them and you should start a journal of when these things happen, such as the date, and the duration of the phenomena. For example, did this happen for ten minutes or two hours. Question your daughters about what they saw and what was said to them. Jack, who knows what is going on or what will happen. There may be a real purpose to this and I think time will give you a clearer picture of what this is all about. Keep me posted because I am very interested in this phenomena."

Les and I left Judy's office with the girls and agreed to do what she suggested. We both wanted to get to the bottom of this and knew that it would take a lot of work.

CHAPTER 17

DIRE PROPHESY

2001

It had been awhile since we visited Dr. Davies. The twins were fine and growing like crazy and more importantly, their behavior seemed to be normal. Annie was doing very well with her therapy and she actually started to say a few words and focus more on her activities. She seemed to be more interactive than before, but she still manifested autistic tendencies. Everything was fine with me but Leslie had not been feeling well and was nauseated for a few days, so she went to the doctor. Les had good news when she came home from the doctor appointment.

"Jack, guess what? The doctor thinks I am pregnant. He told me to get a home pregnancy test kit and see if it reads positive."

"Well, we shouldn't be surprised after all, we were told about this ahead of time," I replied.

We both laughed and Les went in the bathroom to take the test. Sure enough, the test was positive. Leslie called her gynecologist for an appointment.

Dr. Carlin confirmed that Leslie was pregnant and said she was due around December 15th. We were very excited and had hoped that Allie was right about a baby brother. Dr. Carlin said she wanted to see Leslie in four weeks and do an ultrasound to make sure that everything was going well. Leslie came home with the news and we told the girls that mommy was going to have a baby and it would be close to Christmas.

• • • •

"I asked Santa for a baby brother and he is going to bring me and Annie one. Sophielia said so," said Allie.

Les and I looked at each other. "Allie, have you seen Sophielia lately?" I just realized that Allie said the lady's correct name for the first time.

"No daddy," Allie replied.

Leslie had started to dream about her mother again. She dreamed that her mother was rocking a cradle with a baby in it and the baby was covered with a blue blanket. Her mother was saying to the baby what a big boy he was and how he weighed nine pounds at birth and would grow up to be very strong and healthy. She was also singing to him in the dream just the way she sang in dreams Leslie had when she was pregnant with the twins. Leslie took that as a sign that it would be a healthy baby boy and was very excited about the pregnancy.

A few months had passed and Les was feeling great. The morning sickness had subsided and everything was going well. It was August 2001 and the summer was hot and sticky. Thank God for air conditioning. I was wrapping up some work for Kevin Leary and Les and I were thinking about taking a vacation. We were talking when we heard Taffy barking upstairs.

I went up to check on the girls and there they were staring at the window where the sunshine was coming through. Prisms danced on the walls, chimes were quietly ringing, and the scent of lavender was present. They were both in that fixed position talking to someone that I couldn't see, and there was the dog sitting right by Annie as I had seen her do before. I heard Annie talk with great clarity. She said that she will do it and Allie said she will tell her daddy what was said. Allie said that they do go to church with mommy and daddy and that mommy is going to have a baby. This incident, or whatever you would call it, went on for about 20 minutes. I watched the entire time and quickly got pad and pen and wrote down in my journal the time, date, and what I observed.

I questioned Allie about what had happened and she told me Sophielia told her and Annie many things.

"She said mommy would have a baby on December 8th and it would be a boy. She said that his name would be Andrew and he would be a beautiful baby."

I asked Allie what Sophielia said to Annie and she said she didn't know because she couldn't hear her. I asked her what else she said, and Allie said something very bad was going to happen soon in New York and I should not go there for awhile. I asked her what it was and she said tall buildings were going to fall down and people would be hurt. I quickly wrote this down in the journal and then I asked Allie if she knew what day it would be and she said no. Allie proceeded to tell me that Sophielia said that those strange-looking people we saw before in that strange place were just looking at us to see if we were ok. I thought for a moment because I didn't know who she was talking about, but then realized it was the beings who had abducted us on Brower Road. *How did Sophielia know about them?*

So many things were running through my mind at that moment. I actually talked to Allie about someone I couldn't see. Someone who I thought was a figment of her imagination. Now I find myself believing in her existence and hanging on to every word. What insanity! I noticed that Annie had left the room when I was questioning her sister and I began to look for her to make sure she was alright. I saw Annie in my office sitting at my desk. She was typing on my computer just as she had done before. I started to read what she was typing and was astounded at what she had written. She wrote that the towers will be hit in September and they will fall. New York will be a disaster. Washington will be attacked. Terrorists will do this. I asked Annie if she could write more about what she was told and she typed: Sophielia said many people will die that day and we will all be sad. Things will change for America and the world.

I immediately printed what Annie typed on the screen. I had to analyze what she had typed to make sense of it. *What towers was she referring to and what did she mean by the towers being hit? There was a bombing in New York in 1993 at the World Trade Center. Would there be another bombing? Is that what she meant?* I asked Annie if Sophielia said anything else and she typed that Sophielia will visit us in a little while.

We had dinner on the side porch that night and shortly afterward we put the girls to bed. Leslie and I discussed what Sophielia had told Annie and Allie.

"Jack, do you believe what the twins are telling us? I know they wouldn't lie, but it's just so hard to believe that an angel, or whatever she is, comes to them and tells them things. I thought you and I would have a normal life like everyone else but obviously that isn't what destiny has in store for us. I wonder if we are going to have a boy? I hadn't thought of names, but Andrew is a good name for a boy. What do you think?"

I looked at Leslie and didn't answer her immediately. I was still trying to digest what happened today.

"Andrew is a great name. That was my grandfather's name and I really like it. You know, I bet we will have a son. Everything that was said came true. Why wouldn't this be true too? Something is really going on here with our family, and I am starting to think that there is a purpose in all of this. I really want to know what our role is in the scheme of things. Leslie, don't you wonder why this is happening to us?"

Leslie replied, "Yes, I have been wondering the same thing. This has gone way past coincidence or a freak thing. Too many strange things have happened to us and I think that they are all somehow connected."

My wife and I talked for several hours about what we had been through, the lost time, Sophielia, Brie, and all of the research I had done for Kevin's documentary. I decided that I was going to go through all of my paperwork from my research and the notes I wrote in the journal, and review all of the things that Brie had predicted, and try to make sense of this. My gut feeling told me they were all connected and I had to figure this out.

CHAPTER 18

9/11

September 2001

It was September 11th, 2001, and I had just finished eating breakfast. Leslie was upstairs with the girls getting them ready for their day. Leslie called me to come upstairs. Allie and Annie were acting strangely. Allie said that something bad was going to happen and she didn't want to go to school. Annie was making loud noises and holding her ears. It was very bizarre. Les told Allie she had to go to school but Allie cried and threw a tantrum. This was really unusual because Allie loved to go to school. She had gone to a nursery school three days a week in the morning. We decided to let Allie skip school and we called Annie's therapist and told her not to come over that day. We didn't know what to make of this but we soon found out what it was about.

I was in my office and I received a phone call a little after 9 a.m. from my brother. He asked me if I was watching the news and I told him no, I was working.

"Jack, you have to turn on the news. The Twin Towers at the World Trade Center were hit by planes. Quick, turn on the news and I'll talk to you later."

I was totally confused by the call, so I went downstairs and turned on the network news. The reporter said a plane had hit the North Tower at 8:46 a.m. and a second plane hit the South Tower at 9:03 a.m. It was now 9:20 a.m. and I was glued to the tv. I yelled to Leslie to come and join me. The news reported that planes were hijacked, the first plane to hit the Towers was American Airlines, flight 11, which left Boston at 8 a.m. The second plane was United 175, which crashed into the South Tower. There appeared to be a great deal of confusion and very little information regarding these crashes. The news media speculated that it was a possible terrorist attack, but couldn't get confirmation on their suspicion. They concluded that two crashes into the towers were certainly no accident and it began to appear as a well-orchestrated attack on America.

Leslie and I watched in disbelief. *How could an attack of this magnitude be carried out on American soil by terrorists?* Questions ran through my mind such as who was responsible for this attack, and why did they target New York City?

I realized at that moment that the things Annie had typed on my computer were in reference to this day. No wonder they were acting strangely. They sensed it was going to happen this morning. If everything she typed was true, there would be another attack in Washington.

The news media had repeatedly showed the attacks of the Twin Towers and the chaos that erupted on the streets of Manhattan. People were running out of the towers and buildings in the immediate area looking for shelter, while others stood and looked on in disbelief. Windows shattered by the explosion could be seen for many blocks and glass and debris were scattered on the streets and sidewalks. Emergency personnel, police, and firefighters were descending on the area. The news also reported that the military was aware of the attacks and had fighter jets in the air. The president was in Florida and was immediately briefed on the situation.

Eric Newman suddenly popped into my head and I realized that he was in Washington. A wave of panic came over me and I immediately called his cell phone. I got Eric on the phone and I told him that he should leave the building and head home.

"Jack, what are you talking about?" Eric said.

"Eric, you have to get out of there and get out of the city. Leave now and get in your car and drive like hell away from the city. I will talk to you later, just do what I say and do it now," I said with real aggression in my voice.

"Ok Jack, I'm leaving now. I'll call you in a few minutes from my car."

"Thanks Eric, you need to trust me on this," I said with conviction.

I continued to watch the news when suddenly they announced that the Pentagon was just hit by a plane. It was 9:37 a.m. when this happened. The plane was hijacked at Dulles Airport and it was American Airlines Flight 77. I immediately thought of Eric and hoped that he had left the building in time. I was shocked and horrified at what was playing before my eyes. It just didn't seem real. *How could something like this happen? How could the most powerful nation on Earth be brought to its knees by terrorists?* It was obvious that we were unprepared for such a horrifying situation. It brought into question just how safe we really are, and just how much the American intelligence community knows.

The phone rang and it was Eric.

"Jack, you saved my life. How did you know? Did you have a premonition or something? Whatever it was, I sure am grateful. I owe you, buddy."

I could hear panic in Eric's voice, and I told him to go home and be with his family.

"Jack, I can't believe these attacks are happening. We really have to get together and talk. Something is wrong here and it's frightening. I will call you tomorrow and we will make plans to get together. My family and I need to come home to Philly. I'm heading home, but I will call you tomorrow. I think I need a few stiff drinks to calm me down. Take care buddy."

"You too Eric. I'll see you soon."

Shortly after 10 a.m. it was announced that there was a plane crash in western Pennsylvania, but they didn't have details at that time. It was believed that it was United Airlines Flight 93. Later, it was reported that at 10 a.m., United Airlines Flight 93 was headed for Washington, but the passengers stormed the cockpit and forced the plane down in Somerset County, Pennsylvania. The passengers of that plane saved countless lives and possibly the White House. Their bravery and unselfish efforts will never be forgotten.

The South Tower of the World Trade Center collapsed at 10 a.m. Eastern Standard Time. The North Tower collapsed at 10:28 a.m. Pandemonium broke out as people screamed and clamored to get away from what was a tidal wave of smoke and ash filling the streets of Manhattan. New York became a war zone as a result of this attack by an unknown enemy. You could see the fear and panic on the faces of those who were in the area of the World Trade Center as they ran for their lives. The Network News estimated that there were thousands of fatalities. Many of the casualties were men and women of the New York Police and Fire Departments.

Leslie and I looked at each other in disbelief. We still couldn't comprehend what was happening.

"Jack, I'm so glad you weren't in NY. I would be out of my mind with worry if you had been there today. I feel sad for the victims and their families. The casualties have to be great and the pain and suffering the families will be going through when they find out their loved ones died as a result of this will be too much to bear."

Leslie's eyes welled up with tears as she talked. The twins sat on our laps and we hugged and kissed and realized how lucky we were to have them here with us, safe and sound. You don't realize how fortunate you are to have family until something like this happens.

This attack was one of the worst incidents in the history of America and the loss of life was estimated at over 3,000. The world rallied around us and mourned our loss as they offered support. Newspapers all over the world expressed their sorrow for this tragedy and it appeared that this disaster brought us together as if we were all members of the same family. 9/11 changed our lives and things would never be the same. None of us would ever feel completely safe again.

The phone rang and it was Kevin Leary calling to say how sorry he was about what happened in New York and to see how we were doing.

"Jack, I am so glad you weren't in New York. I know you go there often on business."

I was silent for a few seconds.

"Kevin, you won't believe why I wasn't in New York. I don't know where to begin, but there is something definitely going on with our family and I have no idea what it is."

Kevin asked me what I meant but I said it would take too long to explain on the phone. Kevin said he was coming to Philadelphia in three days, so we made plans to get together. I told him I would pick him up at the airport and I insisted he stay with us while he was in Philadelphia.

• • • •

My friend, Eric Newman, called three hours later. He wanted to thank me again and said he and his family were coming to stay with his parents for a week. His nerves were shot from this whole ordeal and he needed to leave Washington. Eric's office was located in the section of the Pentagon where the airplane hit and he knew all the people who died as a result of the attack. He said he wanted to come over to see us when he gets in town. I thought for a moment and said Kevin was coming to Philadelphia in two days and Eric and his wife and son should come over for dinner and we could all talk. Eric said that sounded good, so we made plans to see each other on Friday evening.

It was Friday, September 14th, when I picked up Kevin at the Philadelphia airport at 10 a.m. It was really good to see him and speak to him in person.

"Jack, it's great to see you. What's been going on with you? You seemed so secretive on the phone."

"Well, Kevin, I don't know where to begin. You know about the abductions that happened to us, but something else is going on and it involves the twins."

Kevin had a concerned look on his face. "Jack, do they have a health problem?"

I hesitated at first because, how could I possibly tell him about what has been happening.

"Kevin, about a year and a half ago Leslie saw the girls in their bedroom talking to the sunlight that was shining in their window. They were totally oblivious to her presence. Allie said someone named Sofa visited her and Annie. When Leslie told me about it, I chalked it up to an active imagination, but then I also witnessed them in an altered state of consciousness. I contacted Judy Davies about what was happening. We took the girls to London so Judy could examine them. She gave them all sorts of psychological tests as well as a PET Scan of their brains. She told us there was nothing physically or psychologically wrong with the twins. She thinks they might be visionaries."

Kevin looked at me in disbelief. "Jack, what exactly happened to them?"

I told him about the times we had witnessed these experiences and what they told us. I explained that what really convinced me was when they told us about the Twin Towers and the Pentagon attacks.

"Jack, this is crazy! What are you going to do?" Kevin asked.

"I don't know. What does one do when their kids see and speak to someone you can't see and they predict disasters. I suppose Les and I will have to take one day at a time and see what happens. Judy told me to keep a journal and write down everything the twins say. Sofa is actually Sophielia. Allie couldn't pronounce her name so she referred to her as Sofa. I started a journal like Judy had suggested, and the first entry was the twins telling us about the Twin Towers."

"That is bloody amazing! I wonder what Sophielia will predict next?" Kevin said with his usual enthusiasm.

"I have no idea but I'm sure there is more to come from Sophielia," I replied.

CHAPTER 19

KEVIN THE WITNESS

Eric and his family arrived at our house at 6 p.m. Leslie had been cooking and baking the entire day and the house had a wonderful aroma from her efforts. We all had a great time at dinner and Kevin, Eric, and I went upstairs to my office while Leslie and Carolyn stayed in the kitchen. Eric's son, Tim, was playing games on the downstairs computer and Allie and Annie played with toys in the family room. I was glad that I had this opportunity to speak to Kevin and Eric without interruption. We started to talk about the attack of the Twin Towers and Eric questioned me about the call I made to him.

"Jack, how did you know what was going to happen? I assume that you knew by the way you insisted that I leave Washington. It was the scariest call of my life."

I began to tell Eric about Allie and Annie's experiences and how we took them for tests, etc. I got my journal out and read to them what I had written the day they last saw Sophielia.

Eric had a shocked look on his face.

"This is unbelievable. Jack, I could have died in the attack on the Pentagon, but you saved me from that disaster. I've been doing a lot of thinking since that happened and I've concluded that this could have been avoided had the right people acted on the warnings they were given. We never should have been attacked. There was a lot of buzz going on in the intelligence community and they felt an attack was imminent. Someone high up should be held accountable for this. I heard from a colleague of mine today that the administration is working on an act to pass through Congress quickly, which would basically give the government absolute authority over the public and that they could suspend our constitutional rights in the name of national security. I have a really strange feeling about this. They could push anything through Congress now and no one would feel that their rights were violated. That is not good."

"I believe that something is at work here and all of these things are somehow connected. The alien abductions, the twins' experience with Sophielia, and the increase in terrorism worldwide all seem to be saying something. My instincts tell me that we are headed for some very difficult times, and I definitely feel compelled to find out what it means. I have known both of you for a long time and I trust you, and I feel that the three of us were meant to work together on this. We all have contacts with a wide range of people who have a lot of information. I think together we can figure out what is going on. Are you with me on this?" I asked Kevin and Eric.

They both looked at me and said they were in. Kevin excused himself to use the head.

"Jack, I just met Kevin. Can he be trusted?"

"Eric, he saved my life when we were covering a story about the IRA. I was caught in a crossfire on a street in Ireland when he pulled me to safety. We have been close friends ever since. He is a brilliant filmmaker and the best friend anyone could ever have. His loyalty runs as deep as the sea."

"Well then, that's good enough for me. I trust your judgment," Eric replied.

Eric and his family left our house around 11:00 p.m. Kevin and I stayed up till 3 a.m. talking about old times when we were in Ireland and England and about what was currently going on in the world.

Kevin was curious about the twins' visions of Sophielia and pressed for more information about her.

"Kevin, I don't know why she is appearing to them and I don't know what to make of it. Everything she said came true except for one thing, which we will have to wait and see if it happens."

"What did she tell them that hasn't come true yet?" Kevin asked.

"She said Leslie was going to have a boy and his name will be Andrew."

"Did she predict this before Leslie became pregnant?"

"Yes. Allie and Annie were told awhile ago about a baby brother. Recently, Sophielia said Leslie was going to have a boy on December 8th and his name would be Andrew. I guess time will tell if this is true."

Kevin ran his hand through his hair and turned his head, raised his eyebrows and said, "Well, I can't wait to see if it comes true. You have to let me know."

Kevin and I went to downtown Philadelphia the next morning. Kevin had a meeting scheduled with a film distributor and I went down to South Street to check out some stores. I wanted to get the girls something special, but I didn't know what exactly. Their birthday was coming up and I wanted to surprise them. I was walking down South Street when I saw a toy store around the corner in the middle of a little street. It had a quaint looking sign that had "The Storybook Market" on it. I looked in the window and saw some really cool things including a train set running on a small platform, and a window display of the Big Bad Wolf and Little Red Riding Hood.

I went into the store and, I must admit, it was magical. The entire store had toys that had a storybook theme. There was a huge beanstalk in one corner with a big giant at the top and Jack climbing up the beanstalk. Hansel and Gretel were there with a trail of crumbs behind them. Snow White and the Seven Dwarfs were set up in another corner with the wicked step-mother in front of a mirror. All of the figures were anywhere from two feet to four feet tall and were very realistic in appearance. There was a section with twelve beautifully dressed dolls which represented The Twelve Dancing Princesses. That was Allie's favorite fairytale and Leslie and I read that story to her dozens of times. Allie's favorite princess was Elise. I immediately told the store clerk that I wanted that doll. Annie's favorite story was Thumbelina and I did see a tiny doll dressed in a sparkling dress which the shopkeeper said was Thumbelina. I bought that one for Annie. I was sure that the twins would be surprised and happy when they opened up this year's birthday gift.

• • • •

Kevin and I headed back to my house after his meeting. He was excited about his next documentary receiving worldwide distribution without going through the usual drill. He didn't anticipate the same level of success he had with his UFO documentary for the BFC, but felt that it would do well. We changed subjects and began to talk about terrorism and what was going on in the world. We both agreed that Europe was becoming a very powerful force in the world with a lot going on with the European Union. Kevin asked if I would ever cover terrorism again like in the good old days and I told him that may be a possibility especially since terrorist attacks took place on American soil. I confessed to him that I missed the fast pace of journalism covering world affairs, and there were times when I really wanted to return to it. I missed the element of danger and the adrenalin boost I received from it, but hesitated returning to it because of my family.

Kevin and I entered our family room to watch the news. Taffy was comfortably lying on the floor when we came in. All of a sudden, Taffy started to whimper and got up and ran around in a circle as if she was agitated by something. She started to bark and then ran upstairs to the girls' room. I looked at Kevin and he asked what was wrong with the dog. I suspected she sensed Sophielia was coming, but didn't want to say that to Kevin. I went upstairs to the girls' room and there they were, Allie, Annie, and Taffy staring at the sunlight. I grabbed my journal and called down to Kevin to come upstairs.

• • • •

Kevin and I watched as the girls went into their altered state of conscience. Something was different about the light. It appeared to be larger and brighter than on her other visits. The room was filled with colored prisms that danced around the room. It was a spectacular sight, and the scent of lavender permeated the air. Kevin and I just looked on with amazement.

The girls started to have a conversation with the light and I heard Allie say that she would tell mommy and daddy about that. Annie was heard saying yes, I know. The dog was as still as could be. Allie asked the light why she visited her and Annie. Then she asked if she would visit Andrew when he is born. This went on for about 20 minutes and then the light faded, the prisms disappeared, the scent of lavender ceased, and the twins were back to normal.

I asked Allie if Sophielia just visited and she said yes. I asked her why she visits them, and Allie said that they are pure of heart and innocent, and that's why they could see her. Allie said Sophielia was going to visit Andrew when he is born and she will be with mommy when she goes to the hospital. She also wished us a happy birthday and said she would not see us for awhile. She has things to do, angel things. She said it was important to tell mommy and daddy what she said because you couldn't see or hear her. She told us America will go to war very soon.

Annie ran to my office and sat at my computer. I told Kevin to watch what happens next. Annie proceeded to type what she was told by Sophielia and the following appeared on the screen. It said: We will go to war and many people will die and cities will be destroyed. This war will happen in 2003 in the Middle East. This will make terrorists mad and there will be a lot of deaths. America will fall on hard times. People will lose their jobs and lose their homes. Many countries will be angry with America because of this war. She will lose friends and will have many problems. This will be the beginning of the major changes in the world. I will tell you more when I see you again. Be good, girls, and listen to mom and dad. They love you very much, as do I.

Annie got up and ran out of the room. Kevin was silent. I looked at him and saw a very strange look on his face.

"Kevin, what are you thinking?" I asked.

Kevin shook his head and paused a second.

"Jack, I have never seen anything like this. We really have to get to the bottom of it. I think you are right on the money when you said something is going on. I'm going to make it a priority to find out what it is. I have lots of contacts and between the three of us, we should be able to solve this mystery. Someone is trying to tell us something."

Kevin had to go back to the UK, and thanked Leslie and I for our hospitality. He gave Leslie a gift of a very expensive bottle of wine as a token of his appreciation. Leslie thanked him and asked him to come and visit again. I took Kevin to the airport and he reiterated that we had to work together to find answers. He surely seemed enthusiastic about this whole thing and felt there was something of great importance happening.

CHAPTER 20

EUROPE AND UFOs

Autumn 2001

It was Allie and Annie's fourth birthday and we threw a big party to celebrate the occasion. All of our family members and some of our friends were at the party. The girls loved seeing their cousins and opening their presents. The weather was perfect for the kids to play outside and it worked out well because Leslie rented a trampoline and moonwalk for the kids. She also rented a large tent where all the adults gathered to drink, eat, and engage in lively conversation.

Leslie's sisters were in attendance so she took the opportunity to show them the nursery for the baby that we were expecting in December. One of her sisters commented that it looked as though the room was geared toward a boy and asked if that was wishful thinking. Leslie told her that she had a feeling that it would be a boy and left it go at that.

Allie and Annie opened the gifts that I had gotten them at the Storybook Market. They were so excited when they saw the dolls. The girls went to bed at 8:00 and took their dolls with them. Taffy and Freddie followed the twins to their room and slept on the floor beside their beds. Leslie and I crashed in front of the television. We turned on the news network and they were running a story about UFO sightings across Europe. They even had a video that someone in France had taken. It showed a bright object in the evening sky moving at high speed and doing very unusual maneuvers. Les and I looked at each other and both of us said that object looked familiar.

The news continued to report that a group of teenagers in England were playing soccer in a field when they saw a huge, metallic object hovering over the field for several minutes. They said this object was round in shape and had colored lights all around the rim of the craft and it was almost as big as the field it hovered over. It gave off a blinding light and then speeded off across the sky and disappeared almost instantly.

The boys were stunned at the sight of this object but once they gained their composure, they noticed three of their friends were missing. They quickly ran home and told their parents what had happened. Several parents called the police to report what the teens had witnessed. The reporter said the teenagers were questioned at a police station about the disappearance of the three boys who were ages fourteen and fifteen. The names of the boys who disappeared were Daniel Carver, Edward Beasley, and Ian McCullough.

Reports of sightings were pouring in from all over Europe. It turned into a media frenzy and the story dominated the news for several days. People from every country in Europe witnessed unusual events. Animals were acting strangely and pictograms in crops were popping up everywhere in broad daylight, in plain view, with dozens of witnesses watching as they were created.

The network news actually had a camera focused on a crop circle that was in the process, and it was clear to see that there were no human hands at work. You could actually see the wheat flatten and the design take shape. You could also hear a faint humming sound. No one could get within six feet of these crop formations because an invisible force field surrounded the parameter. Scientists were called in to watch this phenomena, but they couldn't come up with an explanation. The force fields around these formations were especially mysterious. Scientists were completely baffled.

Leslie and I became obsessed with the news as this phenomena continued to take Europe by storm. The sightings continued and more people disappeared. Kevin called to tell me that one of the boys, Ian McCullough, was the son of one of his cousin's friends. He said the continent was in panic mode. The governments couldn't give an explanation and people feared for their lives. The streets became deserted and everything came to a screeching halt. People wanted answers but no one had any, not government officials, not scientists, not religious leaders. People began to flock to the churches in large numbers and they held prayer vigils for hours. It was amazing how people turned to religion for comfort and security.

Several days had passed and the appearance of the UFOs had abruptly stopped. The people who had disappeared in those few days suddenly reappeared in places far from their abduction. Many abductees were found wandering in fields and remote areas. Some were discovered in towns and villages unfamiliar to them. None of the people who vanished remembered what happened to them and they were all in a state of confusion when found. A total of 52 people were abducted in Europe, but England had the greatest number of abductees. All persons were taken to the nearest hospitals for a complete physical and psychological evaluation and were later questioned by the authorities. The general consensus was that these people were too traumatized to give any information regarding the circumstances surrounding their disappearance and it was recommended that they receive therapy to help them through their fear and confusion.

Kevin called me to discuss this unbelievable series of events.

"Jack, as time goes on, life gets stranger. We've known all along that something was up, but it seems that things are happening fast, like one thing after the other."

"Kevin, how is that boy, Ian, doing? Is he alright?"

"That's why I called you. Judy Davies has been seeing him and she feels he is ready to be hypnotized. She has the parents' permission, so next Thursday she will put him under hypnosis during his scheduled session. She also got the parents' permission to tape the session and to show the tape to us. Judy told them about you and Leslie's experience, she didn't reveal your identity, and they agreed to let you and I see the tape. Judy will make a copy for me and I will bring it to Philadelphia for us to review. I have some business in the States, so I will bring it then."

"That sounds like a plan, so I will see you in a few days," I said as we ended the conversation.

I told Leslie about the phone call I had with Kevin and she too was excited to see the video. We were hoping that it would provide more insight into why we were taken. We looked forward to his visit, but we had to get back to normal. Our daily routine was pushed aside and the news had dominated our lives for about a week. The truth of the matter is, our daily lives would never be the same. People all around the globe had witnessed these strange events and fear was everywhere. Life on this planet would never be the same again.

Even though there was a lot happening, things did manage to return to normal. The twins were doing well, and so was Leslie. The doctor said the baby would be a nice size. The baby was lying in such a position that she couldn't determine the sex of the baby. Everything appeared to be fine and the doctor said Leslie should have no problems when she delivers the baby. The doctor still maintained that our child would arrive toward the end of December. All of us were eager for the new arrival, and Allie kept referring to the baby as her brother Andy. I asked Allie if she would be disappointed if she got a baby sister instead of a brother. She said no, but she knew for sure it would be a baby brother and she told me that the angels picked his name and it would be Andrew. I suppose I couldn't argue with that, after all, if the angels say so, it must be true.

Kevin called to let me know he was at the airport and he was going to the city to meet some people. I told him I would meet him in Philadelphia that afternoon at the Four Seasons Hotel. We could come to my house and have dinner and then view the tape.

"Jack, you won't believe what is on this tape. I looked at it last night and I was really taken back by its content. I can't wait for you and Leslie to see it."

I was totally in suspense and was so eager to see it. The next few hours couldn't go fast enough for me. I went upstairs to shower and get ready to leave. I told Les that Kevin was coming to dinner and he had the tape with him. She said she couldn't wait to see it. We both acted like two kids waiting to see Santa Claus at the North Pole.

I picked up Kevin, and Leslie had dinner on the table when we arrived at our house. We ate rather quickly because we wanted to see the tape. My wife took the twins up to bed early and then we popped in the tape and watched intensely as it began to play. Dr. Davies started the session by saying that the client was Ian McCullough, who was 14 years old and who was abducted on Saturday, September 29th, 2001. She explained that Ian was going through therapy because of trauma that he suffered from the events that took place that day. She also described the therapy and that she would be inducing Ian into a hypnotic state to see if he could recall what had happened to him on September 29th. She explained the procedure to Ian and assured him he would be fine. His parents were present during this session.

"Ian, do you recall the day, September 29th, when you were playing soccer at Longfields Park?"

"Yes."

"Can you tell me what happened to you at the park when you were playing soccer?"

"I was playing soccer with some classmates when we saw a very bright light all around us. I looked up and saw this huge, metal thing hovering right above us."

"Can you tell me what shape it was and about how large it was?"

"It was round and it was about the size of half of the field. It covered at least half of the field."

"What happened next?"

Ian started to get excited and he cried out, "Oh my God, what is this thing? It's going to fall on us!"

Dr. Davies assured Ian that this was not really happening now and that he was just remembering something.

"I couldn't take my eyes off of this object, but then the next thing I knew, I was inside it and so were Eddie and Danny. We looked at each other and we all said, 'Where are we?'"

"Did you see anyone else there? Perhaps some strangers?"

"Yes, we saw six strange-looking people."

"What did they look like?"

"They were wearing grey suits, and were about our size, but very thin."

"Did any of them speak English?"

"Well, it sounded like English, but it was in my head. I heard a voice in my head. Their mouths didn't move."

"Did any of them speak to the other boys?"

"I don't know."

"Ian, let's concentrate on you. What happened next?"

"Two of these people took me into a room and told me to lay on the table."

"Describe to me what the room looked like and what was in the room."

"I was on the table. I saw gadgets hanging from a long thing that was attached to the table. It looked like things you see at the dentist. You know, a drill and just things hanging."

"Did you see anything on the walls?"

"There were round, glass objects on the wall. They looked like windows, but you couldn't see out of them. I was scared."

"Did they examine you like a doctor or dentist?"

"Yes, they poked me with instruments, but it didn't hurt. I felt something pinch and I yelled and one of the people put his hand over my eyes and I didn't feel anything after that."

"What happened next?"

"They took a sample of blood from me and cut a piece of my hair. They did something to my eye, but it didn't hurt. They did something behind my knee but I don't know what they did."

"Did they speak to you when they examined you or say anything that you remember?"

"I was thinking about these people and what they were doing here and who they were. One of them said that they were from a faraway place. She said they would be back to help us."

"It was a woman speaking to you?"

"Yes, it sounded like a lady, but she didn't speak through her mouth. I heard what she said in my mind."

"Did anyone else speak?"

"Yes. Someone said I was a very good example of a young human being. Someone else said I would transition very well. I didn't know what they meant by that. I thought to myself, what are they talking about?"

"What happened next?"

"I suddenly felt a lot of fear. One of them, it was the lady, put her hand on my head and gently rubbed my head."

"Did she say anything to you?"

"Yes, she said that I shouldn't be afraid because they were here to help people. She said I would be leaving soon and would be home in time for dinner. She laughed at that comment and it made me feel at ease. She reminded me of my mother. I felt feelings coming from her. I couldn't see her smile, but I could feel her smile at me. It was very strange. I can't explain it."

"Ian, what happened next?"

"I was taken to another room where Eddie and Danny were and the next thing I knew, we were in some field. A farmer found us and called our parents."

"Ian, did they say anything else to you before they left you in the field?"

"They said they will be back someday. Changes will happen on this planet and we will need their help. I felt frightened when they said that, but the lady touched my hand and said not to worry because she will be there for me."

"Did this lady have a name?"

"Yes, her name is Miren."

"Ian, when I count to three, you will awaken. One, two, three. Ian, how do you feel?"

"I feel ok."

• • • •

Dr. Davies finished the video tape with the hope that Ian would return to his normal life and not worry about his experience. She told him that he did great and she and his parents would always be there for him whenever he needed someone to talk to.

Leslie, Kevin, and I sat there watching in disbelief. We just looked at each other for a moment and then we all started to talk about what Ian had said. What did they mean when they said he would transition well? What changes would happen? Ian wasn't the only one who felt fear. We all felt a sense of dread watching the tape. Who are these beings and what do they want?

The next morning I took Kevin to the airport so he could catch a flight back to London. We kept tossing our own theories around about why these beings were here but none of them really made sense. Were the changes going to be political, geographical? Was it about a devastating war? We decided to give our brains a rest and not think about this UFO thing too much. Sometimes obsession gets in the way of seeing things clearly.

That afternoon, Eric called me from Washington.

"Jack, did you see what was happening in Europe?"

"Are you kidding me? How could I not know. That was all that played on the news."

"Jack, we have to get together. I have something to show you. You will not believe what I have in my possession. Will you be home on Sunday? I will be at my parents' house over the weekend and I could come over to your place. My mother's health hasn't been good and we're all pitching in to help my dad."

I thought about my schedule and then I said I would be home and he should come over anytime. We made plans to meet at my house in the early afternoon.

CHAPTER 21

THE BELGIUM CONNECTION

I was really intrigued by what Ian had said regarding what the alien had said about him transitioning well. I decided to read the notes that I had taken regarding alien abductions and listen to the tapes from the meeting I had attended in New York back in November 1996. This was a meeting for a support group whose members believed they were abducted by aliens. I wanted to see if there was any reference to a transition. I found nothing that even hinted about a transition of any kind. The people on the tapes spoke about the abduction, when and where it happened, and what was physically done to them but there was no mention of any transition.

I made a mental note to call Dr. Henry in a week to ask him if he had ever heard transition mentioned during any sessions with abductees. I emailed Judy Davies to ask her if she had heard the term transition before Ian mentioned it. She emailed me back saying she had never heard any of her clients mention that word under hypnosis and she was also intrigued by it as well.

I decided to call my Belgian friends, Antoine and Claude, to see what they had to say about the UFO sightings that swept across Europe. I thought they might have some more information from the government regarding this subject.

"Antoine, this is Jack Branden. How are you?"

"I am doing very well, thank you. And how are you and your family doing?"

"We are doing well. The twins are growing and my wife is pregnant and due in December. Thank you for asking."

"So, Jack, did you see what was going on in Europe recently?"

"What do you think? I was glued to the television watching the news constantly. What happened in your country?"

"Jack, excuse me, Claude just walked in my office. I'm going to put you on speaker phone. Can you hear me?"

"Loud and clear buddy. Hi Claude. How are you doing?"

"Very well, thank you. How about you?"

"I'm fine. Everyone here is fine."

"Jack, getting back to your question, we had a lot of sightings, but it seemed as though these aliens really wanted to be noticed. Their crafts hovered over public places like parks and stadiums for 20 minutes at a time during the day. People were frightened and stayed in their houses. The streets became deserted. Businesses wouldn't open and schools were closed. It was eerie," said Antoine.

"Jack, Claude here. There were reports of alien abductions. A few people were hiking on a trail when they vanished for two hours. They reappeared five miles away from the trail in a cemetery. Can you imagine that, a cemetery. It doesn't get much stranger than that."

"Did they know what happened to them?" I asked.

"They were questioned by the authorities, but they couldn't remember anything," replied Claude.

"Hypnosis seems to be a very good tool in finding out what happens to people when they can't remember. Perhaps someone should suggest that to them."

Antoine chimed in, "That sounds like a good idea. We have the names of these people because the government is conducting a large-scale investigation. We will call them and recommend a good therapist who could hypnotize them if they wish to go in that direction."

Claude began to talk. "Jack, you know how truthful our government is when it relates to this sort of subject. Their policy is to be straight-forward with their citizens, and keep them informed as to what is happening no matter how frightening it could be."

I replied in earnest, "Yeah, I really respect them for taking that stand. They have enough confidence in their citizens to think that they can handle the truth no matter what it is. I don't know of any other government who has that much confidence in their people. Listen guys, I know you are at work so I won't keep you any longer. I'm giving you my email address so you can contact me at any time. Keep me informed. I really want to know what is going on. These aliens are becoming more visible and there is a reason. I want to find out what they are doing here."

Claude responded, "Jack, we will keep you informed. It was great talking to you. Stay well and tell your wife to take care and have a healthy baby and take care of those beautiful little girls."

Antoine thanked me for calling.

"We will let you know what's going on here. We are just as curious as you are. Between all of us, we should be able to solve this mystery. Take care."

"Antoine, Claude, thanks so much for your help. I will come to Europe in the near future to let you know what I uncovered. Take care and I will talk to you soon."

I knew, after that conversation with Claude and Antoine, that they would be delving into the mystery of transition. I had whetted their appetite for investigation. I had faith that between all of us—me, Claude, Antoine, Kevin, Judy, Leslie and Eric—we would discover the mystery of the aliens and their intentions.

CHAPTER 22

THE SECRET FILES

I was eager to see Eric and hear what he had to add to the mix of information. He sounded like he had something interesting to tell me, and knowing Eric, it would be very interesting. He has a low-key demeanor and when he gets excited about something, you can bet it is exceptional. Sunday came and Eric arrived at our house around 1:00 p.m. Leslie and the twins went shopping, so I was home alone with Freddie and Taffy. We went to my office upstairs and sat down in the comfortable leather chairs I had positioned in the corners of the room. It was a quiet room with lots of sunlight and privacy which was greatly needed when I was doing work on a piece.

It turns out, Eric had plenty to tell me regarding the information the government had on aliens and UFOs. He proceeded to tell me, in a very enthusiastic manner, what he discovered.

"Jack, you will not believe what I found last week. I was archiving some files in the basement of the Pentagon when I came across a couple of boxes that contained classified information. The boxes had numbers on them which indicated they were top security which required the highest clearance. The president doesn't even have high enough security clearance to look at these files, just to give you an idea of how secret they are. The cartons had UFO printed in very small letters which were barely visible, and that's all I had to see. I started to read some of the files and I discovered that the U.S. government had information as far back as the early 1940s regarding the appearance of UFOs. Many people reported seeing them in rural areas of the country."

I interrupted Eric for a moment to ask him how these files ended up in a declassified storage room. Eric said a high-ranking military official was looking through them and when he was finished, one of his assistants stored them in the wrong area. This person had just started working at the Pentagon a month ago, and didn't realize they had to be stored in the high security area.

"Can you imagine the chances of that happening? I swear it was destiny. I am thoroughly convinced I was meant to find these files. Anyway, I was going over some of the reports and I was shocked to read that the military had known about UFOs and aliens all along and they actually had contact with some of them. Anyway, someone was coming, so I hid the cartons behind other boxes and got out of there."

I asked Eric if he was able to get another look and he said he went back the next day under the guise that he needed to find some records from the accounting department.

"I took my trusty little digital camera with me, that discretely fit in my pocket, and I photographed a lot of the UFO files. I couldn't wait to get home and download them onto my computer so I could read them."

I was thinking to myself what balls he had for doing that. Would he be considered a spy or something if he was caught?

"Eric, weren't you afraid of getting caught doing that?"

"No. The declassified area is open to everyone. These are the files the public can view. The only thing that would appear suspicious is the amount of time I would spend in that area. That is why I photographed the files during my lunch hour. Lucky for me no one was around at that time. That place empties out at noon. Besides, the people who work at the Pentagon have no interest in this area. They are, however, interested in the files they can't access. My colleagues would salivate over the opportunity to view them. We joke about it all the time. We have this game we play when we see a lot of big wheels congregate in the conference room. We all get one guess at what's being talked about in their meeting. Sometimes we find out later what was being discussed and whoever guessed correctly gets all the money in the pool. Sounds childish, I know, but sometimes we have to lighten up over some of this serious national security business."

I asked Eric what else he discovered in the files.

"Well, let's start from the beginning. Some reports were made to the police in 1942 in a little town in Vermont called Breezy Corners. Some of the residents said they saw bright lights in the sky and heard a buzzing sound. This lasted for four days and then the lights were gone. Several residents said they saw dead animals in fields with puncture-type wounds on their bodies. All of the blood had been drained out of them. The police looked into it, but they couldn't come up with an explanation. That was the end of that investigation.

"There were a lot of reports of that nature up till 1947, and then the Roswell incident happened. That took UFO sightings to a whole other level. The reports you heard about Roswell were basically true. The government really tried to cover up what happened, but people couldn't keep silent. Many witnesses told family members what happened when they were on their death beds. I suppose they felt they had to unload the burden of the secret and probably felt at peace afterward."

I told Eric I had heard about the crashed UFOs when I was doing research for Kevin's documentary but, of course, the government wouldn't give me any information and all of the declassified reports I read were blacked out. I couldn't get anything out of the material that wasn't censured. Eric told me the military completely took over the town when the crash was reported by a rancher whose property was the site of the incident. There was debris all over the ranch and the military cleaned it up with a fine tooth comb.

"Jack, the Roswell report stated that the military used intimidation to keep people quiet to the point where they made death threats. They were afraid the truth would get out. Jack, I read about another incident that was not known to the public, which happened in 1951 in a small town in western Pennsylvania. The military referenced this town as Crash Site #3 PA because they didn't want anyone to find out the exact location. A collision involving two UFOs happened during a severe thunderstorm in August 1951. The military actually had possession of two crafts, and custody of five aliens. All but one were dead when they arrived and the one that survived for several hours was taken to a restricted military area in Maryland. Autopsies were performed on these aliens and the autopsy report explained in great detail the physical make-up of these beings. The report stated that they were small in stature, about 48 inches tall, slight build, their skin was grey in color, had large heads with no hair, large eyes, very small noses, and no ears. They also had no reproductive organs, and their other organs were different from humans. The digestive and respiratory systems were totally different."

• • • •

I just sat there quietly because it was difficult to digest all of this information. I knew he was being straightforward with me but it's just so difficult imagining something like this exists. Eric proceeded to tell me that when they made the first incision during the autopsy, a very strong odor was emitted from the body and it actually caused several members of the medical team to vomit and faint. Military personnel were present during all of the autopsies and they were calling all of the shots.

As I listened to him rattling off classified information about UFOs and alien life, I wondered how something like this could remain quiet for so long. I wondered what else the government knew about these aliens. *Were we going to be attacked by them someday? Would it be like the radio broadcast, War of the Worlds? Are we in danger of being destroyed as a race? If that was the case, why haven't they destroyed us already? Or, perhaps they are waiting for us to destroy ourselves.*

Eric continued to tell me that the Secretary of Defense was flown in to view the wreckage and the bodies. One of the aliens was still alive and laying in a hospital bed, which was located behind a huge glass wall. He was very weak and was hooked up to all kinds of monitors. A soldier was sitting on a chair beside the bed talking to the alien. He later reported that the being communicated mentally and told him that he, the alien, would be dying soon. The soldier actually said the being thanked him for sitting with him and said he appreciated his kindness. The soldier related that he felt very sad for the alien and could sense that this being was friendly and not evil or threatening in any way. The being communicated that we were not alone in this universe and that one day we would become acquainted with all of the other beings who exist out there. He said we were like the babies in the universe and that we would soon be ready to take our next step.

At that moment, the alien saw the Secretary of Defense standing on the other side of the glass wall watching him. The alien must have sensed he was a man of great authority because he started to communicate mentally with the Secretary. This being told him that his race had visited earth for thousands of years. He said more would be coming and they would be monitoring our planet and our progress. He also said they would be coming for his body and the bodies of the others. He then expired in the presence of the Secretary of Defense. The Secretary was so upset over this whole ordeal, he started to go into cardiac arrest. Fortunately, there were doctors and nurses there and they saved his life. The report stated that he had a mental breakdown and was never the same. He died shortly after that strange, frightening encounter.

"Eric, what do you think he meant when he said we were the babies in the universe? Do you think he meant we were babies on the evolutionary ladder? That's what I'm getting out of his comment. What do you think?"

Eric thought for a moment.

"I don't think anyone knows for sure what he meant, but, that would be my guess too. I think we are approaching a time when the human race has become very technological and very scientific, but also very destructive. You can't begin to imagine what our military is really capable of regarding the development of weapons and the strategy of defeating an enemy. There are times when I wished I worked in a factory 40 hours a week and didn't work for the Defense Department. There are times when I can't sleep at night because I worry about the threat of war and mass destruction. Consider yourself fortunate that you don't work at the Pentagon because in this case, ignorance is bliss."

"Did you see anything regarding sightings that have happened in the last few years?"

"There is plenty more, but I haven't been able to look at it. I plan on doing that in the coming week provided no one moves the files. I'm hoping no one looks for them or discovers they are in the wrong area till I'm finished with them. I actually hid the boxes behind some other files so they would be out of sight. Jack, had I not seen these files with my own eyes, I wouldn't believe they exist. Doesn't it just sound like something out of a bizarre sci-fi movie?"

"I know what you mean. I never believed in this stuff until I had my own personal experience. Eric, you have to keep me posted," I said as he approached the door of my office.

"Are you kidding, I brought you copies of all the records I managed to film and they're in my car. I'll bring them in for you. Jack, you do understand that no one can know about this, not even Leslie. Carolyn has no idea I did this. She would go into a frenzy if she knew."

"I understand completely. I will tell no one and I do understand and appreciate the risk you are taking by doing this."

Eric looked really tense, but I knew he had faith in my word. "Jack, I knew I could count on you. We need answers before it's too late."

Eric went to his car and handed me some folders which contained several pages in each one. He said he would be coming back to his parents' house in a week or two and would call me. I said I would be looking over these files and will eagerly wait for the others. We shook hands and said goodbye and then I immediately took the folders to my study and locked them in one of the desk drawers. On one hand, Eric felt he had done something wrong, but on the other hand, he felt the public had a right to know the truth. He suspected something very unusual was going on and he wanted to know what it was.

It was five o'clock and Eric had left my house as Leslie and the girls pulled into the driveway. They were carrying lots of shopping bags. Taffy greeted them as they got out of the car and I helped Leslie carry her bags into the house. The girls were excited to show me the things that mommy bought them. They were at the mall for several hours and I knew a lot of money was spent on that trip. Leslie took them to the Disney store and they had purchased lots of Minnie Mouse items such as cups and plates, dolls, and little purses with Minnie and Mickey plastered all over them. It's comforting to know that some things don't change like the Disney characters. I sense they will be around for many generations to come.

• • • •

Les and I put the girls to bed and went downstairs to watch tv. She asked me about Eric and how his mother was doing. I told her what I knew about his mother, but didn't tell her the real reason Eric came to see me. She would be really upset if she knew what Eric did and that I had copies of the files he took from the Pentagon. As we were sitting there watching the tube, a very interesting program came on. It was about ancient history and the possibility of UFOs existing as far back in time as the biblical prophets Elijah, Isaiah and Ezekiel. It appears that flying chariots were common descriptions in biblical times and Ezekiel described encounters with a mechanical device.

Other ancient cultures wrote of ancestors coming from the heavens and drawings in caves in South America and Asia depict beings with strange appearances that looked like beings dressed in space suits. The pyramids in Egypt were believed by some to have been built by beings from the heavens because of the technology that was used to construct them. Two-hundred- and four-hundred-ton blocks were used to build these structures and the precision with which they were built could not have been designed by someone from this planet. The elaborate drawings in Peru which cover over 200 square miles and were made by stones were believed to be land markings for the ancient astronauts. These drawings of spiders, birds, and other animals could only be viewed from high up in the sky.

• • • •

Things that I originally didn't believe existed were starting to occupy a lot of my time. Leslie and I started to talk about this subject.

"Jack, why do you think they have been visiting this planet?" Leslie said as we watched the program.

"I don't know, but I don't think they are trying to destroy us and take over like some people theorize. They would have done it by now. There are a lot of things that I think, but who knows what the real reason is for their presence," I said in a somber manner.

"Well, I believe in God, and I have faith that things will work out for the best and that He will always protect us," Leslie replied.

"Well Les, not everyone has been protected. Violence in the streets is on the rise, wars are still fought, famine still exists, and greed is alive and well. I don't know how protected we really are."

Leslie sat quietly for a moment and then she said, "What I meant was that the planet, as a whole, would be protected. I think we have a certain destiny as individuals and a certain destiny as a planet."

I told my wife that I pretty much agreed with her and that I was really trying to find out what this thing was all about. I also realized that the older I get, the more I realize that I really don't know much at all. I suppose that is why the saying goes, "With age comes wisdom."

The next day I made a call to Dr. Henry in New York. I wanted to call him sooner but just didn't get the chance to do it. Dr. Henry wasn't available, but I left a message to call me at any time. That night he called and we discussed the UFO phenomena that happened in Europe. We specifically talked about the three boys that were abducted in England. I told him about Ian McCullough and the session he had with Dr. Davies while he was under hypnosis.

"Jack, I'm familiar with Dr. Davies and she has an excellent reputation," Dr. Henry said during our conversation.

"Dr. Henry, have you ever heard the term 'transition' during any of your sessions with abductees?" I asked.

"No, I haven't heard that term used during any of my sessions, and I've never heard any of my colleagues mention that term either," replied Dr. Henry.

We spoke for a few more minutes and Dr. Henry told me he would see if he could get some information from his clients regarding transition. He said he would keep me informed if he received any relevant information about this subject.

CHAPTER 23

ANDREW

December 2001

It was December 7th and Leslie's time was drawing near. She had a doctor's appointment at 10:30 a.m. I went with her for this visit because she was too uncomfortable to drive. My wife's feet and ankles were swollen and she felt miserable. The doctor examined her and said that she wasn't ready yet and that Leslie probably had a couple of weeks before she has the baby. Les protested but Dr. Carlin reminded her that the baby will arrive when he or she is ready and Leslie should be patient. Everything looked good except for the swelling. She told my wife to stay off her feet as much as possible and avoid salty foods. She had one of her assistants schedule an appointment for a week later.

"Jack, do you think I will be giving birth tomorrow like Sophielia said?"

I thought for a moment and said, "Yes, I do believe you will be a new mother and I will be a new father tomorrow, and I do believe it will be a boy."

I turned to look at her, because I was stopped at a red light, and she gave me a big smile and said, "I think so too."

I continued the conversation, "And then you can eat all of the salty foods that you want!"

We both laughed and agreed that it would be nice to have a new baby tomorrow.

Leslie had a difficult time sleeping that night. She tossed and turned and kept me awake. She finally settled in at 4 a.m. but I couldn't fall back to sleep, so I went to my office to do some reading. I always liked the privacy of that room. I would sink into one of my over-stuffed chairs and read for hours. I got out some of the files that Eric gave me to read. The more I read, the more astounded I was by the content. Eric didn't tell me about everything that the report contained.

There was a file that had documents from local police in cities and towns from all over the country that were basically missing persons' reports. Apparently, some people had been missing after UFOs were spotted in rural areas and they were gone without a trace. There were people of all ages, religions, and races who had vanished. The FBI initially investigated these reports, but they were soon handed over to a special task force within the intelligence community. This agency concluded that many of these people who were missing, were abducted by aliens. There was a high-level security agency called SIA, Security Investigation Agency, although others call it Saucer Investigation Agency meaning flying saucer, and one of their top people wrote a report about the results of their investigations. The conclusion was that something had to be done to initiate contact with these beings to find out what they were doing with American citizens.

There was another report dated December 24, 1968, which really disturbed me. A General Richard Romanski reported that the SIA made contact with a group of aliens from a star system that we were not aware of at that time. The star system has since been identified as RORY-10. This group claimed responsibility for the abduction of 60 people from the United States and 240 people worldwide. They said that the abductees were safe and would eventually be returned. When asked why they took these people, one of them replied that they could not give a complete explanation at that time, but they were testing a sampling of the human race to see if we were at the proper level of development. The SIA didn't know what they meant by that and the aliens refused to elaborate on it.

I started to read another report dated April 18, 1980, that an agent submitted to the SIA and it stated that most of the abductees from the United States had been returned and each one was thoroughly investigated, examined by doctors and psychiatrists, and some were given polygraph tests.

The report stated that all of the abductees were in fine physical condition, in fact, it appeared that none of them aged at all since their abduction. It also said that many of these people no longer had long-term health problems such as diabetes, asthma, allergies, high blood pressure and other chronic illnesses. One of the teenagers who was abducted in 1957 suffered from polio and was confined to a wheelchair. When he was returned in 1978, he was no longer crippled and walked like a normal person. Two other persons taken were two teenage sisters who were on their way home from a graduation party when they were abducted. The one sister was blind from birth and the other sister had a heart condition which required daily medication. When the sisters were returned eight years later, the blind girl was able to see and the other sister's heart defect had been corrected. A notation was made regarding the sister with the heart defect. It stated that a team of heart specialists examined her and discovered that surgery had taken place to correct her defect. They figured out how the procedure was done and they are now using it for other patients with this condition. Some of the other abductees who were considered mentally retarded from birth were now gifted with an unusually high intelligence.

The psychiatrists gave each person a psychological evaluation and all of them initially suffered from confusion and fear. They couldn't remember what happened to them and the world they came back to had really changed. Some people had been gone for over 20 years and although they didn't age, everyone else around them did. The world became much more technological and their families had different lives. Some people lost spouses, family members, and friends through divorce or death. It almost seemed to me that these advanced beings thought it was ok to take these people because they cured them of their physical problems, but had no concept of the psychological and emotional damage they did by taking them against their will and returning them to a world that was so different from the one they left behind.

As I read one report after another, *I wondered what gave them the right to just take someone against their will and transport them to a place for many years, subject them to who knows what, and then dump them back home to a place that had dramatically changed while they were gone. What gave them the right to make all those other people suffer the torment of losing someone close to them and not knowing where they were or what they were being subjected to? What gives them the right to take someone for even an hour without their consent like they did to me and my family? What authority allows them to do this?*

I must have dozed off to sleep because the next thing I knew, Leslie was shaking me and telling me to wake up. I'm not the most cooperative person when I am being forced to wake up and I said something to that effect as she was shaking me.

"Jack, it's 12 noon and my water broke. I have to go to the hospital. Please get up." Well, that woke me up real quick.

"Les, I have to call my mom to stay with the twins."

"I took care of that already," Leslie said. "My bag is packed and I'm ready to go. Your mom should be here in ten minutes. Hurry up and take a shower, it's showtime!" Leslie said with a chuckle. "Oh, I also called Dr. Carlin. She will meet us at the hospital."

That's my Leslie, always well-organized.

Dr. Carlin was at the hospital when we arrived and Leslie was taken upstairs to be examined. Dr. Carlin checked her and said she should be delivering within a few hours. I was sitting beside Leslie's bed trying to provide the needed support when she started to get excruciating pains. I rang for a nurse, but there was no response. Leslie suddenly became delirious and that scared me. I went into the hallway to look for the doctor and found her at the nurses' station. I told her about Leslie's behavior and she ran to her room. When she entered Leslie's room and saw her condition, she immediately instructed the nurse to help her wheel Les into the delivery room. Leslie was acting unusually strange and holding a conversation with someone, but no one was in the room with her.

I was not allowed to enter the delivery room because of Leslie's condition. I frantically paced the floor the entire time and it seemed almost like an eternity. I felt panic start to radiate from the pit of my stomach and started to pray that everything would be alright. About 45 minutes after she was rolled into the room, Dr. Carlin came out to talk to me.

"Mr. Branden, your wife is doing well, but she is absolutely exhausted and is resting right now. You have now become a proud father of a healthy baby boy. Congratulations to you and Leslie. She was quite a trooper in there. She was talking as if someone was in the delivery room with her so I thought she may be reacting to a toxin that pregnant women sometimes develop before they deliver, but that wasn't the case. She was fine and delivered the baby naturally without any aids. Your son seems to be very healthy, but a pediatrician is checking him now as we speak. He weighed 9 pounds, 5 ounces and is 21" long. He is wonderful! Congratulations again."

"Thank you very much Doctor for all of your help. Can I see my wife now?" I said impatiently.

"You sure can, but I think it would be a good idea to see your baby first, since your wife is probably sleeping."

"I think that is a great idea."

I walked down the hall to the nursery. For some reason, I was very nervous but also very excited to see him. I suppose it was because of what Sophielia had said and how it all came true. She said Leslie would give birth to a son on December 8th. She was right on with those predictions and Andrew was the name we decided to go with if it turned out to be a boy. *I wonder how she knew that?* The twins will be excited to see their mother and new baby brother. It will be interesting to see Annie's reaction to him because autistic children don't interact with others very well.

I was looking through the window of the nursery when I spotted a carrier with Baby Branden on it. One of the nurses was holding him and brought him over to the window. He was so beautiful and looked a lot like Allie when she was born. He was a lot bigger than the twins were at birth. I couldn't wait to hold him. The nurse came out of the room and told me that she would be bringing him to Leslie in about 20 minutes. They had to check a few more things before they deliver him to his mother. I went down the hall to Leslie's room to see how she was doing. She was fully conscious and talking non-stop.

"Jack, have you seen the baby yet?" she asked.

"You bet I have, and he is just great. He reminds me of Allie when she was born, only a lot bigger. He has a great set of lungs, I can tell you that. He was screaming for a moment when they were examining him. The nurse said she will bring him to you in about 20 minutes. Wait till you see him. He's huge compared to the girls. I think he's going to be a quarterback for the Eagles."

We both laughed and Leslie said that he will have to be a quarterback for Notre Dame first. I agreed with that.

Fifteen minutes had passed and the nurse brought Andrew into Leslie's room. She handed the baby to her and my wife's face just lit up with smiles and joy. She checked him out thoroughly and commented that I was right about his size. She was accustomed to tiny little girls but he was anything but tiny.

"Oh Jack, isn't he just adorable? I can tell he is going to wrap me around his finger just the way the girls have wrapped you around theirs."

"He is great, and I think he and I will be going to games and hanging out a lot. I can't wait to get him in little league."

"I think you are getting a little ahead of yourself, Jack. He's no more than an hour old. Little league is a ways off."

Leslie came home with the baby two days later. Allie and Annie were so excited to see him. Allie said that she knew she would be getting a brother and Annie said his name when she saw him. The twins were touching him and giggling at the faces he was making. He probably had gas but they thought it was funny. Annie kissed Andrew so gently on his head. It was very sweet and I managed to get it on film. I took a lot of pictures of our family. My mom and dad and two of my sisters were at our house when we came home and they were so excited to see the baby too. My dad had a fire burning in two of the fireplaces because it was so cold outside. Snow was expected and I was glad Andy was born before the snowstorm. My mother, the saint, and my sisters, Steph and Dee decorated the downstairs for Christmas, which was only two weeks away. Leslie was too uncomfortable to decorate while she was pregnant and I was too incompetent to do it. I offered to do the job, but Leslie cringed when I made my offer. She knows I have no talent for decorating. Leslie was really impressed with the job my mom and sisters did and very grateful to them. My mother and sisters cooked dinner for us and we all sat down to a fine meal. My family left soon after dinner and Leslie fed the baby while I put the girls to bed. It was a long day and we were all very tired.

Leslie and I sat down in front of the fireplace and I told her about how she was talking to someone while she was in the delivery room. She said she was not hallucinating as Doctor Carlin had thought, but that she really did see someone standing beside her who was talking to her. She began to tell me what took place in that room.

"Jack, I saw Sophielia when I was in the delivery room. At first, I saw a very brilliant light, which was so beautiful and bright but it wasn't blinding. Then a young woman, who looked more like an older teenage girl, began to materialize before my eyes. She began speaking to me and she identified herself as Sophielia. She actually held my hand while I was giving birth. She told me that everything would be fine and the baby would be healthy. She said that she would appear to me again and tell me things to do to prepare the children. I asked her what she was referring to and she said that she would tell me later. She said I should not take the children to public places for three months and that we should not have the baby baptized till March. There will be a severe outbreak of influenza soon and many people will become seriously ill and some will die. It is important that you keep the children away from the public as much as possible."

I was almost envious of Leslie because she saw Sophielia. *I wondered if I would ever get the chance to see her.*

"What did she look like?" I asked.

"She was so beautiful. She had a glow around her. She had long, wavy, dark blond hair and was about five feet, four inches tall. Her voice was soft and sweet and she had a beautiful smile. She was very demure in her demeanor. She wore a long, pale blue dress reminiscent of what you see the Blessed Virgin wearing in religious pictures."

"Did she say anything else to you?" I inquired.

"I don't think so. That was pretty much it. Oh, yes, she said you would see her one day because you were becoming more of a believer. She also said I should tell you to be very careful with the information that you were given. It was powerful information that could destroy you if certain people were aware that you had possession of it. Do you know what she meant by that?"

How do I respond to that without telling a lie? How did Sophielia know about the information Eric gave me? I had to tell her something, so I said that she could have been referring to the tape Kevin showed us with Dr. Davies and Ian McCullough.

One week later, all of our families came to see little Andrew. The twins were so great with him and always wanted to help Leslie take care of him. Annie would stare at Andrew and squeeze his hand and Allie would sing songs and tell him how much she and Annie loved him. I heard Allie tell Andrew about Sophielia and how she named him. Annie made a card for her brother and for Leslie when they came home from the hospital. She even wrote a little poem in the card. Annie may be autistic but she can write like a person three times her age. Her poem read, "Little brothers are so sweet and I can tell that you are really neat. You brought us love, you brought us joy, I'm so glad you are our baby boy. Love, your big sister Annie."

My little Annie can't express herself verbally, but she sure can communicate via the written word. She has a real talent for writing and I intend to encourage and guide her in developing her writing skills.

CHAPTER 24

DR. DAVIES AND LOURDES

March 2002

The past few months were very quiet, however, the things that Sophielia told Leslie came true. A terrible influenza broke out worldwide and there were thousands of fatalities. The news reported that this was one of the worst influenzas of all time and vaccines proved to be ineffective. We kept our kids away from public places and had very little contact with others. We didn't send Allie to school and didn't have any therapists work with Annie during this time. We had friends and relatives who were very ill with the flu, but fortunately they all recovered from it quickly, unlike many others who died. One person who was not so lucky was a friend of mine from college, Hector Martinez, whom I hadn't seen in almost 20 years. He was in a lot of my classes and we often went to games and bars together. He left behind a wife and four children and many others who loved and missed him.

Other things were not going very well for our country. The president was in his second year of office and things were not looking good. The economy was not doing well and people who worked in manufacturing were fast losing their jobs. It was like a mass exodus. The Free Trade Agreement had been expanded to include many other nations and this seemed to seal the fate of the manufacturing sector of the United States. Factories were closing in America and those manufacturing jobs were leaving for China in record numbers. You could no longer walk into a store, regardless of whether it was high or low end, and buy many American-made goods. The middle class was eroding and people were losing their homes and going bankrupt in record numbers. It was quickly becoming a sad state of affairs for the American people.

The unemployment rate continued to climb, but I was not in that position. I was extremely busy with assignments and felt a lot of pressure to meet all of the deadlines. So many offers came pouring in since Kevin's documentary, which brought in many opportunities to make a lot of money. Publishers were begging me to write books on the UFO Phenomenon, but I wasn't ready for that kind of commitment. I preferred to stick to short assignments because I didn't want to be obligated to write a book in a short period of time. I needed time to spend on my quest for the truth regarding UFOs and I wouldn't have it if I was writing a book. I decided to go to Europe for a few days and visit some of my connections such as Kevin, Judy, Claude, and Antoine. Leslie said she didn't mind that I went and my mother agreed to stay with Leslie and the kids and help out while I was in Europe.

My first stop was London. I arrived at noon and checked into a hotel near Dr. Davies' office. I had called Judy before I left the U.S. to see if she would be available to see me. She agreed to my visit and set up an appointment for 3:00 p.m. I unpacked my bag and called Leslie to let her know I arrived safely in London. After the call, I headed to a café located down the street for a bite to eat. There were few people on the streets, and I thought it was unusual. I began to notice that the air felt cold and the day seemed quite dreary as I walked to my destination. I wondered if there was the possibility of snow in the forecast or maybe it would just turn out to be a damp, bone-chilling day. Perhaps that is why so few people were present in this otherwise bustling area of London.

I arrived at Café George and I sat at a small round table with a plaid tablecloth on it. I looked around the room and noticed that all of the tables had plaid covers but each one was a different color and pattern. I questioned the server about the plaid cloths and she said each one represented a specific Scottish clan. I found that interesting and made a mental note to look up the Scottish clan names when I got back home to see if our name was among them.

I placed an order for fish and chips and was pleasantly surprised at how delicious the meal turned out to be. I made another mental note to visit this café the next time our family came to London. I think Leslie would really like this place. She is a designer by profession and would love to see the various plaids and the quaint décor of this café, not to mention the cozy atmosphere it offered.

I finished lunch and made my way to Dr. Davies' office and was right on schedule. I was there only a minute when I was warmly greeted by Judy.

"Jack, it is so great to see you," she said as she hugged me.

I was very surprised by her greeting because she has always been rather reserved and was not the type of person to hug or kiss anyone in greeting.

"I have so much to tell you. I cancelled all of my appointments for the rest of the day just so I would have the time to update you on things."

"I can't wait to hear what you have to say. You sound so enthusiastic," I replied.

She asked me to have a seat and offered me some tea and pastries.

"So, what is it that you have to tell me?"

"Well before I get started, I want to know how your family is doing. I have a little something for the baby."

Judy pulled out a box from behind her desk and handed it to me. It was a large box wrapped in blue paper that looked like a water color blue and it had lots of curly ribbons tied around it.

"Thank you Judy. You are so thoughtful. The baby is doing very well and the twins and Leslie are just fine. The twins constantly pay attention to Andrew; he's sort of like a new toy. My mother is staying with them while I'm in Europe."

"Jack, I'm so glad to hear that everyone is doing so well. You are very fortunate to have such a wonderful family. How is Annie doing?"

"Annie is coming along well, but you know how it is with autism. She still has autistic behavior, but she is doing very well with her therapy and they expect her to go mainstream when she enters first grade. She has been tested to see what level of intelligence she is at and I am happy to report that she tested well above her age group. She is very smart and so is Allie. How is your family?"

"Everyone is fine. My kids are in college and my husband has been recovering from surgery and doing well. He had a blocked artery, but everything went well and he is recovering beautifully. Jack, I have something to tell you about Ian McCullough. He started to have a nosebleed during one of his sessions. His nose was bleeding like a water faucet that was turned on. I had him lay down on the couch and I managed to stop the bleeding. I examined his nose and I saw something sharp sticking out of the inside of one of his nostrils. I pulled it out with a pair of tweezers. It looked like a tiny shard of glass and I didn't think anything of it at the time. I asked Ian if he broke a glass object or was around broken glass and he said no. I washed this object with soap and water and had a strange desire to look at it under a microscope. It looked really unusual under magnification. It appeared to have a honeycomb pattern which I thought was strange so I gave it to a friend of mine who works in a crime lab. She said it was made from an unknown substance and it emitted a very low frequency which was almost undetectable. Here's the weird part. Edward Beasley and Daniel Carver were missing for two days after I had taken this object out of Ian's nose. They were both away from home at some sporting event. Ian wasn't missing at anytime and he was away on holiday with his family in Scotland. Jack, I think the object I took out of Ian's nose was a tracking device."

That worried me because that means that we could have a device in each of us. That would explain why Leslie had more than one lost-time experience.

"Judy, if this is true, then my wife, my daughters, and I could have tracking devices in our bodies."

That was a frightening thought knowing that we could be taken at any time.

"I know and that is why I wanted to see you and explain this to you. You and your family have to be examined for something like this. You could have an object anywhere in your body."

I sat there in her office in shock. *Now I understood why people were taken repeatedly and why they were so paranoid.*

"Judy, I really appreciate you telling me this information. I can guarantee you that we will be checked for this."

"Jack, I think a CAT scan would detect something like a tracking device. I took the liberty of checking the scans we took of your daughters and I noticed something in their arms above their elbow. I think it may be an object like the one Ian had in his nose. Do you have a doctor that you can trust who will remove these objects?"

"I do have a cousin who is a doctor and I'm sure she will take care of this for us."

"Good and if you like, you can send it to me and I will have Jillian check it to see if it is the same type of object that was removed from Ian's nose. Jillian's husband is a scientist who formerly worked for the government, but is currently working independently and he and Jill are really curious about the object I removed from Ian."

"Sounds good to me but can you trust these people?"

"Implicitly!" she said.

I got up to leave Judy's office and I thanked her again for everything. She's a terrific person and I felt lucky to know someone like her. *Now I had something else I had to spring on Leslie. Wait till she hears what Judy had to say about this tracking device. It almost seems like you will never be free of them once you are taken. It's sort of like being under house arrest. I wonder if anyone else had discovered these implants in their bodies? I didn't hear about this before when I did my research for the UFO documentary.*

• • • •

I went back to the hotel to enjoy dinner with Kevin Leary and his wife, Jane. It was so great to see them. We talked about what was going on in our lives and I showed them pictures of the kids. Jane made such a fuss and said our children were absolutely beautiful. Jane excused herself to go to the restroom when Kevin asked about the twins and if they had anymore encounters with Sophielia. I told him that the twins hadn't seen her since he was at our house. However, more things came true that Sophielia said to them. I told him Sophielia said we would have a baby boy and name him Andrew and that came true. They also said Sophielia would be with Leslie when she gave birth and that came true. Leslie saw her and spoke to her when she was in labor and when she delivered the baby.

Kevin looked amazed. "Jack, let's hope she was wrong about war with Iraq. Do you think that is a possibility?"

"I don't think so. What reason would the U.S. have to invade Iraq? The terrorists were members of Al Qaeda who were mainly from Saudi Arabia and Iraq would be a fool to attack us. I gotta admit, though, everything Sophielia said came true."

"Yeah, that's scary. Her track record for predictions has been 100%. I hope she is wrong this time for all of our sakes. A conflict with Iraq would be a catalyst for war throughout the Middle East and you know what that would possibly lead to, World War III," Kevin said with real concern in his voice and I nodded in agreement.

I started to talk to Kevin about Judy Davies and what went on with Ian McCullough during a recent session. Kevin told me he knew about the object Judy removed from Ian's nose and he was really interested. Jane came back from the restroom and joined in the conversation. She said she knew Jillian Richards and her husband Dennis and said they were good people who could be trusted to give us a straight answer about what that object might be. Kevin said he never heard about tracking devices in people, but thought it made sense considering that some people claimed to be abducted several times during their life.

That gave me the chills because that told me we have no privacy at all and people could be taken away, against their will, at anytime. It also means that you could never hide from these beings. They would know where you are at all times. It gives a new meaning to big brother. This is worse than the government. At least they can't track where your physical body goes although they could track everything else you do like phone calls, plane reservations, computer activity, credit card activity and who knows what else.

I told Kevin that I heard the U.S. government knew about aliens and UFOs for decades and that they were heavily involved in cover-ups. That didn't surprise Kevin at all and he told me he had sources in the British Intelligence that confirmed the United Kingdom was well aware of UFO activity and alien encounters. Both governments refused to release the truth to the public. Some believe it was because the government feared mass panic and that would lead to total chaos everywhere. *Can you imagine what Wall Street would do if the government said aliens and UFOs were real?* The stock market would crash in a heartbeat.

Kevin, Jane and I ended the evening at midnight. I told them I was traveling on to Belgium to see Claude and Antoine the next day. I also planned to do a little shopping for Leslie, my mother, and the kids. I know how they look forward to receiving presents when I return from a trip.

I went to bed early that night, because the plan was to get up by 7:00, do a little exercising, and leave so I would arrive in Belgium by the afternoon. I planned to have dinner with the guys and then head for Paris the next day.

• • • •

It was a cold but sunny day in Brussels with temperatures hovering in the thirties. I was eager to see Claude and Antoine because we had much to talk about. I checked into a hotel, unpacked, and went downtown to buy some Belgium chocolates for Leslie and my mother. There appeared to be more activity on the streets in Brussels than the day before on the streets of London. It could be due to more agreeable weather in this city, which didn't have a threat in sight for inclement weather.

I came back to my hotel room a little later and called home. Leslie answered the phone and she told me everything was fine and proceeded to praise my mother for being such a tremendous help to her by tending to the twins while I'm away. I told her that I had a surprise for her and that I missed her and the kids very much. We talked for about ten minutes, and she ended the call by wishing me a safe trip home.

The phone rang soon after I hung up with Leslie and it was Antoine. He called to let me know that he and Claude were in the lobby of the hotel.

I went down to meet them and we went to a French restaurant around the corner called Jacques to have dinner.

"It is so great to see you, Jack. A lot has happened since we last talked," said Antoine.

"You seem very excited, so this must be good," I replied.

Claude chimed in, "Oh, it is. By the way, how is your wife and children? I remember you told us Leslie was pregnant and due in December."

"Everyone is doing very well and we now have a son named Andrew. I have some pictures here with me."

"Oh, you have a beautiful family," said Antoine.

"Indeed you do. You must be very happy," exclaimed Claude.

"I'm a lucky man. How are your families doing?"

"My family is wonderful. The children are grown and my wife and I are doing everything we always wanted to do but couldn't when the children were young. We have been having the time of our lives," said Claude.

"Well, unlike Claude, I still have a young child at home, but all is well and everyone is healthy and happy."

"I'm glad to hear that. There is nothing better than a healthy, happy, family," I replied.

"I agree with you on that one," replied Claude.

The three of us spoke about our families and a few other subjects, but then the conversation steered toward the true reason why Antoine, Claude, and I planned this meeting.

"Jack, do you remember when we told you that some hikers were abducted and you suggested hypnosis?" asked Antoine.

"Yes, I do."

"Well, we contacted them because, as you know, our government has been conducting a full investigation. We recommended hypnosis as you suggested, and some of the abductees agreed to it and the sessions were recorded."

"They all basically said the same thing, which was, being taken up into a craft of some sort, being subjected to a physical examination, having vials of blood taken, and then being returned. However, one of the abductees actually asked questions once she overcame her fear," explained Claude.

"Yes, can you imagine that, asking questions? She asked them where they were from and they said they came from a planet unknown to those on Earth. She asked them if they were watching us and the being replied that they were and have been for thousands of years. She asked why they were so interested in us, and he said it was because we were all connected in ways people on Earth could not possibly know and that some day we will know what the connection is when we understand the clues. She asked why they had made their presence known at this time and he said that there will be changes that will take place on Earth and we will need their help in order to survive. Humans will have to accept their help and not be afraid of them. He said they had to be returned and they were all released into the cemetery," said Antoine.

"Did she say how he communicated with her?" I asked.

"Yes, by mental telepathy because, according to her, they didn't have much of a mouth and it never moved," said Claude.

"It appears that mental telepathy is the form of communication they use. That is the most communication I have heard about between the aliens and the abductees. She said all of this under hypnosis?"

"Yes."

"What do you think of this, Jack?" Antoine asked.

"I think it's probably true. I don't think they are here to harm us or take possession of our planet. I think they would have done that by now if that was their intention. I just want to know what will happen that will warrant their help in order for us to survive. Is it a war that will threaten annihilation? Is it unimaginable destruction as the result of devastating natural disasters? Do we have to accept them in order to be helped? What were these clues he referred to? That was an interesting piece of information, clues."

"We also found that to be interesting. Jack, you said you had something to tell us," said Claude.

"Oh, yeah, Judy Davies was having a session with one of the teenagers who disappeared in England and his nose started to bleed profusely.

She examined him and saw something sticking out of his nostril. She pulled the object out with a pair of tweezers and it looked like a tiny shard of glass. She had a friend, who worked in a crime lab, examine it and she said it was made from an unknown material. Judy thought it might be a tracking device because the other two boys were abducted again but Ian wasn't. The second abduction occurred after Judy removed the object from the boy's nose."

"That would explain why people were taken more than once. Can you imagine being tracked and having someone know where you were every minute of your life?" Antoine replied.

"I hope my wife doesn't hear about that. She would want one of those in me so she could track my every move," Claude said jokingly.

We all laughed and agreed with him. The three of us had a great time talking about the comment regarding clues and said we would all start looking for them. *The question is, what does a clue look like and are we ever going to figure this out?*

• • • •

The next morning I went to Paris and checked into the Carlson Hotel. I planned on taking the flight to New York the next day. I thought I would do a little sightseeing because Paris held a lot of fine memories for me. Leslie and I were married here and it was one of the best times of my life being there with her. I was sitting in a small café having coffee, when I heard some women talking about their trip to Lourdes. They were Americans and their accents sounded like they were from the Philadelphia area. I turned and excused myself and asked them where they were from. They replied that they were from Manayunk and Conshohocken and that they were touring Paris, but were in France to visit the shrine at Lourdes.

I introduced myself to them and proceeded to tell the ladies that I grew up in Philadelphia and asked them if they were familiar with my sisters' art gallery. They got all excited and introduced themselves to me and said they knew about the gallery. One woman said she was well-acquainted with it and spent a lot of money there. They complimented my sisters on the fine art that they carried and the beautiful paintings and sculptures Dee and Steph had done. I asked them about Lourdes and they said that they visited the shrine yesterday. They asked what I was doing in Paris and I told them I was visiting friends in Belgium and was getting a plane out of Paris for New York.

"You should really go to Lourdes. You get a special spiritual feeling when you go there. A friend of mine had a daughter who had MS and she drank the water from Lourdes and was cured. She hasn't had any symptoms since she drank the water in 1978," Margaret said.

"Yes, it's wonderful there. You can bathe in the pool of water. There were thousands of crutches, canes, and other things that people left there who were healed. I highly recommend that you go there. You won't be sorry," Catherine said.

Then she asked me how long I would be in Paris and I said I was leaving to go back to the States tomorrow. Margaret reiterated that I should go to the shrine, and assured me that I had plenty of time to do so and will still be able to catch my plane tomorrow.

I thanked them for the information about Lourdes and said I would think about it. They got up to leave the café and said it was a pleasure meeting me and they hope they see me and my family in Manayunk some day. I said likewise.

I began to contemplate Lourdes and they succeeded in convincing me it was the thing to do, so I made arrangements to go. I arrived at Lourdes that afternoon and immediately went to the shrine where the famous waters flowed. There were pamphlets lying around with the history of Lourdes, so I picked one up and started to read it. In 1858, the Virgin Mary appeared to a peasant girl named Bernadette Soubirous in a small grotto called Massabielle. Bernadette was told by the beautiful lady to dig in the earth in front of the grotto and after some time, a puddle of water appeared. It later turned into a spring for which it became famous for possessing healing powers. The next thing I noticed were the countless numbers of crutches, wheelchairs, and other pieces of equipment that were abandoned there because of miraculous cures.

• • • •

The Basilica of Lourdes was so beautiful and there was a definite ethereal quality to this holy place which you felt the moment you entered. It certainly was a peaceful sanctuary where faith and hope flowed like the water from the miraculous spring. People with physical challenges were seen everywhere drinking the water and bathing in the pool where the spring water continuously flowed. I took a drink of the water and much to my surprise, I felt transformed. I can't explain it, but I really felt alive, uplifted. I took another drink and I felt a wave of joy flowing through me. It was like my body became really lightweight and I could float. It felt like every cell in my body was awakened and I felt liberated. At that moment, I remembered what Brie had told me when I was in her shop. She said I would visit a religious place in France and it would change my life and that I would see things more clearly. *I wonder if this is what she was referring to?*

I was quite taken back by the reaction I had to this sacred place. I never expected to feel this way. *Who would have guessed that this would be the highlight of my journey?* I decided that I would take a bottle of water home with me so everyone else could drink this miraculous elixir and feel the way I did. I was especially hoping that Annie would be cured of her autism. I was aware of the fact that not all people were cured by this water, but I could certainly hope it would cure my Annie. I knelt in prayer at the shrine and asked the Blessed Mother to watch over my family and to help Annie. I also asked her to give me guidance in life so that I would always do the right thing, and to give me the eyes to see the truth and enlighten me on my quest for answers. I left Lourdes with a new sense of being. I was certain my life had a specific purpose and I knew I would discover what that purpose was very soon.

I was back in my hotel room having dinner when I felt compelled to call Leslie. I just had to tell her about Lourdes and how I felt after drinking the water.

"Leslie, I'm so glad to hear your voice. I really miss you and the kids."

"Jack, I miss you too. Are you coming home tomorrow? The girls are here, say hi to them."

"Hi daddy, I miss you," said Allie. Leslie held the phone up to Annie.

"Hi dad," Annie blurted out.

"We all miss you. Jack, hurry home to us," Leslie said.

"I am homesick for you guys and I've only been away a few days. How's Andy?" I asked.

"Andy is teething and he is a little restless. He's been up some nights and your mother was so kind to get up with him and let me sleep. She is the greatest!"

"I agree with you there."

I paused for a moment and then I told Leslie that I visited Lourdes today. I told her about the women I saw in the French café and how they were from Manayunk. I told her that I was talking to them when they insisted I visit Lourdes. They had been there on a pilgrimage and they highly recommended it to me. One woman said that you receive a certain spiritual feeling when you go there and she was so right. I told my wife about how I felt when I walked into the Basilica and how I felt when I drank the water. I told her I have a bottle of the water from Lourdes to bring home. Leslie was very excited about that and wished me a safe trip home and they will all be waiting for me. At that moment, it felt really good to be so loved. That was a feeling I hadn't experienced until I married Leslie. I know marrying her was the best decision I ever made, and I keep reminding myself that I am the lucky one because she agreed to be my wife.

CHAPTER 25

THE LOURDES EFFECT

I returned home the next evening and I was really tired. I suppose it was jet lag, but none the less, I was exhausted. Leslie, my mother, and the girls were waiting for me. Andy was asleep in his crib. I felt like a king returning home from battle. The hugs and kisses were overwhelming. My senses seemed to be heightened since I drank the water at Lourdes and I had this very strong sense of love surrounding me. Freddie and Taffy also greeted me at the door. My hands were full and Leslie helped me with my bags.

We went into the kitchen and I gave everyone their presents. I gave the girls their dolls and they screamed with delight. They really liked them and quickly ran off to their rooms. Next, I gave my mother the cameo I had purchased at The Harvest Moon and she was speechless. Tears began to well up in her eyes and she said, "Oh, thank you so much." My mother grabbed me and kissed me and whispered that this cameo looked just like the one her mother had and it brought back pleasant memories that she had forgotten.

Leslie was looking at me as if to say, where is my present? I pulled out a box and gave it to her. She carefully unwrapped the box and gasped when she saw the bracelet that was inside.

"Jack, this is beautiful. Thank you so much."

Leslie gave me a big hug and kiss and handed the bracelet to my mom so she could look at it.

"Thank you, thank you," she said with much enthusiasm.

Leslie and my mother were talking to each other about the jewelry and I almost forgot that I had a box of Belgian chocolates for each of them.

"Oh, by the way, I have one more present for each of you," I said as I pulled out the chocolates from one of my bags.

My mother gushed over the chocolates.

"Oh Jack, Belgian chocolates. They're my favorite. You are such a thoughtful son, God bless you. I love you so much."

Then she gave me another hug and kiss. Leslie chimed in to say basically the same thing, except that she said I was absolutely, positively, the best husband.

My dad came to pick up my mother and we talked for awhile before they left for home. Leslie and I went up to bed and I whispered to her that we will have to go out on the town so she can wear her new bracelet and maybe she could buy a new dress too. She said she was long overdue for a night out and the sooner, the better. She sounded a little stressed out, so I asked her if she was ok and she said yes but she needed to get out of the house and do something fun. I told her that we would go out soon and have a great time.

The next day Leslie was unpacking my bags when she discovered the bottle of water from Lourdes.

"What's this?" she asked.

"It's the water I got at Lourdes. I want Annie to drink some and see if it has an effect on her."

I began to tell Leslie about my experience at Lourdes and how awakened I felt after I drank the water. I also told her I felt different in that things seemed more clear to me. I told her I didn't know how long this would last, but I was hoping I would feel like this for the rest of my life.

A few minutes later, Allie and Annie came downstairs and were ready for breakfast. I poured a glass of water for Annie, which was from Lourdes. I couldn't wait to see if it had an effect on her. I told Leslie to give Annie some bacon so she would get thirsty. Sure enough, she ate some bacon and drank the entire glass of water.

I must have been staring at Annie to see if anything dramatic would happen because Allie asked me why I kept looking at Annie. I told Allie that I always look at her and her sister because I love them so much. That seemed to satisfy her. I got up from the kitchen table, but I continued to watch Annie. Nothing seemed unusual and she finished her breakfast and went upstairs with her sister to get dressed. I convinced myself not to be disappointed if there were no changes with Annie. We loved her very much just the way she was and that would never change.

The girls were ready for their day of fun and frolic. The kids went outside with Leslie to get some fresh, spring air. Leslie was showing them how to play hopscotch. I was in the house watching Andy. He was really growing and was already five months old and crawling all over the place. He seemed to be more active and curious about things than the twins. He was at that stage where everything fascinated him including wads of dog hair that settled behind a chair. Every piece of lint on the rug that was in his path managed to get shoved in his mouth. I can just imagine what passes through his body and comes out in his diaper. I have a real admiration for mothers. They will do anything for their children including going through a painful labor and changing the most awful, messy diapers. How they manage to change a messy diaper after a kid eats strained peas is quite amazing. I walked in on a few of those changes and I couldn't believe how nonchalant Les was when she was changing those diapers. Mothers deserve some kind of award for all the things they do for their kids. I suppose love is the greatest reward for these women.

Leslie poked her head in the door and asked me if I could make them lunch. I said that I sure could. I looked in the fridge and noticed we had meat and cheese, so I made sandwiches and heated up some soup that Leslie had made the previous day. Then I opened up a can of peaches and put them in a bowl. I put glasses of milk, almond milk, at their plates and a napkin at each place setting. Leslie was impressed and said she would like to hire me.

I accidentally cut my finger on the lid of the peach can and it was bleeding. It was a deep cut, so I cleaned it with peroxide and wrapped some gauze and tape around it. It really hurt but you know how guys are about these things. We pretend that injuries are no big deal. I sat down at the table to join the girls when Annie noticed my finger wrapped up. Some blood had soaked through the gauze and she was staring at it. She reached over and gently grabbed my finger in her hand and smiled. I was surprised it didn't hurt, in fact, it stopped hurting completely. We finished lunch and Allie was telling me all about hopscotch. She and Annie had fun playing and Annie actually focused on the game and played for over an hour. That was quite amazing because autistic children find it difficult to focus on activities for a long period of time and she was no exception.

I woke up early the next morning and took a shower. I got out of the shower and noticed that my gauze bandage was soaking wet so I took it off to put a fresh one on. Much to my surprise, my cut was completely healed and you couldn't even see so much as a mark where the cut was the day before. I thought that was really odd and I showed Leslie how it healed. She just shrugged her shoulders and said, "That's nice." Then she said that she was glad my boo-boo was gone in a mildly sarcastic tone. I quickly put this incident out of my mind because I had things to do.

That night Leslie and I were watching television when Leslie started to complain about a migraine headache. She gets them occasionally and they usually last a long time. Leslie went upstairs to lay down on our bed and that was my cue to take care of the kids. I took Andrew up to bed and let the girls downstairs for another hour before they were taken up to bed. I tucked them in and checked on my wife. She said her head really hurt and she wouldn't be coming downstairs anymore this evening. I went downstairs and resumed my position in my favorite chair in front of the tv and watched the news. The news was covering a story about a woman who was found beaten to death in a field in Iowa. It was a gruesome scene that contained a lot of blood and the body showed many bruises and lacerations. Two teenage boys found her body as a result of chasing after a dog that ran into the field. She was reported missing by her husband a few days before they found her body. They had a reporter interviewing her husband and he said he was looking for her for two days and said he was devastated when they found her body.

I sat there watching this interview and I began to think that this man was lying to the reporter and the thought came into my head that he had actually murdered his wife. I never had that reaction before when I watched the news, but I certainly had one now. I had this overwhelming feeling that he murdered her because he had a lover and his wife confronted him about it. A scene played out in my mind that they argued and I saw that he got so angry with her when she said she was leaving him, that he grabbed a baseball bat and beat her to death with it. I don't know why this scene played out in my head, but it did and it was an overwhelming feeling about this entire murder case.

I continued to watch the news as they switched to a different story about the economy. About 20 minutes later, breaking news appeared on the screen and a reporter announced that new details had been released regarding the brutal death of the Iowa woman who was found by teenagers in a field. The reporter said that the ultimate cause of death of the woman was blunt force trauma to the head. She was brutally and repeatedly hit with an object consistent with the size and depth of a baseball bat. The reporter mentioned that the police had no suspects at this time.

I couldn't believe what I was hearing. I knew she was hit with a baseball bat but, for the life of me, I didn't know why I knew that. A few minutes later, Leslie came downstairs and I asked her if she felt better.

"Jack, the strangest thing happened. Annie came over to me while I was laying in bed and she placed her hand on my head and rubbed it. A few seconds later, the headache was gone. It was amazing."

I told Leslie that maybe Annie has a gift for healing because she held my finger and the next day the cut that I had from the peach can was completely healed and there was no sign of a cut at all. We spoke a few minutes about Annie and then I told her about the murder story on the news and how I had this overwhelming feeling that the husband beat her to death with a baseball bat. She looked at me in an odd way and said something weird is going on here. I said I agreed with her, but had no idea what it was.

The next morning I was eating breakfast and reading the paper. Much to my surprise, the murder case in Iowa was solved. The husband confessed to the police that he had beaten his wife to death because she found out he was having an affair and she threatened to leave him. He claimed that he completely snapped and grabbed the baseball bat that was propped up against the wall and began to hit her with it. I showed Leslie the newspaper and she really looked at me in a strange way.

"Jack, you said exactly that last night. How did you know that the husband did it and killed her with a baseball bat?"

"I don't know. All of the details just popped into my head. It was the weirdest thing. I don't know if this will happen again or if this was just an isolated incident, but I guess we will know in time."

Weeks went by and I found myself having more incidents of knowing the truth about situations. I would see congressmen on the news talking about issues and it would make me sick, because I knew they weren't being truthful with the public. A case in point was the expansion of free trade agreements and not telling the American people that these agreements would result in the loss of thousands of jobs. Instead, they would insist that these agreements would be a wonderful opportunity for our economy to grow by exporting goods to these countries. I sat there thinking, *how could countries whose citizens are paid pennies a day for labor manage to buy goods made in the United States? How could they afford a new SUV or pick-up truck when they could barely feed their families?* I wondered how many people bought that story they were selling.

As time went on, Annie continued to demonstrate her ability to heal, but we didn't know the extent of her healing powers. She could heal cuts and bruises, but she wasn't presented with grave illnesses or injuries that needed healing. Annie's talents even extended to healing our pets. Our cat, Freddie, fell out of a tree and was limping around and crying, so Annie picked him up and rubbed his leg. Within a few minutes, Freddie was running around the yard chasing after the dog. Annie also seemed to be talking more and focusing better since she drank the water from Lourdes. Time would tell if Annie's talent would remain or if it was just a temporary situation.

CHAPTER 26

THE VISIT FROM SOPHIELIA

September 2002

Summer had come and gone very quickly and the twins were disappointed that they couldn't go to the shore anymore. I explained to them that they would be able to go to the shore next summer and it would be here before they knew it. That didn't seem to comfort them, but I told them they would be going to school and kindergarten would be a lot of fun and I reminded them they had a birthday coming up soon. Allie was excited over the prospect of meeting new friends and their birthday coming soon, but Annie had no reaction. She wasn't very sociable because of her autism but she seemed to be improving.

The phone rang and it was Eric calling me from his parents' house. We talked for awhile since we hadn't spoken since the year before. Then he told me he was able to photograph a few more files.

"Jack, the other files that I had originally found in the public storage area were moved, so I created a security clearance in the system for myself and I went to the high security area."

I was shocked that he actually had the guts to do that.

"The security pass worked and I walked confidently into the area with camera in pocket. I saw two men who were talking and I just strolled right by them. No one stopped me and no one looked surprised at my presence. I saw a directory and looked up the SIA. I found the location of the SIA files and proceeded to click away with my camera. Fortunately, no one was around and surprisingly, there were no visible security cameras around."

"Well, I'm always eager to read the files that you manage to get, but, Eric, don't put yourself in jeopardy. I don't want you to get caught and lose your job or worse," I replied.

There was a long pause before Eric answered.

"Jack, I'm willing to take the risk. We have to find out what the truth is and what impact it has on our lives. I had believed in our government wholeheartedly all of my life and I feel so betrayed by what I have discovered. All of the deception that I have uncovered makes my skin crawl."

"Eric, I appreciate your conviction, but the government can be ruthless and it has been known to destroy people without hesitation."

"Jack, we have so much to talk about. You just can't imagine what goes on in this world. When you hear about the power that people have and what they do with it, you will wish you could just relocate to another planet."

I told Eric to bring his family over to my house over the weekend for a cookout and we could discuss what was on his mind. He seamed very disillusioned by something and, as his friend, I wanted to help him with it. He agreed to come over Saturday and thanked me for listening.

Kevin called me moments after I hung up with Eric to tell me he was coming to the States the next day. He wanted to know if we could get together and I told him we could and invited him to stay at our place. I thought it would be great to have Eric and Kevin at my house at the same time because, basically, we were in this together whether the other two knew it or not.

Kevin wanted to do another documentary on UFOs and aliens and he wanted me to produce it with him. That sounded really great because I had so much more material to work with since the last documentary, and I had come around to Kevin's thinking on the subject. The timing was perfect, because I had personal experience and firsthand knowledge of this phenomena. I told him he could count on me because I was itching to do a project like this. During the course of our conversation, I mentioned to Kevin that Eric would be coming to my house over the weekend, and I had a lot to tell both of them. Kevin said he had to go but was eager to see both of us, because he also had a lot to tell us about things he had heard from one of his friends who was a former British Intelligence agent.

I was so excited about the prospect of doing another documentary to the point where I couldn't sleep. I was in my office organizing my material that I had gathered from various sources when I started to read some information I had received from my two friends, Claude and Antoine. I dozed off to sleep for a moment and then I awoke to a glowing figure in the corner. I immediately noticed that the room was bathed in brilliance and there was a scent of lavender. A feeling of serenity permeated it. I got up and walked toward this figure wondering all the time what it could be. I heard a voice softly say my name and a person began to appear in the midst of the brilliant light. She was a beautiful, young woman in a long, flowing lavender dress. She identified herself as Sophielia and I was overwhelmed by her presence. She smiled sweetly and said that she was glad that I could finally see her. It made her happy to know I was now a believer. She didn't have wings like the classic paintings of the angels but she had an ethereal quality about her which led me to believe she was a celestial being.

"Jack, there are things that I will be revealing to you as time goes on, but for now, I will only tell you a few things that will happen. Your daughters have been given gifts from above. They will become healers of the body and of the soul. There are many people who need spiritual healing and your daughters will be instrumental in helping those who are in need. A time will come when people will need guidance to see the truth and you and your friends will be the vehicle for part of their enlightenment. You have become more aware of the truth since you drank the water at Lourdes. That water has allowed you to see things for what they really are.

"You need to know that your country will be going to war with Iraq in March and this will be the beginning of the end of life as people on Earth know it. There will be many changes as a result of this war and it will be the catalyst that will eventually lead to terrorism on a large scale and a much bigger war in the Middle East which will ultimately involve Israel. There is a certain destiny for this planet that will not change but people can change and be saved from the destruction. There are messages and clues all around you and you must find them and reveal their meaning. There are several sources for the clues and messages. There are messages throughout the Bible which are encoded, also clues in ancient texts, and messages in crop circles. There are also similar messages in the pyramids and ancient etchings in caves. Look around you and you will see these things that will lead you to the truth."

I didn't know what to say. Here I was, standing in front of Sophielia, and I had so many questions to ask her, but I couldn't think of one. She said she would be visiting the twins soon but I wouldn't see her again for a long time. She cautioned me not to trust anyone outside my current circle of friends with the information she had given me. She told me that my friends and I were chosen to start a movement on this planet. She said that lies would be spreading throughout the world and many will be deceived, but I wouldn't be one of them. She then told me that I should always have faith and that we were not alone in this universe and there were others watching over us.

In a moment, the brightness began to fade and Sophielia was gone. I sat down in one of the leather chairs in my office and savored the memory of her visitation. I kept replaying all of the things she told me in my head. *The reference to messages and clues sounded familiar. Didn't one of the abductees say something about being told there were clues around us? I think Claude or Antoine told me about that.* I knew I had to check my notes to see if there were any references to clues and messages. I sat in my office looking over all of the information I had been gathering and putting everything in order. I was correct about hearing a reference to clues. One of the abductees from Belgium said that she was told about clues by one of the aliens. *Messages, transition, what do they mean?* I had a hunch that I would be catching on to clues and messages soon. I was driven to do so. I made a mental note to dig out the family Bible and start reading it.

It was 8:30 a.m. when Leslie came into my office to wake me.

"Jack, what are you doing sleeping in your office?"

"I couldn't sleep, so I thought I would catch up on some paperwork. Les, I saw Sophielia last night right here in my office. I saw a bright light and she materialized before my very eyes. She told me a few things. She mentioned that we would be going to war in March and this would be a catalyst that would lead to a much greater war in the Middle East. She said this would be the beginning of the end of life as we know it. She said something that you once said to me, which was the fact that this planet has a certain destiny that will not change, however, people can be changed in order to be saved."

Leslie made a strange face and then asked me if she said anything else. I told her that Sophielia said there were clues and messages all around us and they were in the Bible, crop circles, ancient texts, the pyramids, and just all around us.

Leslie's eyebrow lifted just as it did so many times when she was questioning something I said.

"Jack, are you sure you saw her? You may have been dreaming."

"I thought that too, at first, but the memory is too clear for it to be a dream. I'm sure it was real, but time will tell."

"Jack, this is getting really scary. I hate to say this, but I think we are living in the end times. The thought of that terrifies me but, I must not be afraid because this is what Christians have been waiting for."

I never really thought about that, but she was right. We've been told from a very young age that some day Jesus would come and save us. *What exactly does that mean? Will He be freeing us from the human condition?* I got my journal out, the one that Judy Davies told me to keep when the twins had a visit from Sophielia. I wrote down my experience and recorded all of the things she told me. Sophielia gave me information to build on and keeping a journal helped me to remember all of the things she said to all of us.

• • • •

Many days had passed since I saw Sophielia. I started to read the Bible and so many things became very clear to me. There was a reoccurring theme when I read the prophets regarding the end times and that theme was the rise of the beast and the destruction of the world, and most importantly, the coming of the day of the Lord. The Bible was filled with messages of violence, hatred, greed, and the path that mankind would take to the very end. Amid those negative passages was the message of hope and the promise of a new world for those who remained faithful to the laws of God. A savior was promised and in the end all who survived the end times would witness His glorious entry into this world.

• • • •

I continued to read the Bible, and much to my surprise, there were many encounters with what might be considered extraterrestrial. The very first book of the Old Testament, Genesis, referred to the sons of heaven taking the daughters of man as their wives and these daughters bore them sons. Angels were a prime example of beings who communicated with man in ancient times, but have not been seen by man in modern times. The story of Sodom and Gomorrah was a very good example of a possible nuclear attack to destroy the evil inhabitants of those cities. The angels who were visiting Lot struck down the intruders at the door with a blinding light. The angels told Lot to leave the city with his family and not look back because they were going to destroy it. The Bible states the Lord rained down sulphurous fire upon Sodom and Gomorrah to destroy it.

The prophets in the Old Testament had many, many encounters with what might be interpreted as extraterrestrials. Elijah was taken up in a whirlwind in a flaming chariot with flaming horses. Isaiah was given the opportunity to have close encounters with the Lord and a heavenly visitation. He was given many visions of the future which prophesied the coming of the Messiah and the day of the Lord.

Ezekiel saw a vision in the sky which looked like a huge cloud with flashing fire enveloped in brightness, containing something that gleamed like electrum. He saw living creatures which looked like humans inside this object. He also had encounters with angels who had wheels beside them that moved in all directions and had the appearance of chrysolite stone.

Daniel had encounters with the angel Gabriel, whom he described as having a body like chrysolite whose face shone like lightning, and whose arms and feet looked like burnished bronze. Throughout the Bible, references were made about the Lord coming in the clouds.

Why is it that modern man has not had the honor of being visited by angels who resembled those in the Bible? Is it because modern man would describe them as something other than angels? Why haven't we seen flaming chariots in the sky, or maybe some of us have but they looked more like unidentified flying objects than chariots. Perhaps the people who lived in Biblical times simply didn't know how to describe extraterrestrials or alien crafts. One thing is clear, the Bible is the greatest account of the history of mankind and the best source for discovering man's past, present, and future.

CHAPTER 27

IMPLANTS

The weekend had arrived and Kevin was finally in town. I picked him up at the airport on Friday evening and we drove straight to my house. I filled Kevin in on some of the things that had happened to me recently such as my pilgrimage to Lourdes and my visitor, Sophielia. Kevin was amazed at the things that I started to see since my experience at Lourdes. We started to talk about the documentary he wanted to make, and we talked about the government and how they were suppressing information about UFOs and extraterrestrials.

"Jack, my friend Mick Brant, you know, the guy who worked for British Intelligence, told me that he was in a meeting a couple of years ago with top military and intelligence people and they were discussing the possibility of extraterrestrials making their presence known to all of the world. They discussed how they had been lying to the public about aliens for many years and feared that aliens were literally going to land in parks and fields in the near future. He told me that the government didn't know at that time what their intentions were, but they were very suspicious of them and had very little information on extraterrestrials to draw any conclusions. Someone in the meeting made a comment that the Americans knew more about extraterrestrials and had actual communication with them."

• • • •

"Kevin, I'm surprised the British don't know more. Perhaps they do now since their fear of aliens landing in parks and fields has come true. Did they know anything about who made the crop circles?" I asked.

"They know some of the circles were made by locals, but the real elaborate ones have molecular changes in the plants and they knew humans couldn't have done that. They believe that these formations contain messages, and they have code specialists from the military trying to crack them. Mick was one of the specialists working on the project. He said that when he left BI, no one had cracked the code."

I was wondering why Mick left his job with British Intelligence. I always thought a job like that was a lifetime commitment. I decided to ask Kevin about it.

"Why did Mick leave his job?"

"Well, his wife always feared for his life and she gave him an ultimatum. He had to choose between his job or her and the kids. He chose his family."

"Did he have a problem with the agency when he said he was leaving?" I asked.

"He said he didn't have a problem with them, but he had to sign some legal documents regarding non-disclosure. He told me he wasn't high enough on the security chain to pose a threat to British Intelligence."

Kevin said that Mick had been doing some investigating on his own. Mick's wife was a professor at a university in England and he stayed home with the kids, sort of like Mr. Mom. He studied old manuscripts that had been found in the Middle East, and he had been studying the Bible. He firmly believed that there were hidden meanings in the Bible and other texts. He felt he was getting close to cracking the code.

I also told Kevin that Sophielia told me about messages in the Bible and other places. I told Kevin I would like to meet Mick because we were both on a quest for the same thing. He said he would arrange a meeting soon.

The next day, Eric and his family came over to the house for a cookout. It was exceptionally warm for mid-September. Kevin, Eric, and I were talking about all of the things that had been going on with us. Eric actually told Kevin about the files he copied and how he felt he was being watched by government agents. Someone had been following him and he thought his phone was tapped and his home and office were bugged. He said that men were working on utility poles outside his house and he knew the government took on the guise of utility companies when they were using listening devices on people. I thought at first he was paranoid, but I realized he took a lot of chances and did some bold things in order to get information.

Kevin told Eric about his friend Mick and what he had said about the British Intelligence's stand on UFOs. Eric told Kevin about some of the things he uncovered about our government and UFOs, and expressed his concern for his family's safety because of what he knew. He told us that he thought about leaving the agency and moving back to the Philadelphia area. Eric told us that the last files he snapped contained information regarding a meeting with some aliens and some technology they had given the military. The meeting consisted of handing over the bodies of the extraterrestrials that had crashed in Pennsylvania and they gave the U.S. government some high-tech information on weapons and aircrafts in exchange for the bodies. Eric said there was no indication that our government was aware of the true reason for the aliens visiting our planet. It seemed as though the agency was just as afraid of the aliens as we were because they didn't know their intentions toward us.

I had to man the grill, so I left Eric and Kevin for awhile. They seemed to be engrossed in a serious conversation. Carolyn and Leslie were laughing and having a great time and the kids were playing in the yard. Andrew was crawling all over the grass. He started to scream and Leslie quickly ran to him and picked him up. His hand was really swollen and it looked like he had been stung by a bee or bitten by an insect. Leslie was concerned and wanted to take him to the emergency room. All of a sudden, Annie ran to Andrew and kissed his hand. She began to rub it and she said, "Don't cry Andy." Leslie and I were surprised because Annie doesn't talk much. At that point, the swelling subsided and Andy stopped crying. His hand was completely healed. We were all stunned by Annie's healing powers, although Les and I had experienced her abilities before.

Carolyn was stunned by what she had witnessed. She asked how Annie did that. Leslie didn't know what to say so I interjected and told Carolyn about Annie and Allie's abilities. I didn't tell her about Sophielia but merely mentioned that the twins were born with a veil over their faces and explained what that meant. She seemed to be in awe. The girls went back to playing with Carolyn's son, and Andy was just fine. Carolyn and Leslie went back to where they left off at their conversation and I started grilling again.

I could tell that Eric and Kevin were deep in conversation and I was really curious about what they were talking about. I walked over and said they looked so serious. Kevin told me that he was just telling Eric about some safe houses and where they were located. I asked what they were and he explained that they were houses throughout Europe that were set up by people who helped those who were considered fugitives in their own country. They were housing for people who lived in dictatorships and protested against the government and whose lives were in danger as a result of their political activities.

"Do they live in these houses for the rest of their lives?" I asked.

"No, actually they are there until they are given a new identity. They relocate to another place and start new lives," Kevin replied.

I was curious about this so I asked more questions.

"Who is involved in this? Is it a government program to help people to defect?" I asked.

"No, actually it is a group of individuals who are not connected in anyway with a government. They are true believers in the concept of freedom, and they are wealthy and have the means to pay for new identities and houses, etc. There is an entire network of people involved in this effort," Kevin said.

He continued to explain that it was like a secret society and all of its members were well connected. They had a strong conviction to do what they felt was right and they were willing to take chances to see that people who were oppressed and had the fear of torture and death were helped.

It was getting late and Eric and his family were leaving. He had given me more files to read and said he wouldn't be able to get anymore documents because security was tightened due to the threat of terrorism. I told him to take care and cautioned him not to take anymore chances. Leslie took the kids to bed and Kevin and I retreated to my office. Kevin proceeded to tell me more about the safe houses in Europe. He told me that there were about 50 safe houses in Europe and plans were in the works to set up an additional 50 houses eventually throughout the world. Some of the locations would be in Canada, Australia, South America, and some islands. The members of this elite group of men and women who had come together to set up these safe houses had formed a secret society ten years ago. Kevin told me I would be shocked if I knew who the members were. He did tell me that they were eager to meet with me and they believed that I would be a great candidate for membership.

I was taken back by that statement. I had a lot of questions to ask Kevin regarding this group.

"Kevin, are you a member of this organization?"

"Hell, yeah, I am and you will be too after you meet with these people. I was recently invited to join and I bloody well did."

"How long have you known about these people?"

"Well, I found out about them a couple of months ago when I was working on a project for the BFC. Someone that I had known for many years approached me about having dinner with him and some of his friends. I said I would, and that was the beginning of a life-altering change for me. Jack, they want to meet with you. They have been following your career and they asked me all sorts of questions about you. I told them that you would be a real asset to the group. They are very secretive and they absolutely have to remain that way in order to achieve what it is they need to do."

I asked Kevin who some of the members were, and he declined to reveal their identity. He said I really should meet with some of them and they would answer all of my questions.

"Jack, my trip to the States was specifically to tell you about these people and to ask you to meet with them. I think you are exactly the kind of person that is needed in this organization."

It took me a moment to digest what Kevin was telling me and when I collected my thoughts, I asked him who they were and the name of their organization. Kevin would not reveal the members to me or the name of the group, but he said once again that they were quite eager to meet me. I told Kevin that I would think about it but now was not the time. I had too much going on in my life, but I would consider it in a few months. I could tell that Kevin was disappointed, but he understood. He told me he was meeting with some of the members tomorrow in New York and they were hoping I would be with him. I told Kevin that I wasn't available for a meeting tomorrow, but I would seriously think about a meeting with them in the future, and let him know in a few weeks.

"I hope you agree to meet with them soon because they have a lot of information about what is going on and they have a plan to deal with the problems they foresee happening in the near future. Jack, some of these people were part of the government's think tank. They have a strong sense of what will happen, and they are deeply committed to helping those in need. These are like-minded people who put their money where their mouth is when it comes to preparing for the days ahead."

I was really surprised that Kevin was so impressed with this group. I never heard him go on about anyone the way he went on about this crew. He was always a grounded person with a great judge of character. His assessment of people and situations was always right on, and it was this intuition that made him so successful. You could always trust Kevin's judgment and his word.

"Kevin, you really have me curious and I'm sure I will end up meeting with them. I will call you in several weeks and then we can discuss this further. I'm sorry I can't join you tomorrow, but I have things I have to attend to right now. Les and I are taking the kids to the doctor for a routine physical. We will also be seeing a specialist regarding Annie's autism so meeting with anyone right now is out of the question."

"Jack, that's understandable. I will let you know when I will be meeting with them again and you can decide at that time if you want to attend the meeting. The invitation will still be open."

"Thanks Kevin. I knew you would understand."

• • • •

The next day, Leslie and I took the kids to Dr. Evans for their physicals. Andy was developing at a normal rate, and he was healthy. The doctor examined the twins and everything was fine, but he did notice something which felt like a cyst on each of them. It was located on the upper part of their arm directly above their armpit. He was concerned about it and sent them down the hall for x-rays. He told us not to be concerned because the twins seemed to be very healthy and it was probably nothing. He told us he would have the results in several days. Leslie showed visible signs of concern over that, but I tried to assure her that they were fine.

We had an appointment with an autism specialist, Dr. Matthew Logan, at the Children's Hospital, following the physical exams. The specialist tested Annie to determine the progress she was making with the therapy she was receiving. Dr. Logan reported that Annie was doing very well and we should continue with the program. Leslie and I were relieved to hear it from the doctor. We both thought she was progressing, but we were not trained professionals and were afraid it was wishful thinking on our part.

Dr. Evans called us a few days later to set up an appointment to discuss the twins. Leslie immediately went into panic mode and asked the doctor if the twins had a malignant tumor. The doctor assured her that they didn't have any tumors and said we shouldn't worry. We went to see Dr. Evans the next day. My mother stayed with the kids when we went to the hospital. Dr. Evans greeted us in a friendly manner and asked us to have a seat. He immediately pulled out the x-rays and proceeded to tell us what the spots were on the x-rays.

"Mr. and Mrs. Branden, these x-rays are of your daughters' arms and something very strange appeared on them. There appears to be a foreign object in each of their arms which is not organic in nature. It could be a piece of glass or some other object. The really strange thing about this is that there is no point of entry, no scars and no evidence of an infection. Several doctors and technicians have looked at these x-rays and we all agreed that this is very unusual. It's even more strange that both girls have the same type of object in the same place in their arms."

Leslie and I looked sheepishly at each other. We knew what those objects were, but we weren't telling.

"I would like to remove these objects and have them sent to the lab to be examined."

"Doctor, the twins would be terrified if they were subjected to surgery. We can't allow that," Leslie responded quickly without missing a beat.

The doctor looked puzzled.

"It would be very minor surgery which would only take a few minutes. They should be fine. They would only need a local anesthetic," replied the doctor.

I interjected knowing that we couldn't let just any doctor remove the objects.

"Doctor, we will think about it. It doesn't appear that the twins are in imminent danger."

Dr. Evans agreed that they were not in imminent danger, but strongly advised that these objects be removed soon.

Leslie and I talked about this as soon as we got in the car.

"Jack, I'm sure those objects are the same type of object that was found in that British boy. I believe they are tracking devices and I wonder if we have one in us too."

The same thought occurred to me.

"Les, I think I should have my cousin, Rachel, remove the objects and we can send them to Judy Davies so she can give them to Jillian Richards for analysis. Rachel can be trusted and besides that, she is a terrific doctor."

"I think that is a great idea, Jack, and I think you should call her tonight."

I said I would and then I started to talk about how much Rachel is so devoted to her research and how we haven't seen her in a long time. Rachel had been a doctor for 20 years and was doing research on genetics for the past fifteen years. She worked long hours, was divorced, and had no children. Rachel always said her work was so important that it wouldn't be fair to have children because she wouldn't have the time to spend with them.

That night I called Rachel and actually got her on the phone. It was the first time I didn't get a message to leave my name and number since she became a doctor.

"Hi Rachel, it's your cousin, Jack."

"Jack, it's so great to hear from you."

She actually sounded very excited to hear from me.

"How are Leslie and the kids?" Rachel asked.

"They are fine but I have a favor to ask of you, Rachel."

"All you have to do is ask. What is it?"

She sounded genuinely interested.

"Rachel, the twins have an object in their arms and the pediatrician said these objects should be removed. I don't want the twins to be frightened by some strange doctor they are not familiar with, so I thought you might be able to remove the objects."

"Jack, I would be glad to do it. Has it been a problem for them? Has there been any irritation or infection from these objects? Do they know what they are and how long they have been in the girls?"

She was asking all sorts of questions and I was a little nervous. I told her we didn't know what the objects were or where and when they entered their arms. I didn't want to tell too much or what I suspected because the fewer people who knew our history regarding our abductions, the better it would be.

Rachel seemed intrigued and said she could remove the objects the following week. She told me to bring the girls to her office in Philadelphia and she would examine them to see if she could remove the objects there. She said that judging by what I had told her, it shouldn't be a problem taking them out that day. She was eager to see all of us especially since she hadn't seen us since Andrew's christening. I told her we would be there at her office, and then we could go to dinner afterwards. She said that sounded great and she gave us a time to arrive.

The week passed quickly and we took the girls to Rachel's office. Andrew was staying with my mom while we were in Philadelphia. Rachel was excited to see us, but was disappointed that Andy wasn't along. I told her he gets restless and we dropped him off at my parents' house. We talked for a few minutes and then Rachel examined the twins.

"This is odd. There is no entry point," Rachel said.

I gave her their x-rays from the hospital and she thoroughly checked them.

"I think I can remove these objects now. I'm curious to see what they are since there seems to be no infection and there is no entry point that is visible. That is strange, but what is really strange is the fact that both of them have the same object in the same place."

Leslie and I just looked at each other. We heard this before and knew why there wasn't an entry point and why they both had these objects in the same place.

Rachel proceeded to administer a local anesthetic to Allie and in a few minutes, began to remove the object out of Allie's arm, which was located right below the surface.

"That was easy, wasn't it Allie? Did it hurt at all?"

Allie said it didn't hurt and it only took a couple of minutes for Rachel to remove the object from Allie's arm. Rachel looked at the object under her lamp. The object was triangular in shape and was about a quarter of an inch in length and about 3/16" at the widest part of the object. Rachel looked puzzled.

• • • •

"This looks almost like glass but I don't think it is. It looks like a precision cut. The end is very pointy but it's not sharp. I am really curious to know what the material is that this object is made of. I would like to send this to a lab," Rachel replied with excitement in her voice.

"Rachel, we have a friend who is a lab technician and she said she would analyze the objects. I will let you know what her findings are," I replied.

Rachel repeated the same procedure with Annie. Once again, it only took minutes to remove the object. Rachel looked at the one removed from

Annie and she was really surprised. She picked up the first object and compared the two.

"These objects look identical. How can that be?"

She asked us what was going on and how could both girls have identical objects in them in the same part of their bodies. Les and I felt defensive.

"Rachel, we suspect what happened to the girls, but we can't prove our suspicions. We will discuss this over dinner."

Rachel placed the objects in a small, plastic vial and gave it to me. She had a puzzled look on her face, but didn't say anymore at that point.

We went to a well-known Chinese restaurant in Philadelphia and Les and I told Rachel about our lost-time experiences. I felt we could trust her with this information and I knew she would not judge us or think we were crazy.

"Jack, are you saying that all of you were abducted by aliens from outer space?"

"Yes Rachel, that is exactly what I am saying."

Rachel had a shocked look on her face.

"Rachel, I know this sounds insane, but believe me when I tell you that this really happened. Leslie and I were put under hypnosis and we told what happened to us. We think we all have implants in us and we have a contact in England who has analyzed other implants. She thinks they might be a tracking device. We will be sending the removed objects to her for analysis. We hope we are wrong about this, and that it's just a piece of glass that was in Annie and Allie, but we fear it's not that simple."

Rachel was silent for a moment, and I could see the wheels turning in her mind as she was processing this information.

"This is unbelievable. Do you realize the implication if these are not pieces of glass? You have to let me know what your contact says about these objects."

"Rachel, you understand that this is very confidential and you can't, under any circumstances, tell anyone. We trust you and have every confidence you will remain silent about this matter."

Rachel had a smile on her face that was similar to the smile on the Cheshire cat's face from Alice in Wonderland.

"Jack, you know how secretive I am. You couldn't pry this information out of me with the threat of death."

She laughed wholeheartedly and so did we.

"Yeah, I know how you are and thank God you are like that. You always had a reputation for being secretive. I always thought it wasn't that you had any secrets, but that you enjoyed driving others crazy thinking that you knew things that they didn't know. That always drove your mom crazy. She always hounded you for information about what your brothers and sister were up to. I remember how she gave you the third degree whenever we all went to parties or to the shore. Les, as soon as Rachel got home, Aunt Sue was on her like a flea on a dog. She had to know every detail, but Rachel wouldn't give it up. It drove Aunt Sue mad. She would call my mom and complain that no one would tell her anything."

We all started to laugh because Rachel and I knew it was true.

"Yeah, if I didn't succumb to her torture, then you know I can resist any threats from someone else. I should work for the military."

We continued to laugh and reminisce about the good old days, and at the end of our dinner, Rachel assured us that our secret was safe with her.

The next day, I sent the vial to Judy Davies so she could oversee the analysis. I called her to let her know that it was coming overnight via Speedy Mail Express. Judy was glad to hear from me and told me that something strange happened to the implant that was in Ian. She said that Jillian Richards said she was analyzing it under a microscope and it began to change form before her eyes. It actually disintegrated after 52 hours and nothing remained of it. Jillian was very upset because she didn't have enough time to really analyze it. Jillian and her husband were working together to try and figure out what this thing was made of and how it managed to break down to nothing. Judy said she would immediately give the implants to Jillian so she could check them out quickly and see if she could do a better analysis this time.

The next evening, Judy called me to confirm she received the vial and that she had given it to Jillian. She said she would call me as soon as Jillian had some information. I told Judy that Leslie and I were eagerly awaiting any information she could give us. We talked for a few minutes and then we ended the conversation.

Kevin called me a few minutes after I hung up the phone. He told me about his meeting in New York and reiterated that they wanted to meet me.

"Jack, these people have a theory on where we are going as a planet, and as a race, the human race that is. You would fit right in because you are on the same path as these people. They are a fascinating bunch, and I know you would really want to be a part of this group. Jack, I'm going to a meeting in Berlin next month and I would really like you to come along. Please think about it and let me know by next week."

"Kevin, I can tell you will not let this go. I guess I will have to meet with these people if I want any peace from you."

Kevin laughed and said I was right.

"Jack, you won't regret it. These people will just blow you away."

"Ok, you have convinced me that I have to go to a meeting. I'll let you know if I can make it next month. I have a lot going on with the kids, but I will see what I can do."

Kevin and I ended our conversation a few minutes later.

Leslie put the kids to bed, and we sat and talked about a lot of things. We talked about our future and what kind of world the kids will be growing up in. We wondered if Annie would be able to lead an independent life when she becomes an adult. We talked about what Sophielia meant when she said the twins were special. Leslie and I wondered about a lot of things. What was really nice was the fact that we actually were able to have a long conversation about our concerns without any interruption. We didn't have a conversation like that in a couple years. It made me realize how lucky I was to have such a wonderful wife whom I could talk to and who understood me and tolerated my ways.

A week had passed, and there was no news on the implants I had sent Judy Davies. I decided to give her a call to see what was up with them.

"Judy, this is Jack. How are you?"

"I'm fine and I can't believe you just called. I was just ready to ring you," she said with great enthusiasm.

"Oh, yeah. What's up?" I said.

"Well, Jillian and her husband were looking at the chips, as Jillian calls them, and she decided to put one of them in a biochemical solution in hopes of preserving them so she would have more time to test them. An hour after she put it in the solution, it started to form cells. Can you imagine that?" she said with unabashed excitement.

I wanted to know more so I asked her what she meant by cells.

"Jack, cells as in human cells. They developed DNA. The cells were forming around the chip. Jillian said they were very specialized and she wants to continue to observe this activity to see what forms. She also said it was emitting some sort of signal on a very low frequency. She said her dog was in the lab with her and he started barking and acting strange and that is what made her realize that a signal was being emitted by the chip."

"Judy, this is so scary. How can human cells develop from an object that looks like a shard of glass? This sounds like something out of a science fiction movie. What are we dealing with here?" I said with obvious panic in my voice.

The phone was silent for a moment then Judy spoke.

"Jack, I don't know. In fact, I'm almost afraid to know. Obviously, these beings are way ahead of us and it is frightening to think of what they are capable of doing. I certainly hope they are the good guys. We can kiss our planet goodbye if they aren't the good guys," Judy said.

"Yeah, I know what you mean, but, I think that they would have destroyed us by now if they were evil. At least that is what I would like to think. I believe in God, who is the highest authority, and I believe that He alone decides what our fate is as a planet. I believe that God is pure love, goodness, mercy, and justice. I have to believe that or else I would live in constant fear. What would be the point in living that way? I just feel that there is a higher order who watches out for us and who makes sure things develop according to plan. There are several countries who have nuclear capabilities, and we have come close to pushing the red button, but for some reason no one has done it.

"Remember the accident at the nuclear power plant located at Three Mile Island in Pennsylvania in 1979? I never heard so much panic in peoples' voices when that happened. It dominated the media for a long time. The whole world was watching that power plant and to see how they got rid of the hydrogen bubble. That accident could have been a huge disaster and there could have been an enormous death toll and contamination for hundreds of miles. Somehow we were able to escape that fate and the problem was solved. I believe there was divine intervention with the Three Mile Island incident, and I believe that happens a lot," I said to Judy.

"I clearly remember that incident. All of us in the UK were watching and praying that everything would be alright. I remember asking some American friends about what was going on at Three Mile Island. All of us knew how frightening that situation was for you Americans."

"Well, Judy, keep me posted on the chips. I am a curious person by nature, and profession and I have to know what these things are, what they are made of, and what their purpose is. Leslie and I suspect that we also have a chip in each of us."

"Let me know when you and Leslie are ready to find out. I will be glad to arrange for the MRI and exam."

I chuckled at Judy's comment.

"I'm serious, Jack. I think you should consider it."

I told Judy I would and she said she would call me as soon as she heard anything from Jillian.

CHAPTER 28

ERIC AND FAMILY

2003

Several months had passed and things were really in turmoil. The United States went to war with Iraq on March 20, 2003, just as Sophielia had predicted. The official reason that was fed to the American people was that Iraq possessed weapons of mass destruction. This reason would prove to be untrue as time went on. The public was up in arms about this war. Many felt it was going to be another Vietnam.

This war would end up costing trillions of dollars for the American taxpayer, but more importantly, it would cost the lives of thousands of American soldiers. Families would be robbed of their children, spouses, and loved ones. The death toll on the Iraqi people would be even greater. Hundreds of thousands of Iraqi citizens would become casualties and there would be much destruction in their land. The insurgents took the lives of many on a daily basis with their attacks. This war would drag on for many years and prove to be the ushering in of the end times.

It was an unusual time and strange things were happening. Les and I were concerned about the chips we had sent to Judy Davies. Just as I was ready to call Judy again, she called us to say that the cells around the microchips, as she was now calling them, had abruptly stopped forming. She said she would keep us posted.

I then spoke to Kevin and he immediately brought up the subject of the Iraqi war. We talked about how Sophielia predicted it and how scary it was that it was happening before our eyes. We talked about what would happen next and when Sophielia would make an appearance.

I realized, after I talked to Kevin, that I hadn't heard from Eric in awhile. I tried calling him but he didn't return my calls. I felt something was wrong, so I called his father to see what he knew. His dad told me that Eric was involved with a project at work and he was doing a lot of traveling. I tried to get in touch with Eric's wife, but she too did not return my calls. I began to worry about them. I thought that I should go to D.C. to Eric's house and talk to them in person. I talked it over with Leslie and she also felt something was wrong and felt uneasy. We agreed that I should go and visit them at their home in Virginia.

I left the house at 5 a.m. and thought I would be able to get there before he left for work. I arrived at Eric's house a few hours later and Carolyn answered the door. She looked frightened and quickly did a visual scan of the neighborhood. She asked me to come in and quickly pulled me through the door. I knew at that moment something was seriously wrong.

"Carolyn, what is going on? I have been calling Eric and trying like hell to get a hold of you guys. Leslie and I have been worried about all of you," I said in a very serious manner.

"Jack, I think Eric is in trouble. He thinks the government is trying to eliminate him."

"Carolyn, where is Eric now?" I asked.

"He's in Africa on an assignment. He's checking into reports on some terrorist cells but Eric believes they are setting him up to be killed. He said they discovered that he copied the classified files and they have been putting him in situations that have brought him close to being killed. Jack, I don't know what to do."

Carolyn was on the verge of tears, and I didn't know what to say to her.

"Carolyn, calm down and let me see what I can do. Where specifically is he in Africa?"

"He told me that he was in Libya."

I asked her if she knew where in Libya and she said no. I left Carolyn with a promise to do all that I could and told her I would delve into it and make phone calls to my contacts who could possibly help. I told her she had to keep me up to date on everything and to let me know when she hears from Eric. She said she would and thanked me for coming to see them. She said she felt much better now that she has spoken to me and expressed confidence in my ability to get to the bottom of this situation.

I felt very bad for Carolyn plus I was really worried about Eric. I immediately thought of Kevin and called him on the way home.

"Kevin, this is Jack."

"Jack, how are you?" he said.

"Well, not so good. I hadn't heard from Eric for awhile even though I called him several times, so I decided to pay him a visit. His wife told me he is in serious trouble and he feels the government is out to get him killed. They sent him to Libya to investigate a suspected terrorist cell and Eric told his wife he had a few close calls over there. He couldn't tell her where in Libya he was located. Is there anything you can do to find out his exact location?"

Kevin didn't answer for a few seconds. It seemed like he was thinking about something.

"Well, let me see what I can find out. I'll get back to you sometime today. I'll get on it right away."

Kevin hung up and I continued to drive home.

I arrived home at 3 p.m. and Leslie was outside with the kids and some of the neighbors. We just had a pool installed in the backyard and the kids were having a great time in it. Taffy liked it too. Sometimes she would jump in the pool with the kids. Allie and Annie could swim, but Andrew was still very young for swimming lessons. We always put a life jacket on him so he could splash around in the pool with his sisters. Leslie looked great in her bathing suit, especially after having three kids. I wondered if she was secretly working out. Leslie saw me getting out of my car and invited me to join the party. I passed and went inside to see what I could find out about Eric.

I was signing onto my computer when Kevin called me.

"Jack, I have some information about Eric. I found out he's in Tripoli and Eric's suspicions are correct. The people at the Pentagon know he took the files."

I immediately felt a sense of guilt because he copied those files so I could read them and I also had a sense of dread thinking of what could possibly happen to him because of the files.

• • • •

"Kevin, we need to do something about this."

"I know. He's definitely in danger. I made some calls, and we may be able to get him out of there. I will call you back as soon as I get the word."

I wondered what he meant by that, but didn't ask. I was almost afraid to do that. I told Kevin I would wait for his call.

Kevin didn't call till the next morning. He said he had a plan. He contacted someone who worked for British Intelligence who was connected to someone at the Pentagon and Eric would be coming home tomorrow. I was glad to hear that, but I decided not to tell Carolyn. I didn't want to jinx his homecoming. Kevin came through once again. I wondered who his contact was, but I didn't ask him. I figured he would tell me if he wanted me to know.

Eric arrived home in a few days and Carolyn was thrilled to see him. Eric had acquired a bacterial infection while he was in Africa, so he was on leave from work indefinitely. I convinced him to see my cousin, Rachel, for a complete physical exam. He agreed and he and his family made plans to come to Philadelphia for a weekend. Rachel took blood from Eric in order to do a battery of tests to see what he really had. She felt it wasn't anything serious, but wanted to be sure. The tests came back and Eric had a viral infection. Rachel gave Eric some medication to help ease the symptoms and clear up the infection and told him to go home and rest. That was like a death sentence for him because he couldn't sit still. Eric was always on the run and it drove him crazy to slow down.

Eric recovered in record time and things returned to normal by June. He was scheduled to return to work the following week. Eric and his family decided to go boating at the Jersey Shore before returning to Washington. He called me to say that he and his family wanted to get together with us.

We made plans to get together at our house that Saturday. They were going to the shore on Wednesday and would leave Friday evening. Saturday would be perfect, and the weather was expected to be great.

I received a phone call from Eric's father Friday afternoon. His voice quivered as he told me that there was a boating accident, and Eric and his wife and son were missing at sea. A wave of panic came over me, and my heart felt like it was beating in my throat.

"What happened?" I asked.

"I don't know but their boat was found a few miles off the Cape May shore and they were not on it. The boat was damaged and the Coast Guard felt the unexpected storm they had last night caused the boat to capsize. They were looking for Eric, Carolyn, and my grandson. They found a jacket and some shoes in the wreckage. Jack, it doesn't look good."

It was obvious that Eric's father felt so helpless and extremely concerned about Eric and his family. It almost sounded like a hopeless situation when they found some of their belongings along with the wreckage. Once again I was at a loss for words. I told Eric's dad to keep me informed and offered to help in any way that I could.

• • • •

I immediately called a friend of mine who had a brother in the Coast Guard. I asked him to check with his brother to see what was going on with this investigation. Rodney called me to say that his brother told him it didn't look good. They didn't find bodies, but the boat was severely damaged. They had been searching the ocean and had other boats on alert to keep their eyes open for anything unusual. They suspected that Eric and his family must have drowned because the storm was very bad and they found remnants of clothing to indicate that the family got caught up in this storm.

I couldn't believe what I was hearing. It couldn't be true. Eric and his wife had been through so much and they didn't go through all of their hardship just to end up missing at sea. I just believed they had to be somewhere on shore and they would contact someone soon. A week went by and there was no evidence that Eric and his family survived the storm. Eric and Carolyn's families were devastated. It was worse not finding their bodies and not knowing what happened to them. It would be difficult to have closure if the bodies were never found.

The families of Eric and Carolyn had a memorial service for them a few weeks after they disappeared. Leslie and I went to the services and Kevin was able to be there too. I didn't expect to see him, but I was really glad when he showed up. I invited him to stay at our house while he was in Philadelphia. He accepted the invitation and came back to the house with us.

Leslie took the kids up to bed and Kevin and I had a few beers. We talked about what happened and I told Kevin I felt responsible for their disappearance.

"Kevin, I feel it's all of my fault. If I hadn't questioned Eric about the government and if he hadn't taken those files for me, he would still be alive and well. I feel really bad over this situation. Why did I pull Eric into this obsession I have with aliens?"

Kevin looked at me and put his hand on my shoulder to give me support.

"Jack, don't blame yourself. You don't know for a fact that they are dead. But even if they are, it's not your fault. You asked Eric if he knew anything about extraterrestrials, but you didn't ask him to take those files. He did that on his own and he knew the risk. Jack, please don't blame yourself and carry around this guilt. Eric wouldn't want you to do that."

Kevin is a true friend and probably the closest friend I've got, but his words didn't make me feel less responsible. I sat quietly for several minutes.

"Jack, I'm going to N.Y. to see some of the committee members. I want you to come with me. I think the time to meet them is now. Jack, you have nothing to lose. I promise you that if you go with me to N.Y. to meet some of these people, and you decide that you don't want to become a member, I will never bring it up again. I swear to you I will keep my promise."

I chuckled because Kevin sounded like a kid making a promise.

"Do you triple swear?" I said jokingly.

"I triple swear," said Kevin with laughter in his voice.

"I will do whatever it takes to get you to meet with these people because I am sure that once you meet them and talk with them, you will become one of them."

"You wouldn't be setting me up to become some kind of cult member would ya?" I asked half jokingly.

Kevin laughed with real gusto.

"No, it's not some religious cult. These people don't wear lodge hats or sell flowers at the airport. They don't stick out in a crowd. Now that you mention it, I would pay to see you in one of those lodge hats with the big, hanging tassel. I think you would look good," he chuckled.

I gave it right back to him.

"Yeah, but I think you would look better than me in that hat, especially if you were at the airport selling flowers in that hat. It fits your personality."

We had a few laughs and then retired for the night. I felt better talking to Kevin about my guilt over Eric and his family. I also decided to go to N.Y. with him the next day. I figured that I better meet them and get it over with so I didn't have to continue hearing about this again. I told Leslie I was going to N.Y. with Kevin to see about an assignment. I told her we would be back later that evening. She was fine with it and we left at 8 a.m. for New York.

We arrived in N.Y. at 10:30 a.m. and Kevin told me to go to East 63rd Street near Madison Ave. I found a parking space and we walked up the stone steps of a beautiful brownstone townhouse. The windows had flower boxes and some upper story windows were made of stained glass. Kevin rang the doorbell and a voice came over an intercom.

• • • •

"Who's there?" the voice asked.

"It's Kevin Leary."

A buzzer rang and Kevin opened the door. The inside of the building was somewhat dark in color. There was a lot of natural stained, ornate woodwork in the hall and a wide staircase which was made out of oak. A bright light illuminated the hallway and I noticed a camera attached to the ceiling which was pointed at the door. There were a lot of expensive-looking oil paintings hanging on the walls of the hall. It was a very elegant place.

Kevin and I took a small elevator to the fourth floor. We didn't talk while we were in the elevator. I was thinking about the possibility that I made the wrong decision coming to this place. The building had an air of secrecy about it, I suppose because it was so quiet with a vintage look. Kevin said we're here as the elevator stopped and we stepped out to a small landing with a huge oak door in front of us. Kevin knocked on the door and someone slowly opened it. The door actually squeaked as it was opened and I suddenly saw a vision in my head of an old Dracula movie I saw as a kid.

An older man with gray hair, who was small in stature, opened the door and greeted Kevin and me.

"Luigi, it is so great to see you," Kevin said with enthusiasm.

They hugged each other and Luigi invited us in. Kevin introduced me to Luigi.

"Jack, we finally meet. I've heard so much about you from Kevin. In fact, we have all heard a lot about you. I have been following your career. You are one of the best writers of our times," Luigi said in a thick Italian accent.

"It is a pleasure to meet you, sir, and thank you for the compliment," I responded.

"Well, Jack, it's the truth. You are a great writer and we are very happy that you came here with Kevin."

I didn't know what to make of this. He seemed to know a lot about me and I had no idea who he was.

"Gentlemen, please come into the living room, "Luigi said.

We walked a few yards, and then entered the room. The decor was elegant and the room had rich wood panels covering half the walls with crown molding edging the ceiling. It was obvious someone wealthy owned this place. There was a huge chandelier in the center of the room that contained lots of small crystals on it that sparkled and reflected small, rainbow prisms all over the room. There were oriental rugs on the floor that partially covered meticulously-polished hardwood floors. A huge, carved, marble fireplace graced the west wall, and a large, gilded mirror was placed above it, reflecting the light and image of the grand chandelier. This beautifully-decorated room added a touch of mystery and ambience to this place. The furniture looked like expensive antiques, and there were stained glass lamps on all of the ornately-carved tables. This house obviously belonged to someone with great wealth and power, and I was especially curious to find out who the owner was of such an extraordinary property.

My observation took but a minute or two. I quickly noticed some people entering this room. Six people approached me to shake my hand. Most of them looked familiar to me and Kevin started to introduce them.

"Jack, this is Stephan Heinrich, the well-known German industrialist."

"Jack, it is a pleasure to finally meet you," Stephan said as he squeezed my hand.

A woman was next to greet me.

"Jack, this is Dr. Adrienne Mansfield. She does genetics and stem cell research."

Dr. Mansfield grabbed my hand and said it was wonderful to finally meet me. I returned the sentiment. I felt really strange because all of these people were closing in on me and I was completely taken by surprise.

"It is a pleasure meeting all of you," I said.

Another person approached me with a heavy French accent.

"Jack, I am Pierre Truffant. I have been waiting a long time to meet you. I'm in publishing and own several newspapers in Europe and I have been following your career for many years. I admire your honest reporting and the style in which you write."

This was humbling that a prominent European would admire my work.

"Thank you Pierre. I really appreciate that. I try very hard to get all of the facts and report the truth no matter how unpopular it might be with the public or the government."

There were several other individuals at this meeting and we all were directed to a large room down the hall. It was a conference room with a long table that seated about 14 people. A gentleman I had not yet met entered the room and took a place at the head of the table. He scanned the room and looked at me.

"I would like to welcome Jack Branden to our gathering today. As you all know, Jack is a well-known and highly-respected journalist and author who has received several awards for his writings. Jack, I would like to welcome you to our meeting and I believe I speak for everyone here when I say that we sincerely hope that you join us."

Applause broke out and some said here, here. I nodded in gratitude.

The man sat down, and Kevin leaned over to me to tell me who he was.

"Jack, that's Angus Mathers. He's a former general with the British Army and worked in Intelligence. He founded the organization. Rumor has it he became a spy for British Intelligence and was instrumental in thwarting over a 100 terrorist attacks in Europe."

I thought that was very impressive, and I was really curious about what prompted Angus to start this organization. Angus proceeded to explain that the purpose of the meeting was for the members to meet me and to explain what the organization was all about and to answer any questions.

Angus explained that he started this group because he realized that something strange was going on in the world and he wanted to find out what it was. He was privy to sensitive government information and he noticed that a pattern was forming throughout the world. He said that all of the members were hand-picked by him and everyone who was approached about joining the organization did indeed join. Angus explained that each person added a unique talent to the mix, which contributed to achieving the ultimate goals of the organization. For example, Adrienne Mansfield had been involved with genetic research for over 20 years and she noticed a change in the chemistry of the human body. Hans Northagen, who is from Zurich, Switzerland, studies weather patterns and as of a result of his data, noticed that tornados and hurricanes have become more frequent and more intense with each decade. He also did a study on earthquakes and discovered that the frequency and intensity were increasing at an alarming rate.

Angus began to talk about the report that Jordan Simba, a member from Nigeria, presented regarding the frightening climb in violent crimes and the increase of terrorist acts throughout the world. He continued to say that 20 years ago he was a staunch military man who thought he had seen it all on the battlefield. His opinion changed when he entered civilian life and saw what was going on in the day-to-day lives of people throughout the world. It made him realize that there was a change in the entire climate around the world and he didn't mean just weather pattern change. He decided to assemble like-minded people together to figure out what was happening throughout the planet Earth.

I asked him how many members there were in the organization and what was the name of it. Angus laughed and said there are 29 members, but the name of the organization would not be revealed until I became a member. I asked him why I was asked to join this elite group of people and he said he would discuss that with me at a later date. I really didn't have anymore questions at that moment and Angus ended the meeting.

Angus invited Kevin and I to join him for lunch. Everyone had gone, so we had lunch in the kitchen. An elderly woman prepared the food for us. Angus introduced her as his Aunt Grace. Grace came over to the table and asked us what we would like for lunch. She rattled off various soups, sandwiches, and salads as if she were a waitress in a large restaurant. We gave her our order and she served us our lunch within 15 minutes.

Grace excused herself and Angus proceeded to answer my question regarding why they wanted me as a member.

"Jack, I have followed your career, and Kevin has told me about your family. I also heard about your encounter with aliens."

I turned and looked at Kevin.

"You told him about that? I told you those things in confidence."

"Jack, I know you did, but, before you get mad at me, listen to what Angus is about to tell you regarding his experience with aliens while he was in the military. Then you will understand why I told him about you."

I turned to Angus and asked him what his story was. I was really annoyed and disappointed with Kevin for telling my story to Angus. *His story better be really good if Kevin ever expects me to confide in him again.*

Angus began to speak.

"Jack, I told Kevin what happened to me and he said he had a friend who had a similar experience. He didn't tell me it was you, but I figured it out."

"Ok," I said, and I continued to press for his story. Angus took a deep breath and proceeded to tell his story to me.

"I was stationed in Africa during the 1980s. One night some very strange things started to happen. Four of us were in a remote area of the country where a suspected terrorist group was living and we were using sophisticated devices to eavesdrop on their conversations. Suddenly, we heard animals howling and crying and our equipment abruptly stopped working. All of the lights in the house we were watching went dead, as did the lights in the entire area. Chills went through me and I could feel the hair on my arms stand on end. It was the strangest feeling I ever had considering that I had some harrowing experiences in combat and black ops.

"I told the other men in the unit that something was very wrong and they agreed. The weird thing was, we didn't know what to do because we weren't trained to react to something like this. In an instant, we saw a bright object in the sky and it began to approach us. We looked at it in amazement as it continued to get closer. It began to take on the appearance of some sort of craft. We were aware that it was something none of us had ever seen before. It was really frightening. One of the guys commented that perhaps it was a military aircraft. I told him that my high security clearance allowed me to see all of the latest military craft for the United Kingdom and the U.S. and I assured him that none of them had anything like this craft. The size of this craft alone was beyond earthly proportions. It was massive, probably the length and width of a soccer field.

"This object hovered over us for what seemed like a few minutes and I was able to get a good look at it. It was a huge, round, silver metallic craft with colored lights that were located all around the rim. It also had windows around the entire craft, and I actually saw people looking out at us. Reality set in and I realized that this object was not of this world, because it was hovering about 100 yards above us and it made absolutely no sound at all.

"We stood in disbelief and then we were suddenly engulfed in a brilliant light. The next thing we all remembered was looking around for our vehicle. We were walking around dazed and confused in an area that was unfamiliar to us. The sun was starting to rise when we realized that several hours had passed but we couldn't account for what had happened during that time.

"The four of us were bewildered by the whole experience. We racked our brains trying to remember what happened to us during that missing time. Two of the guys were really traumatized by the experience and refused to talk about it. The other soldier and I couldn't let it go. All of us started to have strange dreams a few months later. The two who no longer discussed the lost-time experience were discharged from the military because of post-traumatic stress.

"None of us reported what happened because we felt no one would believe us, after all, we didn't quite believe it ourselves and what would we report? We couldn't recall what went on after we saw this object hovering over us. Joe and I decided we had to find out what happened and face the truth no matter how disturbing it might be. Joe had a friend who was an amateur hypnotist and he agreed to put us under hypnosis so we could recall what happened that night."

"What happened when you were under hypnosis?" I asked.

"Joe and I remembered basically the same thing. We were standing under this hovering object when a large beam of light surrounded all of us. The next moment we were inside the craft and were surrounded by six individuals who were wearing grey, form-fitting suits that revealed very slim bodies. They were about five feet, seven inches tall and had large eyes, no visible ears, and a slit for a mouth. It looked like the eyes were covered with a thin layer of something to shield them. They spoke to us via mental communication. They asked who was in charge and I said I was the commander. I was taken into a separate room and was physically examined by one of them. A person named Regin spoke to me and said that he was aware of the fact that we were military personnel. He proceeded to tell me that we were all being watched on earth. His species was assigned to monitor Earth and the people living on it. They collect data regarding physical and behavioral changes among the human race and changes to the environment. He also mentioned that others have been visiting Earth for thousands of years and are carefully monitoring our weapons development and nuclear capabilities. Beings from other planets in the universe recognize the potential danger that exists on Earth because humans have evolved to the point where they could destroy the entire planet."

• • • •

"I just sat there on a bench, or whatever it was, and listened to every word he said. He asked me if I was happy. Can you imagine that? I told him that I suppose I was as happy as anyone could be. He told me that I haven't really seen the world or truly looked at people and I had to open my eyes. I thought at that moment that this guy or whatever he was, didn't know what he was talking about. I was all over the world and saw a lot and I thought I knew what was going on in the world. He told me time was running out and he grabbed my hand and held it tightly.

"Immediately, I saw what I had done with my life and I understood what he meant. I had been involved with military situations and got caught up in justifying everything the military did even though a lot of it revolved around deception and power play. I realized that I was completely oblivious to human suffering and to the truth of what was really at the root of the problems of the world. I realized at that moment that governments manipulate people and that there was a handful of individuals in the world who controlled our every move and used people like me to achieve their goal to control the world and everyone and everything in it.

"Regin said I would understand, in time, the evil that exists, and I would feel compelled to do something about it. He told me that something dramatic was going to happen to our planet and that me and others would be instrumental in helping people survive the changes that would take place.

He said I had to brace myself for many catastrophic events that would take place on Earth within the next 25 or so years and that I would have to be strong for others. He also said time would move quickly so we could survive these terrible times. He told me that a day would feel like it was a lot shorter than 24 hours long and the years would pass by quickly, especially when we reached the year 2000. After that, something was placed in my arm and he said that I would know what to do and when to do it. He told me to trust my instincts, because they will help me to choose the right people for the task at hand.

"I asked Joe what he remembered under hypnosis and he said that he was told that changes were going to take place and the world would experience many difficult times. He was also given a physical exam and something was implanted in him. A woman spoke to him about coming disasters and she said terrorism and drug addiction would be the scourge of the new millennium. She told him he would have to help people prepare for the time ahead and he too would know what to do when the time comes. Joe and I decided that we had to find out what was going on and try to help as many people as possible. Both of us had a personal revelation and we realized that our lives were too confined by working in the military. We both left the service and never looked back.

"Jack, do you understand why Kevin told me about your experience? There are those who have been given a responsibility to be the leaders when the time comes. We have been chosen to help guide people when these catastrophic events occur. We didn't ask for this, but we must do whatever it takes to survive. Times are going to get tough and only the strong will survive. I know what the heads of government are capable of, and so I know what these aliens mean when they speak of deception and evil. Take a look around you. Do you see the evil in this world? The violence, the drugs, the pornography, human trafficking, it all points to the greed in this world. Then there's the terrorism. Evil is rampant and it seems so out of control, but let's face it, if you follow the money, you will find very powerful people behind all of it. Then you will know why it is so out of control. Powerful people in high places are becoming very wealthy from this evil and they don't want it to come to an end, but I got news for them—this evil will come to an end and they will be judged for what they have done."

I really understood what Angus was saying and my intuition told me that he was telling me the truth, and I now understood why Kevin told him about us. Fate had brought us all together and there is strength in unity.

"Jack, I hope I answered your questions. Do you have anymore?" Angus asked.

I thought for a moment and then I asked him what was the organization's mission statement.

"Well, some of the things we do include monitoring the climate changes, tracking the frequency and intensity of natural disasters, and tracking the number of epidemics that occur in a certain time period. We try to anticipate the worst scenario and prepare for it. For example, we are buying land in remote areas so we can build housing underground, sort of like barracks to house a lot of people when catastrophes hit. We have safe houses where we hide political activists who are in danger of being killed. We know that, in time, we may have to hide from those who are in power. We have a stockpile of medicine and food for emergency use. We analyze the Bible and ancient texts to see if we can decipher what will happen in the end times. We do lots of things."

I asked Angus how they finance all of this and he told me that most of the members are extremely wealthy and have been financing this project.

"Jack, most of our members are abductees who have basically been told the same thing as me. We all found each other through odd circumstances, but it was destiny that brought us together. This organization was meant to happen just as the end times are meant to happen."

"Angus, I'm curious about the prayer you said at the end of the meeting," I said with a serious voice.

"I could see the surprised look on your face when I started the prayer. All of us in the group believe in God and we pray for His guidance and help. None of us were religious until our experience. We know that there is a higher power looking over us and using us as an instrument to help others through the change."

"You know of a change that is coming but you don't know what it is?" I said questioningly.

"That's right, Jack. We have our theories, but we weren't told exactly what will happen. We were advised to look for clues in order to find the answer."

Wow, that's what I was told by others. Clues, changes, Sophielia said that to me too. I wonder if Kevin told Angus about Sophielia. I will have to ask Kevin later if Angus doesn't mention her.

• • • •

"We have some members studying the Bible and ancient texts from other religions to see if they come up with anything. So far, we believe that we are living in the end times because of the things that are happening in the Middle East and the overall change in morality and in the hearts of mankind," Angus said.

The afternoon flew by and it was 4:00 p.m. Kevin told Angus we had to leave.

"Jack, I know you need to think about our invitation to join. I hope you decide to do so and soon. Please feel free to call me at any time if you have other questions. We really feel you belong in our organization. I believe that destiny brought us together. I would also like to thank you for coming and listening to my story and Kevin, thank you for bringing Jack here."

Angus shook our hands and said to me that he hoped he would hear from me soon.

Kevin and I headed back to Philadelphia. I asked him if he told Angus about Sophielia and he said no.

"Jack, I hope you aren't angry with me. I truly didn't give them your name, just the situation. I do feel that you should join us. You are one of us more than you know."

"I have to admit that his story was compelling and there were many similarities with my own experience. I just don't know if I should commit to something like this. How secretive is this organization?" I asked.

Kevin took a deep breath before he answered my question.

• • • •

"Very secretive. I'm sure no one knows about the organization except the members. Everyone who was approached became a member and everyone said they never heard of this group. Angus didn't tell you everything. You will find out a lot more if you become a member. These people are dedicated to surviving the coming catastrophes and helping others survive as well. They have been instrumental in making people aware of social issues such as the AIDS epidemic, and famine in Africa. Jack, these are people who truly care and do something about injustice in the world."

CHAPTER 29

THE ABDUCTION OF LESLIE AND THE CHILDREN

June 2003

Kevin and I arrived at my house around 6:30. Leslie and the kids weren't home, so I called her on her cell phone, but got no answer. I began to worry because she knew I was coming home this evening and she said she would cook a special dinner for Kevin. I told Kevin I couldn't get her on the phone and decided to give it a half hour.

Leslie wanted to make steaks, corn on the cob, salad, and baked potatoes for dinner but realized she didn't have everything she needed. She rounded up the kids and set off for the grocery store. It was 4:00 p.m. when she left the house for the store. She was driving down Brower Road and the kids were singing in the back seat. All of a sudden the car stalled and Leslie tried frantically to start it. The road was in a wooded area and no one else was in sight. Leslie had a small battery in the trunk of the car that can start the car by plugging it into the lighter. She got out of the car and was rummaging through the trunk when she noticed that the trunk became illuminated with a very bright light. She turned around to look at the source of the light and gasped at what she saw. She mumbled, "Oh no, not this again."

Leslie was sitting in the car when the engine started up again. She thought it was odd that it stopped then started but didn't give it another thought. The kids were sitting quietly in the back seat.

"Mom, did you see that bright light?" Allie asked.

Leslie thought a second as if it was a vague memory, and said that she thought she saw a bright light but was sure it was the sun.

"Mom, Annie and I aren't sitting in the same place. I was sitting behind you and Annie was sitting on the other side of Andy."

Leslie looked in the rear view mirror and noticed that the twins were sitting in opposite seats.

"Allie, did you and Annie change seats when I was looking in the trunk?" Leslie asked.

Just then Leslie realized that she didn't remember getting back in the car after she was rummaging through the trunk.

"No mommy. Me and Annie stayed in our seats. I don't know how we got switched around."

Leslie felt a sudden wave of panic come over her and all she wanted to do at that moment was return home as soon as possible. She maintained her composure and told Allie not to worry about their seats and they would talk about it when they arrived home. Leslie started to have a sinking feeling in the pit of her stomach. She realized that something strange happened to them and it felt real familiar but she didn't want the girls to see her concern.

Leslie realized she didn't get to the store. She checked her watch and saw that it was 5:30. She realized that almost an hour had passed that she could not account for. She began to think that they may have been abducted. She felt a sense of dread as she was driving, but knew that she better get something for dinner. Leslie was close to the store and figured she might as well get the steaks and the other stuff and head home quickly. Her hands were shaking as she helped the kids out of the car.

"Mommy, are you alright?" Allie asked.

"Of course I am, Miss Allie," Leslie replied as she ruffled up Allie's hair and smiled at her.

"Kids, you have been so good today. I'm going to let you pick out a dessert and you can have some gummy bears too. Annie, we can get you some special ice cream that you really like. Would you like that kids?" Leslie asked. She was trying to be upbeat and not show her anxiety to the children.

"Yeah!" the kids yelled.

"I want some moose tracks ice cream!" yelled Allie.

Annie and Andy clapped their hands with great excitement.

"Ok, moose tracks it is. Annie would you like some chocolate ice cream?" Leslie asked.

Annie had to eat a non-dairy ice cream because of her food allergy.

"Yeah!!" Annie yelled in a very excited tone.

"Does Andy want moose tracks ice cream?" Leslie asked.

"Yes!" Andy replied.

Just then, Leslie's cell phone rang.

"Les, where are you? I've been trying to get you for the past thirty minutes," Jack said in a frantic tone.

Leslie was really shaken, but sounded calm when she talked to Jack.

"I'm at the grocery store picking up a few things for dinner."

"Why didn't you pick up the phone when I called before?" Jack said.

"I'll talk to you about it later, but right now, we are shopping. We'll be home within the hour," Leslie said very firmly.

Jack paused because he could sense she was annoyed with him.

"Ok, I'll see you soon. Be careful."

"I will." Les said and hung up her phone.

Leslie and the kids raced through the store in record time and were home in thirty minutes.

"That was fast," said Jack.

"Well, I didn't want you guys to starve to death," she joked. "Hi Kevin, hope you two had a good time in New York."

"It was quite interesting and I will tell you all about it later," Jack said.

Leslie cooked dinner and it was ready in an hour.

"As always, your cooking is superb, Leslie," Kevin said in a very praising manner.

"Thank you Kevin. I always enjoy cooking for an appreciative crew."

"Well, I am very appreciative. I think the real reason I come to the States is for your cooking," Kevin said with a wide grin.

"Flattery will get you another invitation," Leslie replied.

Les put the kids up to bed around 10:00 and then she joined Kevin and I in the family room.

"Where were you today?" I asked.

Leslie had a pensive look on her face. She proceeded to tell me and Kevin about her lost-time experience. She explained how Allie noticed her and Annie were sitting in different seats and she commented on the bright light.

"Leslie, try and remember what happened to you and the kids," I said.

"I can't remember what happened during that time but I'm pretty sure we were abducted. They took us again," Leslie said with emotion in her voice.

"I need to be put under so I can recall the experience," she said.

"Are you sure you want to do that?" Kevin said with a concerned voice.

"Absolutely. They don't hurt us but I need to know why they keep taking me and the kids. What are they doing?" Leslie said in a frustrating tone.

I said I would talk to Judy Davies about this. Perhaps she will be visiting the States and could hypnotize Leslie.

The three of us continued to talk about Leslie's experience and also about our trip to New York. I wasn't going to tell my wife about it, but changed my mind. After all, she was always open and honest with me and I felt I should be the same way. Leslie was really intrigued about this group. She actually encouraged me to join. She trusted Kevin's judgment and her intuition. I was surprised at her recommendation. I thought for sure she wouldn't want me to get involved with people I didn't know. I said I would give it serious thought and make a decision in a few days.

Kevin was returning to Ireland the next day. I took Kevin to the airport in the morning and told him I would call him by the weekend.

"Jack, trust me when I tell you that you won't regret joining these people. We will need support in the coming years and those who prepare will survive," Kevin said as I pulled up to the airport.

"You may be right, Kevin. I'll let you know my decision soon."

"Sounds good. I'll be waiting for your call. Take care," Kevin said as he walked swiftly to catch his plane.

When I returned home, Leslie was making lunch for her and the kids. Allie, Annie, and Andy were splashing around in the pool with other kids. Several mothers were watching them.

"Jack, doesn't your cousin, Rachel, know how to hypnotize people?" Leslie asked.

"Yeah, I think she does, now that you mention it," I said.

"Maybe we could ask her to put me under hypnosis so we can find out what happened to me and the kids the other day. I really want to know what went on during that time and I don't want to wait until Judy Davies can do it."

"You know what? I think that's a great idea. She knows about what happened before and she seemed receptive to what we were telling her. I think she would really like to do it. I'll give her a call and see what she says," I said with excitement in my voice.

That night, I called Rachel and told her about the lost-time experience Leslie just had the other day. I asked her if she would be willing to put Les under hypnosis to find out what happened and Rachel jumped at the chance. She was very excited about it and said she would come to our house over the weekend to do it. She suggested that maybe we should have someone watch the kids while she hypnotizes Les. I said that we would ask my sister-in-law to watch them for a few hours.

Rachel came over the following Saturday afternoon, so the three of us ate lunch before the session.

"Leslie, are you sure you were abducted?" Rachel asked.

"I'm absolutely sure me and the kids were abducted. I can't remember anything that happened for over an hour and even Allie noticed that something was wrong. What does that tell you when a six year old observes she is sitting in a different seat after she sees a very bright light?" replied Leslie.

We all looked at each other and there was silence for a moment.

"Well Leslie, I guess we had better get on with it and find out what really happened in that hour and a half time frame," Rachel said.

"Ok, let's do it," Leslie said.

Rachel told Leslie to lay on the sofa and she proceeded to put Leslie under hypnosis just as Judy Davies did before.

"Leslie, when I count to three, you will start to remember what happened to you and the children last week. One, two, three. Leslie what happened last week when you were on Brower Road?"

"I was driving to the grocery store when the car stopped."

"Why did the car stop?"

"I'm not sure."

"What happened next?"

"I got out of the car to get something out of the trunk. Oh, the trunk's illuminated. What is that? Oh my God, it's so bright!"

"What is it, Leslie?"

"It's a huge beam of light and the entire car is enveloped in it."

Leslie gasped and said, "Oh no, not again."

"Leslie, what do you mean by, 'Oh no, not again?'"

"They're back. They've come for us again."

"Who are they?"

"The aliens. They took us before and they are taking us again. Oh, the children. I must stop them."

"Did they take you and the children?"

"Yes, all of us."

"Where did they take you and the children?"

"They took us to their craft. It's so large, bigger than before."

"How did you get in the craft?"

"I don't know exactly, but it reminded me of Star Trek and being beamed up."

"What happened next?"

"We were all together in a room and one of them told me that he was going to put something in Allie and Annie's arms and this time we should not remove the objects. He said it was important that they have them."

"It was a man doing this?"

"Yes."

"Did he say his name?"

"No."

"What did he look like?"

"He looked like the other beings we saw when we were abducted before. He was not very tall and he wore grey clothing and had big eyes."

"Were there others?"

"Yes, there were about a dozen other beings and they all looked alike."

Leslie was very composed and didn't sound frightened like she did the first time she was hypnotized.

"Did he say what he wanted with you and the children?"

"He just said that the twins need to keep the chips in them so they will know what to do when the time comes."

"What did he mean by that?"

"I don't know but he was very emphatic about it. He said it was urgent that the chips remain intact."

"Did he say anything else?"

"No, but someone else is coming into the room."

"Who is it?"

"It's Miren. I've seen her before."

That name sounded really familiar to me. I started to think about where I heard that name before and then I remembered Ian McCullough. He mentioned Miren.

"Did Miren speak to you?"

"She said the children were growing and they will do very well in the days to come. She said many things will happen and changes will take place, but I shouldn't worry because, in the end, everything will turn out well."

"What did she mean by that?"

"I'm not sure, but I felt she meant we would be having a lot of natural disasters."

Rachel sat there in disbelief. She was actually at a loss for words. She looked over at me with a perplexed look on her face. Leslie seemed very calm and was very responsive to Rachel's questions.

"Leslie, what happened next?"

"We were examined and then, in an instant, we were back in the car, buckled in our seats."

"Did anyone tell you anything else while you were in the craft?"

"Just that I shouldn't worry because everything happens for a reason."

"Leslie, I'm going to count to three and when I say three, you will come out of the hypnotic state and return to normal, but you will remember everything that happened to you and the kids when you were in the craft. One, two, three."

Leslie looked at us and her eyes started to move as though she was remembering something.

"This is really strange. I remember me and the kids being abducted and it is very vivid in my mind. Thank you, Rachel, for helping me to remember."

"I was more than happy to do it. In fact, I feel honored that you trust me enough to share this experience with you."

Leslie looked at me and asked what I thought about this experience. I said that there is obviously an important task that the twins will perform and I suppose we will know what it is when the time comes. They both agreed with my assessment and wondered what it would be. I suppose we will not have the chips removed from the twins this time.

I was thinking about what Miren had said to Leslie about many things happening and changes taking place and it made me think about what the Bible said about future events. Earthquakes, famine, and pestilence would precede the end times. Many other things were predicted to happen and many people had their own interpretation of the book of Revelation. It was clear that the world was changing and the hearts of men were growing colder.

Rachel left our house around 11:00. She thanked us again for allowing her to be part of this experience. We trusted her completely and told her we would keep her informed if anything happens. Leslie went to bed, but I couldn't sleep, so I retired to my office and sorted through papers that were scattered throughout the room. I came across a file that Eric had given me months ago which I didn't read. In fact, I forgot I even had it. I picked it up and it brought back memories of Eric and different times we hung out together. I had a deep sense of loss at that moment because Eric had been one of my very best friends since school and I just couldn't accept the fact that he, Carolyn and their son were dead.

I started to read the file and it basically contained information that was given to the federal emergency personnel. It actually mapped out a plan in the event we were visited by extraterrestrials. It listed instructions such as not to shoot firearms at aliens or their vehicles. It laid the groundwork for contact protocol. They devised a widespread training program to prepare emergency personnel for the eventual alien encounter. It stated not to initiate any action that might be interpreted as aggressive or hostile. They also have a top-secret recovery manual titled SOM101, which outlines the protocol regarding the clean-up of crashed UFOs.

Page after page gave detailed instructions on how to handle every situation imaginable. It was clear that our government not only knew about extraterrestrials, but that they firmly believed these aliens would make their presence known to all of the world in the near future. The report ended with a few comments such as extraterrestrials appear not to be interfering in world affairs and that they don't view them as an immediate threat to the planet.

The report did state that the government didn't know what the intentions of the extraterrestrials were and that they were suspicious of them. They also stated that a special international committee was created to do a study on the subject of extraterrestrials. The United Nations created a manual which outlined protocols for alien contact and France insisted that a study and report be done after Belgium had a two-year period of credible UFO sightings.

I now had concrete proof that the U.S. government, and many other governments for that matter, were well aware of extraterrestrials and the probability that we as a planet would become aware of their existence and possibly have direct contact with them. Of course, I was in no position to make this information public. I could, however, give this information to the public in the form of fiction. I could write stories with all the information I had under the guise of science fiction stories and hope that it made people think and question what the government knows about the subject. It was something that I had to give a great deal of thought.

Kevin called me the following day and asked if I had considered joining the organization. I told him I did and decided, after several discussions with Leslie, that I should join. Kevin was elated.

"Jack, you won't regret this. This is so cool. We'll be in this together, just like old times. Jack, will you be calling Angus about your decision?" Kevin asked with great enthusiasm in his voice.

"Well, I was thinking about calling him tonight."

"Bravo, I'm so excited about this," Kevin said.

We talked for a few minutes and then the conversation ended. I couldn't believe how excited Kevin was. I didn't see what the big deal was about joining. I told Leslie about my decision and that I talked to Kevin and she was very supportive and thought I made the right decision. That surprised me but what can I say, she still surprises me after all this time.

That night, I called Angus and told him I decided to join the organization. He told me that the next meeting would be held in Belgium in November and inquired if I could attend. I told him it should not be a problem and he gave me the details of where and when the meeting would take place. He also cautioned me not to tell anyone the details of where the meeting would be held except for my wife. I told him the secret was safe with me. We spoke for a few more minutes and he said a lot would be revealed to me at the meeting and he would talk to me then.

Leslie and I talked about the meeting. She was fine with me flying to Belgium. I told her the meeting would be held outside of Brussels in November, and also gave the gist of the conversation with Angus.

"Jack, this is very exciting. I can't wait to hear what happens at the meeting," Leslie said with excitement in her voice.

"Les, you know this is between you and I and you absolutely cannot tell anyone about this organization."

"Jack, you should know by now how well I keep secrets. I would never repeat anything you tell me about this matter," Leslie said.

"I know and I apologize for saying it, but in this case, silence is really golden."

"I'm well aware how important it is that these people remain anonymous and my instincts tell me that they are good people who are trying to help the human race."

"I agree with you there. I wouldn't join if I felt they had a sinister agenda and I wouldn't hesitate to leave this organization if I felt they weren't for the common good. I'll be watching closely."

"Yeah, I know you will," Leslie chuckled.

CHAPTER 30

THE GIFTED TWINS

October 2003

A few months had passed when something strange happened. Allie and Annie were in their room playing dress-up and Leslie and I were downstairs talking when Taffy started to bark and run around the room. She then ascended the stairs to Allie and Annie's room. I knew what that meant. It was the ritual that Taffy went through when Sophielia came to visit. Taffy ran into their room and stopped barking. I grabbed my journal and ran up the steps and down the hall to their room. The room was filled with sunlight and prisms danced all over the walls. It was a beautiful sight to behold. Taffy was sitting beside Annie but Freddie, our cat, was in Andrew's room sleeping under the crib. The scent of lavender permeated their bedroom and it had a very calming affect on me. I could also hear the faint sound of wind chimes in the distance which was strange because the windows were closed.

Annie and Allie were now in an altered state of consciousness and talking to Sophielia. I observed their demeanor more closely than before because I was no stranger to this phenomena. The girls had a radiance about them that I had not noticed before and their faces had a joyful look to them. Oh how I wished I was having those conversations with Sophielia. I had so many questions to ask and I knew she would have the answers. Allie murmured, "I will, Sophielia. Annie will too." Annie smiled and started to communicate with the light using sign language. Annie learned sign language in school so that she could communicate better with others.

The altered state that they were in went on for about 15 minutes. The twins told Sophielia what was going on in their lives, but they were silent during much of the apparition. I sensed that Sophielia was telling them something very important during that time. They smiled and Annie made the sign for "I love you" and Allie said goodbye. The chimes stopped ringing, the prisms disappeared, and the scent of lavender was no longer present in the room.

I asked the twins what Sophielia said and Allie told me that her and Annie would soon be given gifts that would surprise many people. Allie said Sophielia told them not to be afraid of how people would react to their gift. I was really curious about that but Allie didn't know what Sophielia meant by that statement. Allie said that she and Annie would see things that would help me understand what would be happening in the near future and help answer the questions I was asking. She said her and Annie would help a lot of people with their special gifts.

Annie ran to my office and sat at my computer, and as before, she began to type what Sophielia told her. She typed that terrorists would continue to attack groups of people and there would be a lot of suicide bombings. The world would be subjected to many natural disasters and diseases which would cause many deaths. The rich would become richer and the poor would become poorer and there would be poverty in the United States. America was on a downward trend and it would cause a lot of unrest in the country. The weather patterns have started to change and this will cause a lot of problems with farming. Crops will be lost and the Earth will dry and become like a desert in parts of the world. 2005 will be a very significant year for several reasons. Israel will make important changes in their country and many will be angry with those changes. There will be more conflicts in the Middle East. There will be severe hurricanes, more earthquakes, and much political unrest. Do not be afraid of the turmoil that will unfold before your eyes. You have guardians who will protect your family from harm, just have faith.

Annie got up from the computer and ran downstairs with her sister. It amazed me how the girls seemed so unaffected by what Sophielia said to them. I suppose it was because they were too young to comprehend the meaning of what was told to them and they were simply innocent messengers. I began to understand why young children were chosen to repeat Sophielia's messages. They were too young to have prejudices and could be relied on to say exactly what was told to them. I often wondered why they were the ones. *What was different about the twins that allowed them to see and hear an angel? Perhaps we would find out in time.*

It was November and I just received a call from Kevin.

"Jack, are you going to Belgium for the meeting?" Kevin asked.

"Yes, I am. Are you going?"

"Oh, yeah, and I'm looking forward to seeing you there. This will be your first official meeting. I hope you're excited about this because this is a bloody big deal."

"Yeah, I know it is and I'm very anxious about it, in fact, Leslie is excited too."

"Well, Jack, you will be surprised when you see who some of the members are in this group. You just won't believe it," Kevin said with enthusiasm in his voice.

"I'm sure I will be. Should I bring an autograph book with me?" I asked sarcastically.

"I don't think that will be necessary. It's not like they're bloody rock stars or famous athletes. They're more low key. They sort of remain in the background, and, of course, this is like a secret society in that all of us haven't revealed the existence of this organization to others."

I was intrigued by Kevin's statement about this group as a secret society. As I thought about it, I realized he was right. I have a lot of professional contacts and most of them are very important people and I have never heard of this group until Kevin told me about it. My curiosity increased and I realized I was more eager to learn about these people than I had originally thought. I must admit that it would be an ego boost to belong to an important, secret organization that had a lot of power, but a power that was used for the good of mankind. So many secret societies which have been made public, have an obsession with control and many times these societies end up very corrupt.

"Well, Kevin, I never considered myself a candidate for a secret society but now you really have me curious. Did you ever think we would end up like this when we were dodging bullets in Northern Ireland or getting rip-roaring drunk in an English pub?"

"Hell no! I thought I would continue to chase down the violent stories till the day I died and continue to get rip-roarin' drunk in Irish pubs," Kevin said with a laugh.

"I thought I would continue my bohemian lifestyle forever, but of course Jane changed that and I don't regret it. Your life really changes when you become a responsible adult and start to think of others before yourself. I never would have guessed that I would end up like this."

"Yeah, I agree with you there. Ain't life a funny thing? It throws you curves all the time."

"Amen," Kevin replied.

Leslie and I were sitting in the family room talking about my trip to Belgium. She said she was taking the kids to the local nursery to pick out some pumpkins and decorations for the front of the house. Halloween was a couple of weeks away and the kids were getting excited about dressing up in costumes and going to parties and going out to trick or treat. Leslie made costumes for the kids and the girls kept pulling them out and dressing up in them. The theme for the Halloween costumes was the wild west. Annie's costume was a cowgirl kinda like Annie Oakley. Allie's was an Indian, Pocahontas, and Andy was a cowboy.

The next day Leslie and I took the kids to the nursery. They were all looking at pumpkins and having a great time when an older woman beside of Allie lost her footing and started to fall down. I went to grab her so she wouldn't fall, but she grabbed Allie's arm to steady herself. I was able to catch her before she hit the ground. She had a look of shock on her face and she just stared into space. I asked her if she was alright but she seemed to be deep in thought and didn't answer me. She started to breathe deeply and gasped. That made me really nervous because I thought she was going into cardiac arrest.

I noticed she was still holding onto Allie's arm.

"Ma'am, are you alright?" I asked again.

She continued to ignore me. Finally, after a minute or two, she turned to me and asked me if this young lady was my daughter. I told her she was and said her name was Allie, short for Alianna.

"Alianna, what a different and beautiful name. I never heard that name before," she said quietly.

She turned to look at Allie.

"Young lady, you have just saved my life and I am very grateful to you. Thank you so much for allowing me to see myself clearly," the woman said.

I thought that was a weird comment and wondered what she meant.

Allie smiled sweetly and told the woman with the bright red jacket that she was welcome.

The woman turned to me and smiled.

"Sir you have an exceptional child. She has a wonderful gift and I am so glad I met her."

I was puzzled by this entire situation. The elderly woman had a very serene look on her face. Tears started to well up in her eyes. She really had me curious and so I asked her what she meant by that. I was hoping that she would tell me what just happened to her. I couldn't help but notice her entire demeanor changed.

"Sir, when I grabbed your daughter's arm, I immediately had a personal revelation. I saw myself for what I had become and I realized that I had turned into a bitter, older person who lost her love for life and who treated others with contempt. I realized in an instant that I have to change because I owe it to myself and to others. I also realized that there was still a lot of life to live and I have plenty of time to make amends to those who I treated badly. I only hope that the people that I hurt with my ill words and rude behavior can find it in their hearts to forgive me."

I didn't know what to say to her at first, but then I smiled and told her that I was sure those she offended would forgive her. She smiled back and turned to Allie and thanked her once again.

Leslie came over to us and asked what was going on. She had seen the woman talking to me and Allie. I told Les that we helped the woman from falling and she was telling us how grateful she was for saving her. I also told her that we needed to talk after the kids went to bed. She had a worried look on her face when I said that.

"Jack, you're scaring me. You said that so seriously. I hope you don't have any bad news to tell me," Leslie said with concern.

"No, it's nothing you should worry about, it's just something I observed about Allie," I replied.

• • • •

That evening Leslie put the kids to bed and we sat down to talk.

"Leslie, the strangest thing happened at the nursery. Do you remember that elderly woman I was talking to?"

"Yes, I remember. She was also talking to Allie."

"Well, she said that she had a personal revelation when she grabbed Allie's arm. She said she saw the kind of person she had become and that she needed to change. She basically said that she hoped those she treated badly would forgive her, and then she thanked Allie for her help. Do you think this is the gift Sophielia told the girls about?"

"Well, I guess time will tell what the gifts are that they received. I wonder what Annie will experience?"

There was silence for a few moments and then Leslie continued to talk.

"It still amazes me, after all this time, that our daughters have strange talents and things they say come to pass. I always thought I would have a very ordinary life, but that couldn't be further from the truth. Our lives are anything but normal."

"Well, I always thought that my life would be fairly exciting. I started my journalism career right out of college and it was one scary experience after another. I knew with that first encounter with the IRA in Ireland that life for me would be anything but ordinary. I never anticipated anything like this, though. Having daughters who experience visitations from an angel, who tell us what wars and calamities will happen in the world, alien encounters, and then approached by a secret society were things that I never would have imagined in my wildest dreams happening to us."

"Yeah, I know what you mean. I always thought people on tv who claimed they were psychic or who claimed that they were abducted by aliens, were a bunch of nut cases. Now I have a different perspective on such things. It's frightening if you really think about it. What is going on in this world? Time is going by so fast and strange things are happening all the time. Look at the political scene around the world. Look at the crime rate and the bizarre behavior that people manifest. There's something going on, but we don't know what it is. It's almost like it's a build-up to a dramatic climax," Leslie said with real emotion in her voice.

We continued to talk for about an hour and then went to bed.

CHAPTER 31

THE COMMITTEE

November 2003

I got up early and started to pack my bags for the trip to Belgium. I was becoming more psyched about the trip with each passing hour. Leslie had all of my clothes and toiletries laid out on the bed so it took only a few minutes to pack my bags. She came in to see how I was doing and to make sure I didn't forget the usual things like a toothbrush, deodorant, and a razor.

"Jack, I think I'm as excited as you are about this trip. I can't wait for a report when you get back. Oh, by the way, don't forget to bring home some Belgian chocolates. You know how I love them and you better bring a box back for your mother."

"Don't worry, I will bring plenty back for everyone," I replied.

• • • •

Leslie and the kids came to the airport to see me off. Leslie looked so beautiful in the autumn sun. I looked at her and the kids and realized how lucky I was and how much I loved them. I was so eager to go to Belgium but, on the other hand, I didn't want to leave my family. I always miss them when I'm away. Leslie leaned over to kiss me and all the kids gave me hugs and kisses. Life doesn't get any better than this. Leslie said I should call her as soon as I get to the hotel and I promised her I would. As I boarded the plane, I turned around to see them watching and waving at me. I never forgot that sight of the twins in their bright red jackets and Andy in his Eagles' jacket and then Leslie in a sleek, black coat. I started to miss them even before I got in my seat.

Leslie decided to go to the farmer's market after they saw me off and promised the kids that they would all go to the Dairy for lunch. The children loved the Dairy. They could get their favorite ice cream sundaes there and the waitress always gave them extra whipped cream. Leslie did her shopping in the market and then they headed for the Dairy. They settled into a booth in the middle of the restaurant when Annie fixed her gaze on a young man sitting across from them. She kept staring at him and Leslie told her to stop. Annie ignored Leslie's request and she began to talk.

"Mom, he's a bad man," Annie said.

Leslie was shocked at what Annie said because she never said many words and certainly didn't comment about people.

"Annie, look at me," Leslie said.

Annie immediately looked at Leslie and said again that the man was bad. Les was stunned at Annie's comment. Andy was playing around with Allie's hair and pesting her, so Allie was oblivious to Annie's comment.

"Annie, what do you mean?"

Annie continued to look at her mother and said that the man hurts people and he lies. Leslie asked her how she knew that and Annie merely said that she just knows he's bad. Leslie once again told her not to stare at the man. She was thinking that this conversation with Annie was the most her daughter had spoken at anytime to anyone. Les was happy about the fact that Annie spoke so much, but she was troubled by what Annie said.

• • • •

I had arrived in Belgium by early evening and then I settled in at the hotel. I called Leslie as soon as I got to my room.

"Leslie, how's it going? I just arrived at the hotel and I'm settling into my room. I miss you guys something awful. Is everything ok at home?"

"Jack, we miss you too. Everything is fine. The kids had fun at the

Dairy. They wanted ice cream sundaes with lots of whipped cream so, of course, I let each of them have one. We all need a special treat once in awhile. How is your room? Is it nice and clean?" Leslie asked.

I told her everything was fine and that the room was great and the weather was perfect. Les began to tell me about Annie's comments regarding a man she saw at the Dairy. I was amazed that Annie spoke so much and expressed her thoughts so clearly. Leslie told me that Annie looked right into her eyes and said that the man was bad. We didn't know what she meant by that but had a feeling that one day we would find out. Leslie and I spoke for awhile and then ended our conversation with a promise to talk the next day. I then called Kevin's room.

"Kevin, it's Jack. I'm on the fourth floor in room 408. Can you meet me in the lobby in about 20 minutes?"

"Jack, glad you got here in one piece. I'll see ya in 20. How was the flight?"

"It was fine, but it becomes more difficult to leave my family with every trip."

"Yeah, I know what you mean. Well, I'll see you soon and we can talk then."

"Sounds good, see ya later," I said.

I met Kevin in the lobby and we went to the hotel restaurant to get something to eat.

"Are you ready for the big meeting?" Kevin asked with laughter in his voice.

"Man, I'm a little nervous. I really don't know what to expect or who to expect. This is sort of like going to the big game, you know, or maybe like goin' to the dentist," I said sarcastically.

"It's not that bad, Jack. Actually, I think you will really be into this thing once you meet everyone and start exchanging ideas with people. You will be amazed at the energy that is generated in the room. These people are some of the greatest intellects of our time and probably the greatest philanthropists of all time," Kevin said.

"Well, I'm as ready as I will ever be," I said with a little reservation.

We ate dinner and stayed at the bar for a couple of hours before retiring for the night.

The meeting was scheduled for the next morning at 10 a.m. in the countryside outside of Brussels. A car was sent to pick me and Kevin up at 9:15 a.m. The scenery was beautiful and the ride was relaxing.

"Jack, did you hear about Fred Delaney's death?" Kevin asked.

"Fred Delaney? The Fred Delaney who was a secret op for BI? The one who infiltrated the IRA back in the 80's?"

"Yeah, that would be the one," said Kevin.

"No, I didn't watch the news this morning. I was running late. What happened?"

"Apparently the details are not available, but there was an explosion in a London townhouse and they believe he was one of the people who died inside the building. The last I heard he was working on an assignment in the Middle East, very top secret. No one knows exactly what his assignment was, but, from what I was told by one source, it was the most dangerous assignment he was ever given."

"Oh, man, that's bad. Do you think the explosion involved the Middle East?"

"I don't know, but there's a strong possibility that it could have been a terrorist attack. The British government is doing an investigation and I suspect we will know the details in a few days."

"Remember when you and I met him in that Irish Pub in Dublin? He seemed like a great guy. Did he have a family?" I asked.

Kevin thought for a moment and then said he wasn't sure. The car that we were driving in pulled onto a dirt road a moment after our conversation ended about Fred. We drove up the private road for about a mile and ended up at a large house surrounded by woods. It was a secluded setting which was well-hidden from the main road. The woods surrounding the property served as a barrier to uninvited guests. A narrow path led to the house, which was quite a magnificent building. As we approached the house, I noticed huge wooden doors with heavy-looking hardware on them. The building itself was made from stone and it blended in with the surrounding woods perfectly. There were tall windows with thick, wooden shutters and ivy covered a lot of the walls.

It had an eerie look to it like something out of a horror movie, but yet it was very beautiful. It gave me the chills as we climbed the steps to the front door. Kevin proceeded to knock the large knocker that was the shape of a lion's head. A minute had passed before someone opened the door. It was a petite, middle-aged woman with short, light brown hair and a heavy accent who spoke very good English. Kevin greeted her and turned to me to introduce us.

• • • •

"Jack, I would like to introduce you to Ivana Petrovich. She is originally from Russia but is now living in this country and this is her home. Ivana had worked for the Russian government as a physicist."

"Jack, welcome to my home. It is a pleasure to finally meet you. I was sorry that we didn't meet in New York. I was not able to attend that meeting, however, I am so glad you could attend this one," Ivana said in a soft voice as she shook my hand with a strong grip.

"It is great meeting you also and thank you for the warm welcome. I'm glad that I was able to come here and I'm excited to meet all of the other members."

"Well, as far as I know, everyone will be here for this meeting. I hope that you enjoy your stay."

"I'm sure I will and thank you again for your warm hospitality."

Ivana smiled and took us down a long hallway which led to a large room filled with many people. Most were unfamiliar to me. People were walking up to us and Kevin started to introduce me to all of them. They seemed genuinely excited to meet me. I was really surprised when I saw who some of the members were in this group. Kevin warned me that I would be blown away when the members were revealed and he was right. One of them was former Senator Jimmy Garner, another was former British Prime Minister John Hailey. It was a who's who of American and European royalty, so to speak. The group consisted of former major political leaders, leading industrialists, renown scientists, and other very powerful people.

Angus came into the room and started shaking hands with everyone. He approached Kevin and I and said he was glad we could come to Brussels. We spoke for a few minutes, and then he continued to work the room. I have to admit that he had a lot of charisma and really knew how to take command of a situation.

We sat down at a very long, wide table and Angus brought the meeting to order. Apparently, the organization was broken up into groups and each group had a specific agenda. One group was acquiring property around the world, another studied the weather patterns and kept track of all natural disasters. Another group analyzed governments and people, and another group was involved in the study of medicine, science, and genetics. Others were involved with studying the ancient texts such as the Bible, the Apocrypha, the Dead Sea Scrolls, and all sacred texts of every major religion. The last group was a rather mysterious bunch of people who investigated UFO phenomena and supernatural events.

Each group presented a brief summary of their reports and then went into separate rooms. Kevin belonged to the last group of members, and I was assigned to that one as well. I was curious about the name of this organization and pressed Kevin for a name, but he refused to tell me. He said we were having dinner with Angus and some others and Angus would give the name then. I figured I could wait a few hours, after all, I waited this long. I was introduced to the others in this group. There was Katherine Reynolds, a professor at Oxford; Jakob Goodman, a former diplomat from Israel; Jordan Simba, a former diplomat from Nigeria; and Maria Haun, daughter of a German car manufacturer, who was currently working at the United Nations.

We went into a room located on the second floor. This estate was amazing and the panoramic views were spectacular. The front of the house was wooded but the view from the back of the house was breathtaking. There were beautiful gardens and rolling hills and valleys that you could see for miles. The sky was a beautiful blue this day and the setting was absolutely peaceful.

The room that we were in felt like a classroom. There were long tables and chairs and blackboards that covered two of the walls. There were charts that you could pull down which had pictures and diagrams of crop circles on them. Erasers and chalk lined the bottom ledge of the boards with drawings and calculations everywhere. The prearrangement of this room gave me a flashback to my early days in Catholic school, and I thought for a moment that I would see a nun coming in with a pointer in her hand giving instructions to the class.

• • • •

Maria started to discuss the drawings on the board and explained that she and the others were trying to interpret the meaning of the crop circles. I asked her what they knew about them and Jakob interjected.

"On one hand, we know a lot, yet very little. Jack, we have been studying this phenomena for several years and we are all in complete agreement that someone is trying to tell us something. There have been crop circles all around the world. Many are man-made, but about 50% are not. We believe it is a higher intelligence that is responsible for the other half of the formations and that they are warning us about something."

Maria chimed in at this point. "See this formation here?"

She pointed to three circles intertwined with each other.

"We believe it represents the trinity and eternal life. I personally feel they are saying life is eternal and a continuous circle."

I thought to myself that it made sense, but I didn't say anything. She pointed to another picture which had a series of many circles in various sizes which were circling a huge center circle.

"We believe this crop circle is a solar system somewhere in the universe. There appears to be many solar system-type crop formations around the world. These formations have appeared for decades; in fact, the first formations were discovered over 200 years ago near Stonehenge," Maria said.

Jakob began to speak after Maria. He pulled down a chart from the board displaying pictures of drawings.

"These are pictures of interesting markings in South America, Peru, to be exact, which can only be seen from the sky. These are not crop circles, but rather images known as geoglyphs which are located on the ground over a thousand miles long, and possibly thousands of years old. They are known as the Nazca lines and consist of birds, spiders, fish, and a monkey that is the size of two football fields. There are also geometric patterns and 800 straight lines that intersect in 62 different points. There is also a drawing of what looks like a man in a space suit which is probably the most interesting of all the drawings. These geoglyphs were created with great precision and without the use of modern equipment. One has to wonder if these were really man-made. How could primitive people manage to make drawings on the ground, some over 800 feet in size, which can only be seen from an aerial view? When would people have the time to do these geoglyphs?"

"It's a mystery to me," I replied.

Maria continued to show us more pictures of formations and presented a brief history of when they were first reported, and how sightings have increased over time. She then discussed man-made circles, commonly referred to as hoaxes. She and Jakob had hundreds of pictures of crop circles and each was dated according to when they were reported and where they were located. It was mind-boggling to see so many formations and so many different designs.

Kevin began to enlighten us on the subject of crop circles that were not man-made. He said there were several elements that proved which formations were not man-made such as molecular changes within the grains, radio activity being detected within the circles, and the manner in which the crops were bent without breakage. Kevin also said that there were two very strange things that they found when formations occur. One is that the seeds were missing from the grain that forms the circles, plus most of the wheat and cornstalks had areas that look as though heat was radiated from the inside, sort of like the effects of a microwave oven. I found that interesting since I had not previously heard that information.

We spent several hours looking at these formations and brain-storming about them. I asked Maria if I could have a copy of these pictures and she said she would make copies for me during our lunch break. I wanted to study them at home when I had more time to digest them. I also wanted to let Leslie see them and receive feedback from her. I was sure that there was an intelligence out there that was trying to tell us something but no one could figure out what it was.

The afternoon passed quickly and everyone left Ivana's house by 4 p.m. Kevin and I were going to have dinner with Angus at 6 p.m., so that gave me time to take a shower and call Leslie. Leslie said they were all doing fine and not to forget the chocolates. Sometimes I think she has a one-track mind. I told her about the other members and told her about Jimmy Garner and John Hailey. She was impressed, but said if Paul McCartney or Elton John were members then she would really be impressed. I laughed and told her she was beyond hope.

Kevin met me in the hotel lobby and we went to a restaurant around the corner where we met with Angus.

"Good evening," Angus said.

"Good evening to you, Angus," I said.

"How did you enjoy your first experience as a member of the group?"

"I found it very interesting and look forward to more of these gatherings. By the way, what is the name of this crew?"

Angus laughed. "I knew you would ask me that. Jack, the name of our group is 'The Committee.' Not very original I'm afraid."

"It may not be original, but you could certainly mention it around a group of outsiders and they would probably think you were talking about a charity event committee or something like that."

"I think it's bloody brilliant. You are exactly right, Jack. You could talk about 'The Committee,' and no one would know you were discussing a secret society who doesn't appear on any government radar," Kevin said with conviction.

"So, Jack, what did you think about your teammates?" Angus asked.

"They seem like great people and very knowledgeable on the subject of crop circles. Do you know Mick Brant?"

"I have not had the pleasure of meeting him but Kevin has mentioned him many times. I know he is a code cracker and left British Intelligence awhile ago, but I'm not sure he would fit in with the group. I fear that too many members would jeopardize our anonymity. Kevin keeps in touch with him and Mick has been very open with his findings."

"I'm sure you're right about the membership. The chances of leaking information about the organization to others increases with every new person who joins. That's why you are the last person we will bring into the Committee," Kevin said in a serious tone as he looked at me.

"I don't know what to say. I feel so honored that you have invited me into the fold."

Angus casually gazed around the room, observing the customers and the waiters and waitresses. I thought he may have seen someone he knew or felt someone was watching us.

"I'm a people watcher and it is probably because I was trained by the military to always be aware of the environment you are in and the people who are around you. You always have to be prepared for an attack. I know that sounds paranoid but I know what governments are capable of and I know they have their own agenda which is sometimes counteractive to the common good. You would be amazed at how many people work in intelligence and what their covers are. We are working on very important issues that governments don't want ordinary people to be aware of and they might view us as a threat. I don't know if you are aware of this, but governments are well aware of aliens and UFOs but they don't know what the aliens want on this planet. They fear what they can't control. They fear annihilation.

"Angus, do you think that, 'cause I sure don't. Why would they wait to finish us all when they could have taken over centuries ago and would have had a lot less of a mess to clean up?" I asked.

"I feel the same. It wouldn't make sense to wait till the world population was in the billions and most of the natural resources were depleted," Angus replied.

"Well maybe they have this tremendous source of energy they want to sell us. Couldn't you just see it. Little grey people on tv peddling the newest source of energy and partnering with the big oil companies. Isn't that the American and European way?" Kevin said.

We were all laughing at that because we could picture it.

"How about selling their form of government to us on tv the way the evangelists sell religion on the screen? That would be entertaining," I said.

"Yeah, couldn't you just see the male aliens dressed in Italian suits and the females made up with high heels and red lipstick? That would be something to see," Kevin said laughing.

"All joking aside, I think they have been sent here to watch over us and help us in our darkest hours, sort of like guardians," Angus said.

"What conclusions have you come up with based on the information that Committee members have uncovered?" I asked as I looked at Angus.

"We have concluded that the Earth is changing and that we are probably approaching a new age but before we enter that new age, many catastrophic events will happen. We believe the coastal areas will disappear due to the melting of the glaciers and polar ice caps. We also feel hurricanes and tsunamis will contribute to this. We think that islands will rise and continents will split and some land masses will disappear forever. We think the poles may begin to shift in 2012 due to the strong gravitational pull that will be created when the sun aligns with the center of the Milky Way. Jack, we may be approaching the next step in the evolution of the Earth and mankind. The signs are there and the prophecies are starting to be fulfilled."

• • • •

"Israel has been a nation since 1948 and the prophets have foretold that this will happen in the end times. Many other things have happened that were foretold in the Bible but many are yet to unfold. We feel there will be so many natural disasters that governments won't be able to deal with it. People all over the world will reach a boiling point. Wars will erupt everywhere. We believe that there will be a severe shortage of basic needs such as food, shelter, and clothing. It will be every man for himself, so to speak. Chaos will run rampant. Much blood will be shed. A new world order will emerge where a corrupt leader will rise. Martial law will be in effect throughout the world. We believe that our darkest hour is close at hand," Angus continued in a very business-like manner.

"Angus, you're scaring me. I can't imagine things will become that grim. I have children and I hate to think that there will be no future for them," I replied.

"Jack, these things will come to pass but there will be hope. All major religions teach that there will be a renewal, a rebirth, after this dreadful period. Evil will reign for some years but it will be destroyed. We have to prepare for this terrible period and survive it. That is why I have assembled some of the greatest minds on this planet to join forces to get us through this tribulation."

"This whole thing is bloody awful, but I just know we can get through this. Jane and I have already bought some land in Montana where we are planning to build a house well hidden in the mountains."

I began to laugh because the thought of Kevin living in a place like Montana was really funny. This guy is as urban as they come. Dublin, London, and New York, are the kind of cities he has always lived in and I couldn't picture him living in a place as rural as Montana. I suddenly had a vision of him in a cowboy hat, riding a horse and yelling yee-haw.

"Kevin, you're joking, right?" I said.

"No man, I'm not. Jane and I decided to buy 100 acres because we feel it would be a good place to go when the shit hits the fan. The cities will be filled with mass hysteria and we don't want to be around when that happens. I'm not afraid to die, but I don't want to check out like that. We are building a house up against the base of a mountain and there are a lot of trees to hide it. You should think about doing the same. There's plenty of land in that area of America."

We talked for a couple of hours and then went back to our hotel rooms. The next day we would all return to Ivana's house. I called Leslie and everything was fine. The kids were playing and Les let them talk a few minutes. I told her I would be leaving for home the next day and she said she would meet me at the airport. I told her how much I missed them and she said they missed me too.

The next morning I met Kevin in the lobby and we left for Ivana's house. The ride was great, because it was another beautiful day and the countryside had a tranquil effect on me. We pulled up the driveway and I noticed there were fewer cars than the day before. I was told that some had to leave to take care of business. Angus brought the meeting to order as members were talking about the war in the Middle East and what a costly disaster it was becoming. They said that this war would drag on for several years and would be the catalyst that would lead to a great world war which would be the final battle. It all comes down to the Arabs and the Israelis and things were happening according to Biblical plan.

Jimmy Garner brought up the famine and the AIDS problems in Africa and expressed a desire to do something to help the situation. He wanted to organize a campaign to raise money for humanitarian efforts to give medical and food assistance to Africa. Angus reminded him that we all had to keep a low profile, but said we should all think about this and come up with a way to give aid without making it public. He also reminded us that we have to concentrate on the future and not allow the present state of affairs to distract us from our mission. After all, things will be far worse down the road than they are today.

Some of the Committee members gave reports regarding weather, civil unrest around the world, and financial information. Apparently, this is a cash-rich group and they have quite a treasury of money stockpiled in the Swiss banking system. A property report was given and the Committee now owned 63 properties worldwide. Most of these properties were located in rural areas around the world but some were in heavily-populated cities such as Los Angeles, New York, London, Copenhagen, Munich, and Paris. There were a lot of properties in Canada and the United States in Kentucky, Vermont, and Montana. Some of these properties were occupied by people who were on the run, but about half were vacant and were being prepared for the end times. Some of the buildings were built underground and were fully equipped with alarm systems and very sophisticated surveillance equipment. They contained a lot of features used in the military.

The meeting ended and Kevin and I headed back to the hotel. It was

3 p.m. and I knew I had better buy some Belgian chocolates for Leslie or she would kick me out of the house. The hotel was located downtown, so I found something for everyone in the shops located within a few blocks of the hotel. I picked up toys for the kids and some chocolates for Leslie. That will make her happy.

• • • •

I arrived at the Philly airport the next afternoon and was greeted by Leslie and the kids. They were as excited to see me as I was to see them. We exchanged hugs and kisses and went home. The twins were asking where their presents were and I handed them a large bag filled with goodies. I reached in another bag and pulled out some things for Andy and the kids went into the family room to play with them.

"Thank you daddy," said Allie, Annie, and Andy.

I grabbed Leslie by the waist and kissed her.

"Well, where's my present?" Leslie asked.

"Oh sure, that's all you care about."

"Oh, you know I'm glad you're home. You know I miss you when you're gone," said Leslie.

"I don't know about that. I think you like when I come home because I always bring you expensive chocolates," I said jokingly.

"That's not true, but I do love those Belgian chocolates," Leslie said with a big smile.

"Good, because that's what I got you," I said as I handed her a 2-pound box of chocolates wrapped in paisley paper with a gold ribbon.

"You are the best!" she squealed.

Leslie and I put the kids to bed and then we sat down and talked about the meeting. I showed her the copies that Maria Haun made of the crop circles and I began to tell Leslie what the Committee knew about them.

"Jack, this is fascinating. What do you make of them?"

"I don't know, but I'm sure going to try to find out. I really do believe there are messages in these formations."

"I agree with you. Some of them are quite elaborate and I don't see how people could make something like this," she said as she pointed to a formation that consisted of over 100 circles with geometric patterns.

I was really tired and we called it a day. I left the copies on the dining room table and told Leslie I would put them away the next morning.

I came downstairs early the next morning to find the twins looking at the photos of the crop formations. Annie was rearranging them in a different order.

"Annie, what are you doing?"

She looked up at me and smiled. Allie said that they were putting the pictures in order. There were eight photos of crop formations across the table and the first one was a formation with three rings entwined.

"Daddy, this picture is the Trinity. The Trinity has no beginning and no end."

I was surprised at her response.

"Allie, how do you know about the Trinity?"

"Sophielia told us."

Annie proceeded to pick up the last photo and looked at her sister. It seemed as though they were communicating mentally. This photo was a large, solid circle like the sun or moon and part of another solid circle partially emerged from the first one.

"Daddy, this one means that the universe is pulling apart to make two universes. See, one is coming from the other one," Allie exclaimed.

Once again, I was shocked at what she was saying.

"Allie, did Sophielia tell you this too?"

"No daddy, Annie told me."

Once again, I was stunned by what she was saying to me.

The twins ran upstairs to get dressed and Leslie came downstairs with Andy. I told her what Allie had said and she was just as surprised as me. I knew in my heart that there was something or someone trying to tell us something and now it was confirmed. The twins came downstairs and I asked them about the other photos, but Allie said they didn't know what they meant but told me that I would find out soon. Now I was really curious about this whole thing. *How would I discover the meaning of these formations?*

CHAPTER 32

MARCH 2004

A few months had passed and I was no closer to understanding what the formations meant than when I first brought the copies home from Belgium. I had them spread out on a table in my office in the same order as the twins had arranged them. I looked at those pictures dozens of times but nothing made sense. I was almost frustrated by the entire situation and wanted desperately to figure out what they meant, but perhaps they didn't mean anything at all. Perhaps they were a result of a vortex. I decided that I would abandon this project for awhile and concentrate on the book I was writing. I had been working on a novel about a murder mystery and my publisher had reminded me of the deadline for the book.

I finally finished the book, and Leslie and I decided to pack up the kids and go to New York to see my publisher. We thought we would make a weekend of it. We went to the publisher's office and then headed for that huge toy store on Times Square. The kids were having a great time looking at all the toys and we ended up buying a ton of stuff for them. It was a lot but at least it would keep the kids busy while we were in the hotel room. I have to laugh at Leslie whenever we travel. She always brings sheets along and lays them all over the hotel suite so the kids can sit on the floor and play. She's so concerned about cleanliness in public places.

• • • •

Les and the kids were settled in for the night, so I went out for a walk. I was walking down Fifth Avenue when I decided to stop in at St. Patrick's Cathedral. I always liked going into St. Pat's when I lived in New York. I made a point of visiting it whenever I felt alone or stressed out from the job. The beauty and serenity of this sacred place always had a tranquil effect on me and always restored faith and balance to my inner self.

I went into the dimly-lit cathedral and noticed that only two other people were there. It was eerily silent as I walked around the place, looking at the marble statues of Christ and the saints. An overwhelming sense of peace came over me as I walked along the sides of the church, so I stopped to light a candle at a figure of Jesus and to say a prayer. The strangest feeling came over me and suddenly I knew at that moment that even though difficult times were coming, we would somehow survive it and move on to a much greater time. I knew we would be saved.

I returned to the hotel and found the kids asleep and Leslie sitting in bed reading.

"Les, the most unusual thing happened to me when I went for a walk. I stopped in at St. Patrick's and I felt so at peace in there."

I continued to tell her of my experience and how I felt hopeful of the future even though I knew we would be subjected to very terrible times.

"Jack, you sound like you had a profound experience. You're scaring me," Leslie laughed.

"Les, I'm serious. We'll be ok," I said in a serious tone.

"Well, I'm glad you feel that way. I always felt that way," Leslie replied with a big grin on her face.

• • • •

We returned home from our visit to New York and I headed up to my office to file away papers I had received from my publisher. I noticed the copies of the crop circles were still spread across the table. I started to look at them and all of a sudden my mind began racing with thoughts of what these formations represented. Ideas began to swirl around in my head and a theme began to emerge.

The Trinity was a strong theme along with life being eternal. I looked at a formation that consisted of many circles which formed a shape that looked like the letter Y, but more like a wavy Y. The circles didn't line up in straight lines but rather in a wave pattern. I sensed that it was a bacteria which would become a deadly plague to the world. I felt that many would die from it, perhaps tens of thousands. There was also a thought of the Earth going through a lot of turbulence before a major change takes place. I saw the death of an age, followed by the birth of a new age, along with the birth of new planets and a new universe. Looking at one of the photos of a large circle with many small circles coming off the large one, I felt the message was the expansion of the universe.

Allie told me that one of the formations represented the universe splitting into two. I had the same feeling now when I looked at that very photo. I got the feeling that there was a parallel universe to our own and things happen in that universe that affect our own. *Could this really be true, or was I just losing my mind?* I felt a sense of panic come over me as I thought of the implications. I realized, perhaps for the first time, that our planet was poised for an extraordinary event in the near future and we needed to prepare for it. The Bible spoke of a time of tribulation and the book of Revelation gave us an indication of what would happen. I started to understand what the book really meant and that it wasn't completely written symbolically.

Leslie came into my office and we started to talk about the pictures of the circles. I explained to her what my thoughts were regarding each one. She stepped back a little to look at them from a distance.

"Jack, I think your assessment may be correct. I can see a pattern here. That Y-shaped formation is scary. It does look like bacteria. I wonder if Rachel would recognize it. You should make a copy and send it to her," Leslie said with a serious tone.

"That's a great idea and I think I will send Judy Davies a copy of all of these formations to get her idea on what she thinks they represent," I said.

"Sounds good to me," Leslie said.

Leslie and I decided to go to Manayunk that afternoon while the twins were in school. My wife was looking for some artwork to hang on the living room walls, so we stopped in at my sisters' gallery. Steph and Dee were glad to see us and they really fussed over Andy. Leslie picked out some artwork, and we decided to go to lunch at the little café at the end of the street. This place has the greatest Philly cheese steaks and my wife loves the atmosphere. My sisters started to tell us about a buying trip they made to London and they began to tell us about a real cool shop with a really unusual shopkeeper named Brie. Les and I looked at each other and then Les began to tell Steph and Dee about her experience at the Harvest Moon.

"What a small world we really live in," said Dee.

"Smaller than you think," I replied.

Leslie and I picked up the twins at school and headed home. Les started to make dinner and I helped Annie with her homework. Allie was in the family room playing with Andy. She relishes the role of big sister and likes to teach Andy different things. Allie is great with Annie too. She always looks out for her and takes the time to communicate with Annie. She has been a tremendous help pulling Annie out of her autistic shell.

I was helping Annie with her speech therapy when she said, as clear as day, "Daddy, where is Sophielia?"

I was stunned by what she said. I paused for a moment and then spoke to her.

"Annie, I don't know where she is or where she comes from."

"Heaven."

Dumbfounded by Annie's ability to speak clearly, I managed to ask her where Sophielia came from and she said in a very clear voice that she comes from God. I drew my face close to Annie's face, looked her straight in the eyes and told her what an amazing girl she was and how I loved her so much. She smiled at me and then got up from the table and ran off to her sister and brother.

Leslie had just put the kids to bed and we were sitting in the living room talking about my sisters when the phone started to ring. Leslie picked up the phone and started to talk to the person who called. I could tell by the conversation that it was Kevin. Leslie handed the phone to me and told me it was Kevin.

"How are you?" Kevin said in a loud voice.

"I'm fine, everybody's fine, how are you and Jane?"

"We are just great and glad to hear you, Leslie, and the kids are doing well."

"Jack, Mick Brant and I are coming to the States and we would like to get together with you. We plan on being in your area sometime in May. What does your schedule look like?"

"I'm open in May. We don't have anything specific planned except for Memorial Day weekend, which is at the end of the month. What's up?"

"Well, Mick has never been to Philadelphia and we were going to New York on business, so we thought we would drop by to see you."

"Sounds great. Let me know what day you are coming by and I'll make sure I'm here. Leslie can whip up some fancy, gourmet food for us or maybe some burgers and fries. It'll be great."

"Leslie doesn't have to go crazy with the food. Burgers and fries will be perfect for us guys. Mick and I are burger kind of guys. Hey, we plan on being there Saturday, May 15th. It will just be Mick and I. Our wives will not be coming this time."

"Ok, sounds good. I will be here. What time do you think you will be here?"

"We'll arrive in New York on Thursday, and then drive down in the morning and should be there by noon."

"Great, I will make sure you're well fed that day. Leslie bakes a lot so I'm sure she will have something special for you guys."

"I better stop eating a week before we come. You know how I love her cooking."

"Yeah, I know you do and she loves to cook and bake. She'll be excited to see you. It has been awhile."

"I know it has. I'm looking forward to coming to your house and seeing you guys. Mick is eager too. He never had the opportunity to really look around New York, and we plan on seeing the sights. We may even go on a tour of Philadelphia if we have time."

"Well, if you need a tour guide, I'm your man," I said.

"I'm sure we will take you up on that offer."

We ended our conversation and Leslie asked me why they were coming to the U.S. I told her Kevin said they would be here on business, but I didn't press for more details. I'm sure there is a good reason for their visit. Mick has a bunch of kids and he doesn't like to be away from them very long. That was one of the reasons he left British Intelligence.

CHAPTER 33

THE HOUSE IN VERMONT

May 2004

The time passed by quickly since I spoke to Kevin. It seemed like the weeks flew by in the blink of an eye. Kevin and Mick were coming to our house the next day and Leslie had been cooking and baking up a storm for the past few days. Leslie smacked my hand as I took a piece of chocolate cake.

"Jack, there won't be anything left for your friends," Leslie said as she took the cake plate away from me.

"Come on Les. You know I'm addicted to your stuff. I can't help myself. It's not my fault you are such a great cook."

"Please, spare me the excuse. Practice a little self-control, at least till your friends leave. You don't want them leaving with an empty stomach, do you?"

"You're right. I promise to leave the goods alone. I can't wait till they get here. I'm dying for some of that pasta."

I walked over to Leslie and whispered in her ear that I would buy her a really nice present if she would let me have a piece of her lasagna. She smiled and whispered in my ear that I couldn't have any lasagna till tomorrow and that I would be buying her a present since she put so much effort into making him look so good to his friends. Somehow she always turns things around and comes out the winner. How do women manage to do that?

Kevin and Mick arrived right on schedule. It was noon on Saturday and the weather couldn't have been better.

"Hey guys, it's so great to see you. Come on in," I said as I led them into the dining room.

"Jack, how are you? How's life been treating you?" Kevin asked.

Mick walked toward me and shook my hand.

"Jack, great to see you again. It's been awhile," Mick said.

Leslie walked in and greeted Mick and Kevin. Leslie had met Mick a few years ago when we were in London. Kevin gave Leslie a big hug and said how great it was to see her. Mick shook her hand and thanked her for having them at her house. Just at that moment the twins ran into the room. They yelled at Kevin and he stooped down to greet them. Annie and Allie got hugs and kisses from Kevin, and Leslie introduced them to Mick. Mick pulled some candy out of his pocket and gave it to the girls. They were delighted and ran off to the family room.

Leslie brought Andy into the dining room. Kevin marveled at how much he had grown. Mick gave him some candy too and remarked about our beautiful children. Mick was like Mr. Mom after he left BI and he has a great rapport with children. Kids gravitate toward him. He understands them so well and I guess it's because he has a few of his own.

"Life has been really good. My book is doing well and I've been busy writing articles for *INM*," I replied.

Kevin smiled and said that he and Mick have been busy too. Leslie excused herself and went back in the kitchen. She was preparing lunch for everyone.

"Jack, we couldn't wait to get here. Mick has been working on codes and he thinks he's found something."

"Yes, I have found a code that works with the Old and the New Testament of the Bible. I also think I have interpreted a lot of the crop formations," Mick said with great enthusiasm.

Kevin began to tell me that he and Mick bumped into each other at a pub in London and Mick told him what he discovered.

"Jack, if these codes are correct, then we are in for some frightening times starting very soon."

I thought to myself that I had that very same feeling lately.

"What have you discovered, Mick?"

"I was sort of playing around with different codes that were used in the military and I did a combination of them. It's kinda complicated but I came up with one that yielded some amazing results. The Bible is chock full of predictions and many have already happened, and that is how I know this code works. It contains information regarding all of the world wars, the deaths of John and Robert Kennedy, the dividing up of Germany and the fall of the Berlin wall.

"Every major world event that has taken place is in the Bible. The French and American Revolutions are there and it gives dates of when they took place. Names, dates, places, events, and people are in there. The incident with the Twin Towers is even in there too. It is unbelievable! I used the same system with the Dead Sea Scrolls and the Apocrypha and it yielded the same results."

"Did you obtain any information regarding future events?" I asked.

"I sure did. If the codes are correct, the world will experience a horrible cycle of extreme weather starting soon. They predict a series of hurricanes in the U.S. starting in August and going through September followed by a Tsunami the end of 2004. There will also be several hurricanes that will devastate the southern part of the United States and islands in the Atlantic in 2005. Predictions range from natural disasters to political upheaval. Lebanon and Syria will have major problems which start in 2005. Iran will become prominent in world affairs and trouble will be brewing with Israel and the surrounding Middle East countries.

"The U.S. is in for terrible times. There will be an economic crisis where Wall Street will basically crash and a severe recession will follow immediately afterwards. This should take place in 2008. One of the predictions stated that a major earthquake would split up California and will have a devastating effect on the world economy. There was also mention of a comet hitting the earth in 2030 which would cause mass destruction worldwide. The rise of the anti-Christ was in the codes. It just seemed to me that everything started with the destruction of the Twin Towers in New York. That appears to be the turning point where things start to get ugly on an international level."

Kevin chimed in at this point.

"I agree with you, Mick. Things really began to happen after the Twin Towers were hit. It was the catalyst that got the U.S. into war with Iraq, even though the war was started as a result of incorrect information."

"I'm sure it's all a part of the plan, the beginning of the end. Look at all the things that are happening in the world. It's like it is coming unglued. The problem with global warming, the wars, the violence on the streets, and the drug cartels. Look at how people kill a bunch of people and then end up killing themselves. It's all leading up to something," I said.

"Jack, you haven't heard all of it. Mick, tell him about the crop circles," Kevin said.

"Oh, yeah, I've been studying them and they too have messages."

I looked at Kevin because I had been studying the crop circles and wondered if Mick had arrived at similar conclusions about them. Mick began to discuss his interpretations of the formations with real conviction.

"Jack, I believe they are describing an alien agenda. It looks to me that we are not alone. An intelligence is behind some of these formations and I don't think it is of this world. I've studied hundreds of them and they tell a story of coming events. They are similar to the Biblical codes, containing messages of war, pestilence, disease, but they seem to spell out the splitting of the universe and the birth of a whole new existence. They also seem to point to a parallel universe."

"So, it sounds like the crop formations and all of the other codes kind of point to the same scenario," I said.

"I think so. The codes describe events leading up to the end times and I suspect the crop formations describe what will happen when the end of the current times come and the new age arrives. There is a lot more to be discovered with the codes and crop circles, but for now, we have to be prepared and help others when the tribulation starts to gain momentum."

I was intrigued by what Mick had said. I concluded much of the same things when I studied the pictures of the crop formations, plus Allie had told us a lot of the same things that Sophielia told her and Annie. It seemed that all sources pointed to time running out for this world as we know it and action needed to be taken quickly to prepare for the rough times ahead.

Leslie entered the room and said that lunch was ready. She served our lunch in the dining room while she and the kids ate in the kitchen. Kevin and Mick raved about Leslie's cooking.

"Jack, I heard your wife was one of the greatest cooks on the planet, but now I know firsthand it's true."

"I know she is. I have 15 extra pounds on me to prove it," I replied.

"I am designating her as the official chef when we all end up in some compound. Jack, make sure there is plenty of food and whatever else Leslie would need to feed all of us. We will all be fat and happy while the world crumbles around us. She will definitely be in charge of the food distribution," said Kevin.

"I don't even want to think about that, but I know I can't ignore it. We have been chosen for a specific purpose and we can't ignore our obligation to serve others when the time comes," I said very seriously.

"Amen to that, brother," Kevin said.

Kevin and Mick left by 4 p.m. and returned to New York. Kevin said that he and Mick still had things to do there but he would be getting in touch with me soon. That night Leslie and I talked about what Mick said about the codes and the crop formations. We both agreed that something was going to happen in the near future, and we had to prepare for it. We decided that we would purchase property in a remote area, possibly in Pennsylvania or upstate New York. We both agreed that it would not be wise to mention this to any of our family members, but when the time comes, we would have a place for everyone to go so they would be safe and survive the end times.

I was checking out properties for sale on the web, and I came across a great place on the border of Pennsylvania and New York. The description of the house and land was appealing and I mentioned to Leslie that maybe we should check it out. She agreed, and so I called the real estate broker who had it listed on the internet. I made an appointment for Leslie and I to meet with the agent the next Saturday.

Leslie and I drove up a very long driveway fairly hidden from the road. It was definitely a house deep in the woods and well hidden from public view. I was thinking that perhaps that was good since the reason for buying this property was to stay out of sight in the event we needed to lay low. The house was a nice size, 2,500 square feet. It was made of stone and had a lot of the same features our house had such as fireplaces and hardwood floors. The house definitely needed work, but Leslie thought it was a great house and she seemed to envision what it would look like with renovation. She was excited about it, but I reminded her that we had a few other properties to look at and we had plenty of time to shop around.

After checking a dozen or so properties, we finally decided on a house in Vermont. This particular house was a log and stone building that dated back to 1876. It was situated on a 25-acre tract of woodland nestled away in the beautiful mountains of Vermont. Leslie loved it and I felt it would be a great investment and would serve us well in the event we had to retreat to a secluded place. It had three large fireplaces, and some wood burning stoves, and there was plenty of wood on the property to keep those fireplaces burning for years. The house was 3,000 square feet, with a huge kitchen, four large bedrooms, and three full baths. The attic was finished, and it was also large enough to accommodate several beds if necessary. Beautiful gardens surrounded the house and a small pond was in the back, which had some fish. This place was a real find and I had a good feeling about it. My instincts told me this was the right house for us, so we pushed for an early settlement.

Leslie and I picked up the kids at my parents' house on our way back from Vermont. They were kind enough to keep them while we were gone. My mother loves having the kids and my dad really gets a kick out of Andy. He comments about how big he is getting and how he will be a football player one day.

We finally arrived home from picking up the kids when the phone started to ring as I turned the key to open the door. I quickly ran to pick it up in the event it might be an emergency.

"Hey Jack, how is everything?" Kevin said in his thick Irish accent.

"Everything is great. Leslie and I just bought a house in Vermont. Oh man, wait till you see it. It's tucked away in the mountains on 25 acres of land. There are trees everywhere, however, there is a clearing in the back of the house. It is well hidden from view. You have to drive around winding roads and then you have to drive up a long, narrow, dirt driveway to get to the house. The really cool thing is that it's close to Canada. You know how we like Canada. It is a great place," I said with great enthusiasm.

"I didn't know you and Leslie wanted to move. The house you live in is great. What made you decide to move?"

"Oh, yeah it is a great house and we're not moving out of it. We love it here and our families live within 30 minutes of us. We just wanted to buy a place that we could use as a vacation home, but we also wanted to invest in a place that we could go to in the event we had to leave here quickly."

"You mean sort of like the place I have in Montana?"

"Exactly. You never know when we will have to make a hasty departure, and we then need a place if things get out of hand," I said with a very serious tone.

"Yeah, I know what you mean. One can never be too prepared. Shit happens."

"So, what's up?" I asked.

"Well, you know we have a Committee meeting coming up next week and I was thinking about asking Angus if Mick could be invited to join. What do you think about that?"

"That's kinda weird that you should say that because I was thinking the same thing. We really need a guy like him on our team and I think he can be trusted. I am really impressed with the progress he has made on cracking codes and he sure is knowledgeable about the way the intelligence community works."

"He knows a lot about that and he knows how to work the system without detection."

"Kevin, the question is, do you think he would want to join our crew?"

"Definitely. He was complaining to me about how bored he was at home all the time. He loves staying home with the kids but he feels his talents are wasted. As a member of the Committee, he would be perfect 'cause he could do all of his work from home, but still be a part of a dynamic team that is working on an extraordinary project that would utilize his talents. I think he would jump at the chance to work with us."

"The other question is, would Angus welcome him into the fold? You know what he said that I was the last person allowed to join the Committee and how the membership has to remain small so there are no security leaks."

Kevin sighed. "Yes I know, but I think we could convince him what an asset Mick would be. He is brilliant and we can't let him slip away. We really need to let Angus know what Mick has been doing and how he has cracked codes."

"I agree with you, in fact, maybe you should call him and discuss it with him before we have the meeting," I suggested.

There was a pause, as if Kevin were deep in thought.

"Good idea. I think I will call Angus tomorrow and discuss it with him. I just have to think about how to approach him about letting Mick join the group."

Kevin paused for a moment and then his voice took on a very serious tone. "Mick really is a trustworthy guy and I know he would be totally dedicated to our cause," Kevin said as he emphasized the word trustworthy.

"Sounds like a plan. Good luck with Angus," I said as we ended our conversation.

"Thanks. I'll see you next month in Germany, but I will let you know how it goes with Angus."

• • • •

Kevin called several days later to tell me that he talked to Angus regarding Mick becoming a member of the Committee, but Angus was not convinced that Mick would fit in with the group. After a lengthy conversation, Kevin and I agreed to double-team Angus when we got to Germany for the meeting and convince him that Mick would be an enormous asset to our team. We also discussed many other things going on in the world regarding the Middle East, finances, and crime, just to mention a few. We ended the conversation with the belief that we could convince Angus to expand the Committee membership by one more person.

CHAPTER 34

MEETING IN MUNICH

Leslie and I took the kids to our new retreat in Vermont over the weekend. When we returned, Kevin called and I told him we just returned from Vermont. He asked all about the house and the area where it was located. I told him Les and the kids loved it there and our pets seemed to like it too. It certainly is a quiet, tranquil place where only the sound of nature could be heard for miles. I told Kevin I would have to acclimate to the silence and isolation since our house outside of Philly is always noisy with the sound of neighbors and family members. Our pool is a magnet for the neighborhood kids all summer long and our family and friends prefer coming over to watch football in the Fall and visit during the holidays.

Kevin and I ended the conversation with plans for our trip to Munich the following week. Both of us were staying at the same hotel and all of the members would meet at Maria Haun's country home outside of Munich that Wednesday. I hadn't been to Germany in several years, and was looking forward to the trip. I would only stay there for four days, because I didn't want to leave my family any longer. Leslie is always good about trips that I have to make, but I hate to be away from her and the kids. It never ceases to amaze me at how much I miss her when I'm away even after all of these years. I sure am grateful that I can work from home and help her with the kids. Annie and Andy can be a real handful at times, but Allie is a great help to Leslie.

I was all packed for my trip and ready to leave. Leslie and the kids went to the airport to see me off. I kissed everyone and told the kids to be good and listen to mommy while I was gone. I whispered to Leslie that I would have something special for her when I returned and she said she would have something really special for me and winked and gave me a huge smile and a very long kiss. I was hoping her and I were on the same wavelength regarding what she would have for me. We could really use a night to ourselves without kids around to dampen the mood.

I was already hoping the next four days would go fast so I could return home to her. As I got in line to board the plane, I looked back and waved. They all waved back and Leslie threw me a kiss. All I thought about during my flight was how much I loved my wife and how amazed I was that I ended up married with kids and loving every minute of it. I never envisioned myself staying in one place for very long when I was younger and always pictured myself as the kind of guy who would travel constantly and be totally into my work. Love and romance would always be just a sideline. Funny how your perception of life changes when you fall in love. I wouldn't change my life for anything.

My plane touched down in Germany several hours later and I immediately headed for the hotel. I asked at the desk if Kevin Leary checked in yet, and they said he did and he left instructions to tell Jack Branden that he is to ring his room as soon as he arrives. It just happened that Kevin's room was two doors down the hall from my room, which made it very convenient for us. I called Kevin a few minutes after I entered my room and we made arrangements to meet in 30 minutes.

"Hey man, how was your flight?" Kevin asked as we walked down the hall.

"It was good but long, as usual. Hey, let's grab something to eat. I'm starving," I said.

"Yeah, me too. I could use a couple of beers."

Kevin and I exchanged small talk as we went down to the first floor of the hotel. There were four other persons on the elevator, so we chose not to discuss anything regarding the Committee with others present.

• • • •

We decided on a restaurant around the corner from the hotel. It was a small place, but it had a great reputation for good food and service. We arrived and were immediately seated at a table, located towards the back of the room. There were several tables that were not being used, in fact, it appeared like a slow night for business. We were given menus and our order was soon taken.

Kevin began to tell me about the conversation he had with Angus regarding Mick.

"Angus is not open to bringing anyone else into the group. He made it clear when you joined that you would be the last member brought into the fold. I tried to convince him of Mick's value to the organization, pointing out his talent for breaking codes that no one else has ever been able to do, but he just wouldn't budge on his position."

"That's too bad, because I think it will turn out to be a huge mistake if he refuses him membership. We clearly have a void in that area and Mick would fill it. Why is he being so close-minded about him?"

"Who knows. Time is running out, and you and I have to convince him that Mick should be one of us. If he doesn't agree to let him join the Committee, then you and I will have to come up with a plan to have Mick work with us without Angus knowing and without letting Mick know about the Committee," Kevin said in a very frustrated voice.

"Yeah, we have to keep Mick on our side and engage him in work that we're involved in. He is way too valuable to us to just let him go. We can always work independently from the group and take the information we have acquired on our own to them and sort of incorporate it into group projects."

"That sounds good, but I would prefer that Mick was part of the group," Kevin replied.

"So would I, but if Angus shoots us down, then we have no other choice but to work on our own with him. The group will benefit from the information we get from him and ultimately it will help many, many people. We have to look at the larger picture and do what is best. Our goal is to try and ride the storm that is coming in the best way possible and help as many as possible to ride that storm with us."

Kevin nodded his head in agreement.

"Does Mick have any idea at all about the group?" I asked.

"Not a clue."

"Well, then I think we could work with Mick independently and achieve the same result. Angus may get suspicious of us if we push too hard for Mick. You know Angus gets paranoid at times."

Kevin was silent for a few seconds. I could see the wheels turning in his head.

"You know, he does get paranoid, but I think it's because of the training he had in the military. It's second nature to him. But, I think you are absolutely right about Angus becoming suspicious of us if we keep pushing for Mick. I think we should let it drop and not double-team him as we had originally planned.

"Where is it written that everything we do has to go through the group? We can pursue interests on our own as long as it's for the common good. It's expected that people within a group won't agree on everything, and it's normal for people to pursue other interests even when they belong to a particular organization. It doesn't mean you're being disloyal to that organization. In fact, it will be a benefit to them," Kevin said with conviction.

"That's what I'm thinking. Our intentions are not to be deceitful. Our intentions are to do what is best for everyone. It's unfortunate that Angus doesn't see it our way, but he is the founder of the Committee and it is his prerogative to pick and choose whomever he wants. We can always leave the group if we don't like the way things are going," I said.

"Well, I don't know how easy it would be to just leave the Committee once you are a member. No one has ever left the group. I would think that if someone would leave they would be completely cut off by the others and communication of any type would cease to exist," Kevin replied.

"Wow, I never even thought about that but I could understand why they would do that. I'm sure all of the members would be suspicious of the person who left and would be concerned about any breach of confidence regarding the Committee. Not only that, I think Angus would have that person watched to make sure that the Committee's anonymity wasn't compromised."

"I don't think it would be good for that person. I don't think Angus would physically harm anyone because of leaving, but I think he would make it clear that any information given out about the group and what they are involved in would be met with a high price to pay. He has a lot of friends in high places and he could make life miserable for someone if he wanted to," Kevin said with a serious tone.

Kevin and I ate dinner and then returned to the hotel and decided to hang out at the lounge for awhile. Soon after we sat down at the bar, several other Committee members walked in and came over to us. We immediately shook hands with Steven Heinrich, Adrienne Mansfield, Jimmy Garner, and John Hailey. They all said they were staying in the hotel and that they had just arrived in Germany that afternoon. Steven lives in Germany, but he had been in Spain for a week on business. It had been awhile since we had a meeting, and everyone seemed eager to go to Maria's house.

It was getting late and our little party started to break up. Kevin and I left the bar around midnight and we agreed to meet in the hotel lobby the next morning at 8 a.m. We planned to grab breakfast and then head for Maria's house. The others said they would see us there around 10:30 a.m.

I called Leslie to let her know everything was ok and to find out how things were at home. Leslie said she was glad I called and assured me everything was fine. She told me that Andy pinched his finger in the door but it wasn't broken, just bruised. We talked for about 20 minutes and as we were ready to end the conversation, I told her that I loved her and not to forget that fact. She assured me that she wouldn't, and that she really loved and missed me. I told her to kiss the kids for me.

Eight a.m. came quickly and I was in the lobby waiting for Kevin. He appeared a few minutes later and we grabbed some breakfast and headed for Maria's house. We arrived at 10:30 a.m., right on schedule. All of the members had arrived before us and were gathered in the large foyer. Maria's place was beautiful, with the high ceilings and oriental rugs. She had fresh flowers in huge vases stationed everywhere and their scent was very fresh, sort of like a flower shop. Maria is quite an animal lover, so she had several cats strolling freely inside and outside the house with two very large German Shepherds sitting guard in the foyer when we arrived. I had to laugh when Kevin told me their names were Tiny and Mini.

Angus greeted all of us in the foyer and invited us to join him in a room down the hall. He began the meeting and everyone gave their reports as usual. Hans Northagen got up to give his report regarding weather patterns. He looked very intense as he began to address the Committee members. He cleared his throat and began to speak in a deep voice. "It is my belief that the time period between August 2004 and October 2005 will be a period of great disasters. The conditions are present for very destructive hurricanes in the southern part of the United States. I also fear there may be an earthquake in Asia which could devastate that part of the world. I anticipate, based on new data, that it will be a year of violent storms."

Hans paused for a moment and then continued.

"A lot of rumblings have been detected below the Earth's surface in the northwestern region of the United States and in Hawaii, so we may see some volcanic eruptions and earthquakes in the near future. There have also been signs of possible volcanic action in Iceland."

Hans finished his report and it was clear that what he had to say about the coming year or two was grim. It became one of the dominant subjects of conversation the next few days.

Angus closed the meeting at 5:00 in the afternoon by discussing the financial aspects of our group, and said that we remain financially sound. The Committee hadn't purchased any properties in the past year, but Angus was looking into buying survival equipment for the properties that were located in remote areas. He felt that the times warranted preparation, and he wanted all the buildings to be ready in the event we had to seek emergency shelter. He also said we would meet the next morning to discuss a very important situation that was brought to his attention yesterday. He was planning to meet with a gentleman who had details regarding this matter and he would share them with us tomorrow.

Kevin and I returned to the hotel and had dinner in the restaurant. Both of us were disturbed by the dismal picture that Hans had presented regarding the weather patterns.

"Jack, weren't you and Leslie thinking about a trip to South Carolina at the end of the summer?" Kevin asked.

"Yeah, we were but I think we'll have to pass on that little vacation. I don't want to take any chances going there if the southern coastal region will be battered by hurricanes. There are plenty of other places we can go for a vacation. Maybe we will go to Canada or Nova Scotia. We've never been to Martha's Vineyard, so we could go there. I heard that it's a really nice place to go."

"I heard Martha's Vineyard is very nice, too. Jane and I thought about going there sometime."

It was getting late, so we headed back to our hotel rooms and said we would meet in the lobby at the usual 8 a.m. time. We were going to Maria's house for another Committee meeting at 10 a.m. and we wanted to grab something to eat before departing. I called Leslie as soon as I got back to my room and told her what Hans had said about the hurricanes and weather in general. We both agreed that South Carolina was definitely not a place we wanted to visit this year, and I said we would discuss another vacation spot when I returned home. Leslie thought that sounded good and we ended our conversation.

The next morning, Kevin and I had breakfast at the hotel restaurant and took off for Maria's house. The weather was awful and I really didn't want to be there. Angus began the meeting with some disturbing news he had recently received regarding the practice of genocide in some African nations, and expressed a desire to do something to help the people who lived in those countries. Angus appeared to be very solemn as he spoke.

"I am deeply disturbed by what is happening in Africa. Sources tell me that evil forces are at work to eliminate large populations on that continent and an epidemic is brewing that will achieve their goal. From what I understand, a bacteria is going to be let loose on the northern African population in the near future, as an experiment to see how many people would die in a given area in order to determine how effective this bacteria would be for the use in germ warfare."

The information that Angus shared with us was certainly deeply disturbing. It was difficult for me to comprehend why human beings would deliberately kill other human beings and have absolutely no remorse about it.

"We need to organize aid workers to help stem the extent of the mortality rate. We can't stand by and do nothing. We need to talk to doctors who are confidants and find out how we can prevent mass genocide," Angus said to the group.

Angus adjourned the meeting for lunch, so Kevin and I took the time to check our voice mail. I didn't get any calls, but Kevin received a voice mail from his wife. Jane had called to tell him that his brother Liam had suddenly taken ill and was in the hospital. Kevin called Jane and was very distraught by the conversation, because he and Liam were close. Apparently, the doctors were not certain as to the nature of his illness. He was running a high fever and had some boils on his legs, and was in a lot of pain. Jane said they were going to run tests to see what they could discover about his illness. Jane said she would keep Kevin posted on Liam's condition.

"Jack, I am really worried about my brother. He never gets sick, not even a cold."

Kevin's voice sounded different. I could sense he was upset but tried not to show it. Liam was Kevin's younger brother, and Kevin always looked out for him.

"I just don't have a good feeling about this. I always knew when my brother was in trouble and I was always there for him. This just doesn't feel right."

I tried to assure Kevin that his brother probably had the flu or something ordinary like that, but it didn't seem to calm him down. He really had a sense of impending doom about his brother.

• • • •

Kevin and I skipped lunch and returned to the room where the meeting was taking place. Angus was there and started to take a silent head count to see if everyone was present. He appeared to be extremely distressed. His face was white as if the blood had been drained from him and he seemed to be fidgety, like a person who was nervous about something. When we were all seated, Angus told us he needed to address the subject that he spoke about earlier regarding the African situation. He began to read a startling report from the World News that appeared on television before noon. It was in regard to an epidemic that had broken out in Sudan and was sweeping across Africa. Medical professionals believe it is a new strain of bacteria and they are dispatching aid workers to Africa. His voice sounded very grim as he continued to read.

"Thousands have died as a result of this new strain and it is believed that perhaps as many as a million people will die before this is identified. The symptoms start out as boils on the legs and arms and is followed by a fever that reaches a high temperature which causes the individuals to go into convulsions. When the convulsions cease, blood, and puss begin to excrete out of the boils and they die. They don't know how long the incubation period is for this bacteria. It is a new strain that is very aggressive and spreads rapidly. They aren't sure at this point if it is spread from personal contact or if the bacteria is airborne, however, death occurs within a couple of days after the symptoms begin."

There was a long pause before Angus spoke again. He seemed to be struggling with his composure. I had never seen Angus so emotional and I started to feel that something was really wrong because Angus is normally a rather reserved person and was not prone to show great emotion. Angus began to speak with a trembling voice.

"I have feared this day was coming but I thought we would have more time. As I had reported to you this morning, I was just told about the rumor yesterday and immediately shared the information regarding the testing of germ warfare with all of you. I didn't know the bacteria was already released to the public. According to the news media, it is expected to reach epidemic proportions. We must all take extreme precautions and curtail traveling as much as possible. It is crucial that all of our members remain in good health because we have very important work that must be done. I will be consulting with doctors to find out if a vaccine can be developed quickly. Some of our members will be working to organize aid workers to help with this situation."

The meeting ended on a sad note and all of our members wanted to return to their families immediately. All of the news outlets worldwide were reporting the story of the epidemic and the rising death toll. The illness was a great mystery and a name was not yet assigned to it because no one could identify it at this point. I suddenly remembered the pictures of the formations I had gotten from Maria Haun when the Committee met in Belgium and remembered the Y-shaped formation that I thought looked like a bacteria. *Could this be what the formation was conveying and that it's a bacteria that is a threat to the world?*

Kevin and I got the first planes back to our homes so we could be with our families. We were concerned that the airports would shut down if the illness reached Europe. We both took precautions to wash our hands and avoid contact with others as much as possible. Kevin was deeply concerned his brother may have this illness and wanted to return to Ireland to see how Liam was feeling.

• • • •

The flight back to the U.S. seemed to be endless. I couldn't wait to get home and be with Leslie and the kids. No one appeared to be ill on the plane, so I believed I was safe, but concerned none the less for my well-being. I felt a great deal of relief when the plane flew into Philadelphia and

I heard our kids yelling for me as I got off. What a great feeling it is when you return from overseas to such an enthusiastic reception. Life doesn't get any better than this even though it was shadowed with the possibility of a pandemic.

CHAPTER 35

MESSAGE IN THE CIRCLE

October 2004

Several months had passed since the mystery illness took its toll. It had been identified as a bacteria, similar to the Black Death, that killed an estimated 100 to 200 million people worldwide from 1346 to 1353. This epidemic was named the Black Epidemic because the bacteria was a close relative to the *Yersinia pestis*, which was the bacteria that was responsible for the Black Death. Both bacteria are spread by fleas that are carried by rodents but this one took on the characteristics of a pneumonic plague, which can be transmitted person to person from blood, coughing, or sneezing, and both are deadly. Modern medicine had been able to identify the bacteria and contain it so that the death toll was much lower than when the illness had originally appeared.

The epidemic started in Sudan and spread through Africa. The death toll had reached 250,000 by the time it spread to the Middle East, killing an additional 100,000 people. Syria was the worst hit in the Middle East, accounting for one-third of the casualties in that region. India and China had substantial losses at a total of approximately 225,000 combined. Europe lost 40,000 citizens to the epidemic and North America lost 30,000. South America had lost approximately 15,000 citizens, but Australia and New Zealand were unaffected by this illness and only a handful of their citizens contracted the bacteria. Scientists worked day and night to identify the strain to come up with a plan of action to help prevent the spreading of the bacteria and treat those who were exposed. Their efforts paid off and the epidemic was contained and a successful plan of treatment was implemented. A vaccine was developed and no new cases were reported for weeks. The CDC believed the worst was over and were confident the vaccine would be effective in preventing the spread of this illness.

• • • •

Leslie and I were extremely stressed because of the epidemic and so we decided that we would take a mini vacation with the twins. We originally planned on a vacation in South Carolina but decided not to go after hearing Hans' report on weather patterns. We decided to go to England because we thought the girls were old enough to appreciate the trip. Leslie wanted to go to London and do some serious shopping, but we also wanted to see Judy Davies and visit Brie at the Harvest Moon. Kevin's brother Liam was recovering from his illness, so we knew we wouldn't be seeing him this time. We were all happy to know that Liam wasn't sick from the Black Epidemic and that it was actually pneumonia. It turns out that the boil on his leg was actually an ingrown hair that had become infected. What a relief to know he was recovering well from his illness.

We checked with my cousin Rachel to see if she felt that traveling to Europe would be safe and she thought that it would be, so I booked a flight for Leslie, the twins and me to leave for England on a Friday morning and come home the following Tuesday. Les and I decided to leave Andy at home with my mother. She would stay at our house for a few days while we were in England and take care of Andy and our pets.

The flight from Philadelphia to London was calm and we arrived at our hotel at 5 p.m. Leslie quickly unpacked our suitcases and we went to dinner in the hotel restaurant. We were all tired so we actually went to bed shortly after dinner. Allie and Annie were quiet, which is unusual for the twins. Allie said she was excited to visit London and wanted to see the really big toy store in Piccadilly Circus. I was taken back by that because I never talked about Piccadilly Circus and was curious as to how she knew about it, so I asked her. Allie told me she heard about it on tv. Who would have guessed?

It was 8 a.m. and we were ready to start our day of sightseeing. Leslie wanted to go to Regent Street to see Brie, so we went out for breakfast first, which took us till 10 a.m. The stores don't open till 10 a.m. so the timing was perfect. We took off for the Harvest Moon to see Brie. We opened the door and immediately smelled the familiar aroma of vanilla and cinnamon. MMMM!!! That place has the most delicious aroma. It reminds me of the cinnamon buns they sell at the mall. Brie greeted us with her usual warm, friendly enthusiasm and gave all of us a hug.

"I can't believe how you girls have grown," Brie said with great excitement.

"We can't believe it either. They constantly grow out of their clothes. They are costing us a bloody fortune," I said with laughter in my voice. We all laughed over that comment.

Brie showed the twins a collection of beautiful crystals and Annie picked up a light pink one that fit in her palm perfectly. She was truly mesmerized by it and didn't want to give it back to Brie. Brie told her that it was a gift for her and gave Allie a pink crystal also and told them that it was a belated birthday present. She told the twins in a very soft voice that these are magic crystals and they will know what to do with them as time goes on. I was really intrigued by her comment but didn't ask what she meant by that. Leslie glanced at me when Brie said that to Allie and Annie. I think it piqued her curiosity as well.

Leslie asked Brie if she could do a reading for her and she said yes. They went off to a back room and were there for about 15 minutes. When Leslie came back, she had a smile on her face, so I assumed Brie told her some good news. I chatted with Brie for a few minutes while Leslie walked around the store. She saw several items that she wanted to buy, so Brie rung them up and off we went to the next few stores. Till it was all said and done, we spent several hundreds of dollars for items from three stores. A lot of the items that we purchased for family had to be shipped because there were too many to carry on the flight back home. Some of the small toys we got for the kids were going home with us. Allie and Annie would make sure of that. No way were those two going home empty-handed and they wanted to make sure their brother had something too when we arrived home. That's what I love about them—they always think of their brother.

The following day we saw Judy Davies and she too commented on the girls and how they had grown. I asked Judy if she had counseled any abductees recently and she told me that things have been very quiet on that front and, in fact, it seemed to be eerily quiet. Ian McCullough and his friends hadn't been taken since the last time and she didn't hear of any new sightings or abductions

"Jack, do you think the aliens have abandoned us for a new and younger species?" she said laughing.

"Maybe. We seem to have a lot of drama going on with the human race and they are probably tired of it. It's maybe like the same old soap opera to them. They probably need something new to analyze so they don't get completely bored. I think we've become tiresome to them."

"You are probably right, but I confess I don't miss them. They really frighten the people that they take on board their craft," Judy said.

"I know firsthand what you mean. I've been there and it is a frightening experience."

Leslie and I spoke to Judy for awhile and then we left her office. Judy is an extraordinary person who is at the very top of her profession. She has helped so many people put their lives back together. She sure is a great person.

Leslie, the girls, and I headed back to the hotel. We were somewhat exhausted from our whirlwind vacation, which took us to some of the greatest stores, museums, and cathedrals in all of England. We decided to change things up on our last day and tour Stonehenge and some of the places where crop circles were known to appear. I was hoping the twins would get to see at least one crop circle before we left England. We contacted a guide and booked a private tour of these sites. We were excited about this particular trip, but little did I know that this brief excursion would turn out to be the highlight of all of my visits to England.

Friday morning started off with some foggy weather, but it began to clear around 9:30 a.m. Our tour guide arrived at the hotel at 11 a.m., so that gave us plenty of time to order a hearty breakfast before we began on our journey. We were all excited, but the twins seemed to be more eager than me and Leslie. I wasn't surprised because kids are usually more excited about new adventures than adults.

Our tour guide was waiting in the hotel lobby for us and he immediately shook our hands and introduced himself. His name was Manfred Layton and he explained all of the details of the tour to us before we left the hotel. He said that he had taken a party of five on a private tour a few days ago, but there were no new formations and he said he hoped we wouldn't be disappointed if we didn't see any because Stonehenge alone was worth the tour. I assured him that we wouldn't be disappointed, and I brought my camcorder along to film Stonehenge. It would be a bonus if we saw a crop circle. Fred, as the tour guide wished to be called, was relieved to hear that. He said some people become irate when there are no pictograms to view and actually ask for a refund. I assured him we wouldn't be like any of those people and told him not to worry.

The drive through the English countryside was so relaxing. Allie and Annie were quiet as they looked out the windows, observing the surrounding area. Allie pointed out some sheep to Annie, which both found fascinating. Stonehenge was close, in fact, we could see part of it in the distance. We arrived at our destination and Fred parked the car in a lot close to Stonehenge. Many people visit these ancient ruins. It is considered one of Britain's hottest tourist attractions. It is also one of the great wonders of the world, and is Europe's best known prehistoric monument dating back to 3,000 BC. Stonehenge is located in Wiltshire, England, home to many crop formations that have appeared through the years in surrounding fields. It is said to be a very magical place, which we soon found out firsthand.

As we approached the ruins, I heard Allie ask Annie if she felt that. I turned to Allie and asked her what she meant by that comment.

"Dad, I felt a tingly feeling in my arms and legs," Allie said.

Annie acknowledged that she felt it too. We continued to walk to the ruins and stopped in the center of the structures. Suddenly, I felt energized to the point of feeling euphoric. I looked at Leslie and I could tell by the expression on her face that she felt it too. I thought to myself that it felt like a high from drugs. We all felt exhilarated. I looked at our tour guide and told him he was right about Stonehenge. It was well worth the trip.

We stood in the center for several minutes and during that time, the twins began to spin around and they both started chanting something unfamiliar to me. It wasn't English but it didn't sound like any language I ever heard. They stopped the spinning and chanting after a couple of minutes and fell to the ground. Leslie and I immediately ran to their aid and picked them up. I had Allie and Leslie had Annie and we both asked if they were ok. Allie said she was fine and Annie shook her head yes to Leslie's inquiry.

We were starting to leave Stonehenge when I stopped and realized I didn't take any video. I told Leslie and the twins to go back for a minute so I could get some footage of them at the monument. I filmed them outside the structures and then we walked off to the parking lot. We saw a group of people gathering at a field across from Stonehenge as we were leaving, so we decided to check out what was there. Much to our amazement, a pictogram was formed in the field located on the other side of the road. It was very long, perhaps the length of a football field. We couldn't really see what it looked like from the ground so we climbed up a hill nearby that Fred pointed out to us. The pictogram consisted of a long pendulum with a huge triangle at the top and a large circle at the bottom of the formation. We had a great view of the design so I filmed it for a few minutes.

Fred suggested that we take a drive to another location in Wiltshire to see if any crop circles were there. We ended up at Etchilhampton Hill in Wiltshire and noticed that there were white spheres of light swirling around a field. We decided to climb up a hill so we could get a better view of them. The spheres navigated the field very quickly and it was clear something extraordinary was going on. Much to our amazement, a circle began to form before our very eyes. I quickly turned on the video camera to record the spheres creating the formation.

Allie and Annie immediately reacted to this event. This pictogram was quite different from any I had ever seen. It was a disc-shaped formation with many tufts of wheat standing up and it was about half the size of the other pictograms we saw across from Stonehenge. It almost looked like a code of some sort. Allie and Annie almost went into a trance-like state and Leslie and I looked at each other with great concern. Annie turned to Allie with a wide-eyed look and said, "They're coming." Leslie and I looked at each other and I then asked Annie in a perplexed voice, "Who is coming?" Allie turned to me and said in a very serious manner that the Angels are coming.

Just as she said that, the tufts of wheat began to flatten out and blended in with the disc-shaped formation. Fortunately, I had recorded the entire event. I had the disc shape with the tufts of wheat and I also had them flatten out and blended into the formation. I immediately thought of Mick Brant and decided that I would send it to him. Something really strange happened in that field and I needed to know if Mick could extract some information from this crop circle. I couldn't wait to get home and download the video onto my computer so I could send it to Mick and Kevin.

Fred took us back to our hotel, and I thanked him for serving as our tour guide and gave him a huge tip. He was grateful and said that this was the best tour he ever gave and that he never saw a crop circle being formed and was very excited that he got to witness an event like that. He also thanked me for the tip and said it was a pleasure being our tour guide and that we were the best tourists he ever encountered. I thanked him for the compliment and said we may see him again sometime down the road. We shook hands and Fred departed the hotel.

We arrived home late the next day and all of us were exhausted from the flight. My father picked us up at the airport and told me that Andy was a really good boy for them and they thoroughly enjoyed watching him. He updated me on a few things that were going on in our family as we drove home. My mother was so happy to see us and gave all of us hugs and kisses. I presented my parents with a gift from England, which was a Waterford crystal, and after a few minutes, they left for home.

It was great to see Andy, and the twins hugged him and gave him some small toys we had purchased while on our trip. The kids went right to bed because they were sleepy and Leslie and I went to bed shortly afterwards. I was really tired from the flight but I couldn't stop thinking about the crop formation that I filmed. I was extremely eager to send it to Mick and Kevin. I was quite sure a message was contained within the tufts of the formation.

I woke early the next morning and made a pot of coffee. Everyone else was still in bed sleeping so I quietly went to my office to download the video I took of the forming crop circle. I emailed it to Mick and Kevin with a note saying that we had witnessed this circle, and to take note of the tufts of wheat disappearing into the body of the circle after a few minutes. I also stated in the email that I felt there may be a message in this formation and to please let me know if there is one. I was so eager to hear from Mick and hoped he read my email quickly so he could get back to me that very day. I had a lot of things to do, but this video took priority over everything else.

• • • •

Leslie and the kids got up about an hour after me. We all sat around the kitchen table and ate breakfast. Leslie and I talked about our vacation in England, but we mainly discussed Stonehenge and the crop formations. Allie and Annie sat quietly as Les and I discussed the video I took of the forming crop circle. After a minute or two, Allie proceeded to tell us that the Angels are coming. I asked her why she said that when the circle was forming and why is she saying that now? Allie said that the circle was telling her and Annie that Angels are coming. I was curious about what she was saying, but I didn't understand what she meant and wondered if she understood what she was telling us.

"Allie, do you know what that means?" I asked.

"Yes daddy. The Angels will be coming to see all of us," replied Allie.

I remained confused by her comment.

Night had fallen and it was 8 p.m. Eastern Standard Time when I got a call from Kevin.

"Jack, how was your trip?"

"It was great and thanks for asking. Did you get my email with the video attached of the crop circle?"

"Are you kidding me? Of course I did, and Mick got it too and immediately started to work on it. He was so excited that he called me to come to his house."

"Was he able to decipher it?"

"Yep, and he is here with me so he will tell you firsthand what is in the message."

"Jack, this is Mick. How are you?"

"I'm doing well. How about you?"

"Well, I'm doing well, but I gotta tell you that I am really excited about this video that you sent. Turns out, it's binary code and I was able to decipher it. There is a message in this disc formation and it's in English. The tufts of wheat form the binary code and it was interesting to see them flatten out after a few minutes. It almost seemed like the message was for your eyes only. Anyway, the message is as follows: contact is imminent - be prepared - we are guardians who speak the truth - we abhor deception and violence - observation of planet Earth continues."

I was speechless for a moment. This was beyond incredible. A message from aliens regarding contact? Mick asked me if I was still on the phone. I told him I was but I had a momentary loss for words. Mick had the entire conversation on speaker phone so Kevin was aware of my comment.

"Jack, you at a loss for words? That's a first," Kevin said.

"I know, but do you realize what the implications are? They're ready for contact. My question is when, where, and how? Mick, do you feel confident that you deciphered the message accurately?"

"Yes, I am very confident that this is exactly what the message states. Binary code was the only code that made sense. I tried a couple of others and they didn't spell out anything. I am sure this message is about contact."

Everyone was silent for a moment. The message that was contained in the formation was beyond what any of us could comprehend.

"I wonder how they're going to make contact? It's not like they can call on the phone or send an email," I said.

Kevin began to give his take on the subject.

"The ball is obviously in their court. They know where you are so they will be the ones to make the first move. I'm sure they already have a plan mapped out for contact. You just need to be open to it, whatever it is."

"I'm sure you are right and when it happens, you and Mick will be the first ones to hear about it after I tell Leslie."

Kevin chuckled.

"You better tell your wife first or you will be in some deep shit."

They all laughed over that comment.

The conversation ended with a lot of questions that had no answers. The thought of a Being from another planet wanting to make contact with a human was monumental, not to mention historical. This was like something out of a science fiction book or movie—something that you fantasized about but never thought it could actually happen. I felt a wave of anxiety come over me at the thought of a meeting with an alien. Once again I wondered when it would happen, and where this contact would take place. I realized at that moment that I couldn't obsess over this or it would drive me crazy.

Leslie had just put Andrew to bed and was ready to give the twins a bath. I told her I wanted to discuss the conversation I had with Mick and Kevin after the girls go to bed. She was aware that I sent them an email with the video attached that I took at Etchilhampton Hill in Wiltshire, England.

"Jack, was Mick able to get anything out of that formation?"

"Yes indeed, and I will tell you all about it when the girls are in bed."

Leslie was beaming with excitement and it was obvious that she couldn't wait to talk about it.

"I can't wait that long. Tell me now. Come on, I'm really excited about this," Leslie said.

"Ok, I get it. I was excited too so I will tell you all about it now. Mick said that the tufts of wheat formed a binary code and it contained a message in English."

I paused and Leslie pressed for more details. She could barely contain her excitement.

"What did it say?"

"It said contact is imminent - be prepared - we are guardians who speak the truth - we abhor deception and violence - observation of planet Earth continues."

Leslie stood with her mouth and eyes wide open for several seconds. I never thought I would see her at a loss for words. She seemed to be in shock and had difficulty articulating her words. Finally, she blurted out that this was unbelievable. She demonstrated a range of emotions from surprise to elation.

"Jack, this is amazing! They want to have contact with you. It must be you since we were basically the only ones present when the disc and the code were formed. The fact that the message blended into the circle to eliminate the message is also an indication they wanted only us to see it. Don't you feel sort of privileged knowing that we were the only ones who got the message?"

I thought for a moment and then I said to Leslie that we assume they will contact one of us but it is possible that the message was for someone else such as Fred, our tour guide. Just because we didn't see anyone else doesn't mean others didn't witness the formation with the message.

"Jack, we have a history of abductions. We know they exist so wouldn't it be logical to make contact with one of us?" Leslie said.

"It would be logical, but it doesn't mean it will happen to us. We have to wait and see. As Kevin said to me, the ball is in their court and they know where we are so we just have to kick back and let them make a move if indeed we are the ones they wish to make contact."

Allie and Annie were in the hall waiting for Leslie. Allie walked over to Leslie and I and said Sophielia told her and Annie that Simon will be talking to daddy.

"Allie, who is Simon?" I asked.

She looked at me with a big smile on her face.

"Daddy, Simon is one of the angels. He watches over us."

I didn't know what she was talking about so I questioned her further.

"Allie, is he with Sophielia?"

Allie thought for a few seconds.

"No daddy. Sophielia said Simon sent a message and you will meet him soon."

I thought about what she said but it wasn't clear to me. Leslie looked at Allie and asked her if Simon made that circle in the wheat field that daddy got on his camera and she said yes. Leslie turned and looked at Jack.

"Jack, now you know who sent the message and now you know that Simon will make contact with you."

Allie interjected and repeated something she and Annie said when they saw the circle and tufts of wheat in the English field.

"Daddy, they're coming. The Angels are coming."

And so it begins . . .

Soon to be released . . .

COMING OF
ANGELS

BOOK 2

CONTACT

M. J. BANKS